Death of a Warrior Queen

DEATH OF A
WARRIOR QUEEN

S. T. Haymon

St. Martin's Press
New York

Library of Congress Cataloging-in-Publication Data

Haymon, S. T.
     Death of a warrior queen / S. T. Haymon.
        p. cm.
     ISBN 0-312-06950-2
     I. Title.
PR6058.A9855D46   1992
823'.914—dc20   91-34610
                                                                      CIP

First published in Great Britain by Constable and Company Limited.

First U.S. Edition: January 1992
10 9 8 7 6 5 4 3 2 1

1

They came to the coast by narrow roads that snaked between fields of barley and heathland where the bracken along the verges bent to the stir of the car's passing, Jurnet handling the Rover with a conscious delicacy as if afraid that the jolt of a single pothole could be enough to fracture irretrievably the fragility of their reunion. He let his glance slide momentarily towards the passenger's seat and felt his heart leap with incredulous joy at the sight of Miriam's bronze hair streaming in the breeze from the open window, her smiling face beneath.

So far, so good, he reassured himself, even if, after a year's separation, it was no use pretending that nothing had changed. Everything had changed, whether for better or worse remained to be discovered. Everything, that was to say, except his love for the woman at his side. No: even that was altered; neither augmented – which was not possible – nor diminished, but altered in quality by the year-long fear that she was never coming back. Even in the old days, locked in each other's arms on the old brass bed that jangled a tambourine *obbligato* to their couplings, he had never felt completely certain of her, and now – ? The very fact that, returning to Angleby from Israel two days before, she had opted to go to her flat in the trendy converted warehouse down by the river in preference to his own crummy pad spoke volumes. The fact that, forty-eight hours later, they still had not gone to bed together spoke encyclopaedias.

For a moment of perverse nostalgia he was suffused with longing for the past year, for the bitter-sweet pleasures of separation, of Miriam in the desert setting up the knitting project which was to be an extension of her thriving business in Angleby: no rows, no misunderstandings, a time of dreams that always came out the way you wanted.

The sight of a church in a field, no village in sight, its round tower of dressed flints striking sparks off the sun like a lighthouse sending its beams out over an empty sea, sent his mind off at a tangent. That morning's *Angleby Argus* had carried an item about a ceremony at another church in the county, a consecration of its ancient ring of bells which had been recast and rehung. A prosperous church it had looked from the picture in the paper, not like this starveling standing half-ruinous among the young corn. Jurnet, with his usual affection for the losers of this world, favoured the abandoned church with a commiserating nod, reflecting that the *Argus* man, in his report, had omitted what must have been the most significant part of the occasion – that moment when the bell-ringers, hands on the tufted sallies, had waited sweating for the signal to launch the new, the inevitably different sound on to the waiting air. Would the reborn bells ring true, tumbling up there in their refurbished tower? And his reborn relationship with Miriam – how was that going to sound in its new incarnation? A dying fall or the firing of all bells together in one glorious clang?

Miriam twisted in her seat, pushing her hair back from her face.

'And now,' she said, 'suppose you tell me why we're *really* going to Lanthrop.'

His eyes resolutely on the road ahead, Jurnet said: 'I told you. This chap Abbott. After what he told me – Druid temples, shades of Boadicea and all that – I thought you'd be interested. And then, you've never been to Lanthrop beach. They only opened it up to the public while you were away, and it's incredible. I thought we could sunbathe afterwards, have a swim if you felt like it – '

Conscious that there were altogether too many excuses, and even more aware that there must never more be any lies, small or large, between them, he began again. 'Paul Abbott. A bit of a joker. Came into Headquarters to ask if there was anything in the laws of England to stop him taking a Kalashnikov to blokes who came on to his site with metal-detectors while he was down the village having a few jars in the local, and buggering his whole operation by digging things up out of context, to say nothing, for all he knew, of making off with Ancient Brit bits and pieces worth a king's ransom. Did we have any better ideas on how to discourage the bastards, and if so, could I possibly see my way to coming down to the dig myself and giving him the benefit of my expert advice on the spot?'

8

Jurnet stopped abruptly, all the unsaid things lying between them, heavy as lead. Such as, chiefly, 'Once a copper, always a copper.' Even on their first day back together, here, as usual, was Detective-Inspector Benjamin Jurnet, Angleby CID, taking precedence over the lovesick swain enraptured to have his beloved home at last. But amazingly, as a swift look, fearful of the worst, told him, Miriam actually nodded, as if he had passed some test. Perhaps, he thought, scarcely daring to hope, she too had changed during the long time away – or perhaps it was OK to be fuzz, a dick, a man under authority, so long as the deaths you were investigating took place in the year dot, the blood and guts long bio-degraded; by which time they were archaeology, a respectable way of earning your living, not like bloody murder.

The countryside had changed subtly, an alien presence undermining its bland orderliness. There were stretches where the barley lay about like a tousled bed. The roadside trees which had hitherto spread their canopies with calm impartiality leaned to one side as if flinching away from an invisible enemy. The air that came in through the car windows had a bite to it.

Miriam lifted her lovely face and said: 'The sea.'

Nothing much seemed to be going on at the dig, if that indeed was what it was. If Jurnet had not followed Paul Abbott's detailed instructions for finding the place, he would have passed it by without a second look: a builder's site, perhaps, with a couple of prefabs, a deep trench, an area of shallower excavation, and a pervading sense that here was yet another bit of England done to death for no good reason. Miriam, however, pointed to where a young man, bare to the waist, his fair hair cropped close to the skull, knelt on the bare earth dreamily shifting soil about in a sieve, every now and again replenishing supplies with a fresh trowelful taken from a seemingly endless store. The young man's mind did not seem to be deeply engaged in the operation, which was not surprising, considering the girl who stood at the gate watching him, her breasts protruding between the upper bars.

'Excuse me,' Jurnet said, finding it hard to keep his own eyes off these astonishing appendages as their owner turned towards him, the taut nipples, visible through the thin fabric of her singlet, swivelling round like guns in a battleship turret homing in on their target. 'Is this the dig?'

9

Before the girl had had time to give more than an ungracious nod in reply, a man came out of one of the prefabs, waved a greeting and made his way towards the gate, his glasses glinting in the sun. He took them off, revealing a comfortable face atop a plump, comfortable body clad in dilapidated shorts and a sweater that looked itself like an ancient artefact.

'Hi!' he hailed the newcomers, contriving a brief appreciative summary of Miriam before turning to the girl at the gate. 'You still here, Sandra? Don't you know that down at the Co-op customers are going mad for a sight of your lovely hands ringing up at the check-out?'

'I'm off sick,' Sandra declared with satisfaction. 'The fresh air'll do me good.'

'Sick! You look bursting with health to me.'

'It's me chest,' the girl explained, speaking in the solemn tone she clearly felt proper to the subject. 'Delicate. Me mum says I was always the first to catch anything, even when I was a baby.'

Since the chest in question preceded the rest of her body by a distance such as to make it a matter for prurient speculation in the village as to how far art might or might not have been called in to bolster up nature, this propensity for being first did not surprise the girl's hearers. In any race to catch a germ Sandra could be relied on to come in busts ahead.

Turning a smiling regard on the twin globes, Miriam said generously, 'Your chest looks fine to me.'

'Nice of you to say so.' After a brief consolatory glance at the older woman's less spectacular equipment, the girl turned her attention back to the young man.

'Fancy digging up a Druid temple!' she commented. 'It makes you think.'

'The first thing it could make you think', Paul Abbott, unimpressed, corrected her, 'is that the Druids didn't build temples. The second is that if you are determined to spend your days taking my workers' minds off their work, you'd better come in and sign up as a volunteer yourself and be done with it.'

A look of suspicion overspread the girl's features, which were undistinguished and comically prim above the swelling abundance below.

'Volunteer for what, would that be?'

'For sifting through the soil, principally, like young Ian over there is doing at this moment.'

'It looks mucky.'

'It *is* mucky, not to say unpaid except for a few quid pocket money, unhealthy and incredibly boring, even while it does fill every crevice of your soul with improbable but impassioned hope.'

'Oh ah?' At the word 'impassioned' the look of suspicion deepened. The girl sighted along the line of her breasts to the young man kneeling in his hole in the ground. Even at that distance the message was received loud and clear. The young man went bright red and began to jiggle his sieve with uncharacteristic vigour.

Sandra turned down the power, turned away and said: 'I'll think about it.'

Promising coffee in the prefab, Paul Abbott ushered his guests round the rim of the excavation.

'We nearly overshot,' Jurnet replied to an inquiry as to whether he had had any difficulty finding the way. 'Your directions were first-rate. It's just that I was expecting a hive of activity.'

'Ah! That's because half the kids who do the donkey work have gone into Angleby with Pete, my assistant. Once a week he takes our finds in to the Museum, where they've given us house-room to store our stuff pending the definitive report. They're hoping, incurable optimists that they are, that we'll turn up another Snettisham hoard or another Sutton Hoo ship burial and that then they'll have first call before the B.M. gets its predatory paws on it.'

'Any chance of that?'

In reply the other shrugged his shoulders humorously.

'What they'll say when they see our latest consignment of minced sherds and unidentifiable lumps of iron I can imagine – which is why I leave the deliveries to Pete. He has gorgeous eyes and the assistant curator all but swoons at the sight of him. This time he's taken some of our little darlings along with him to hear a lecture on the storage and safe-keeping of archaeological material. Somehow we have to get it into their heads that bits of Roman glass ought not to be thrown away under the impression that it's only another bottle of 7-Up. The rest of our workers – and I use the term in affectionate amusement – are either down in the village drinking their lunch in the Norfolk Hero, our local watering-hole, or else – ' pointing in the direction of the woodland which fringed the further edge of the irregularly shaped open space ' – they are taking their break over there amongst the brambles, copulating.'

'Brambles? Sounds a mite uncomfortable,' Jurnet suggested.

'Hides like rhinoceroses,' Paul Abbott assured him cheerfully. 'Requirement of the trade. Guatamalan cactus, Kalahari thorns, Norfolk brambles – it's all one to the likes of us.' The man put his glasses on again and pushed a hand through his thinning hair. 'I can't think what it is that makes archaeologists so randy, unless it is that being dunked as we are, as unprepared as an infant at the font, into the immensities of the past encourages a neurotic anxiety to get the best out of our own pitiful little crumb of time before the lights go out for good and all.'

He raised his glance to where the young man Ian continued to sieve soil with the air of a somnambulist.

'That, if you can believe it, is our security guard for the day. Doubt if he'd notice if a metal-detector nipped in and nipped off his balls.'

Jurnet let his gaze roam round the field which, besides the woodland Abbott had mentioned, was bounded along the lane by a straggling hedge, and on the remaining two sides by iron railings through which it was possible to discern lawns and a long drive leading up to what, judging from the many chimneys overtopping the intervening greenery, was a house of substance and character.

He said: 'You don't need me to tell you that, on an open site like this, posting people and dogs round the clock is your only real hope of keeping out intruders. Unless, of course, you put a chain-link fence round the entire perimeter.'

'Hannah's going to love that!' Abbott exclaimed, going on to explain that Hannah was Mrs Milburn, whose property it was, and who already had enough to put up with, having her paddock turned into a disaster area, without the added visual insult of security fencing. 'Assuming we could fund it out of our grant, which we can't.' Something in the way he said 'Hannah', the two unpromising syllables infused with a subliminal warmth, alerted Jurnet's receptors, hypersensitive in that area.

Miriam chimed in: 'I must say, if this were my place, I'd never let anyone do this to it, even if they gave me a cast-iron guarantee

12

to turn up Queen Boadicea and her chariot with the scythes on the wheels still in working order.'

The archaeologist screwed up his eyes in good-humoured pain. 'That bloody Thornycroft! The only place, my dear girl, you'll find that particular hunk of baloney is on Westminster Embankment in sight of Big Ben. Unfortunately for Victorian sculptors, the actual Ancient British chariot was mostly wicker-work, made for speed and manoeuvrability, not for boring public monuments. The Romans had never seen anything like it – which is why it nearly cost them the province of Britannia.'

With an endearing, schoolboy awkwardness which took away all offence, the man went on: 'And I hope you won't think me fussily pedantic if I say that the old girl's name was Boudica, not Boadicea – Boudica which, ironically enough, means Victoria. As to Hannah – Mrs Milburn – giving permission,' he ended, 'she didn't. It was her husband. Seemed to think there was some kind of cachet in it, get him accepted as a patron of culture and so on, and she went along with it as, I fancy, she went along with anything he'd set his heart on.' Perhaps to cover up an imper-fectly disguised jealousy: 'He's dead, poor sod. Accident last year. Wrapped himself and his Jag round a tree on the bypass. Unfortunately, he had their five-year-old daughter with him at the time.'

There was a short, embarrassed silence before the archae-ologist finished: 'Funny the way no amount of digging down to the past, the one and only reality, compensates for the pain of the illusory present. Still, as things have turned out, I think it's done Hannah good to have us around. Taken her mind off what's happened.' With a shake of the head and a rueful smile: 'Though that's a bloody silly thing to say, if ever I heard one.'

The three of them stood looking down into the trench, the ar-chaeologist with proprietorial affection, Jurnet and Miriam in some confusion as to what reaction was expected of them. All that was visible across the sandy face exposed to the air was a wide band of rusty black, the detritus, surely, of a tremendous burning. At last, feeling that some observation was called for, Jurnet confessed: 'I'm afraid I'm as bad as that young lady at the gate. I also thought we were going to see a Druid temple – the remains of one, anyway.'

13

'Please don't feel disappointed,' Paul Abbott begged earnestly, 'or think I've got you down here under false pretences.' He looked sombrely down at the black slashed across the excavation like a geological insult. 'What you see there, I do assure you, knocks any tonnage of ancient masonry into a cocked hat. What you are looking at, my friend, vibrant as the day it was perpetrated, is the Romans' revenge.'

The black, thought Jurnet, grew even blacker. A trick of light undoubtedly. At his side, Miriam gave a small involuntary shiver.

'As I said,' the archaeologist went on, 'the Druids didn't build temples. They communed with their gods in groves of oak trees, a much more poetic conception, even in the English climate. Their divinities were the forces of nature and therefore it was in nature, in the open air, that they must be sought, and hopefully found.' For a moment he regarded his visitors with a certain severity before the good-natured rotundities of his face reasserted themselves. 'How I do go on!' He smiled in disarming apology.

Jurnet, always one to give credit for expertise and commitment in whatever field of endeavour – even an ingenious villian evoking his reluctant admiration – warmed to the man.

Nodding towards the trench he asked: 'They burned the trees down – is that it? After they'd put down Boadic – Boudica's rebellion?'

Paul Abbott nodded. 'They burned them down, reduced the lot to carbon, that essential element of death and life. Given the technology of the day, can you imagine the effort it took to cut down and utterly destroy a grove of fully mature oaks, not so much as an acorn left to tell the tale?'

'You'd have thought, a bloody war just over, they'd have had better things to do with their time.'

'Oh no! It was the most important thing. When we talk of the Druids, we're not talking about woad-painted savages, you know, but about a class of subtle men, the one unifying force in a narrow tribal society; philosophers and politicians, custodians of the national magic. Without the Druids there would have been no rebellion. Destroy them and their groves, and the Romans made sure there would never be another.'

Miriam went to the very edge of the excavation; gazed long and hard at the black band.

14

'It's horrible,' she pronounced at last, rejoining the two men. 'When I think of all that Boudica [*trust her to get it right first time!* Jurnet smiled at his love in unalloyed congratulation] had to go through at the hands of the Romans – the way she was flogged, her daughters raped – ' Miriam paused, overcome by the recollection.

'Oh ah, as they say in these parts,' Paul Abbott rejoined mildly. 'Undoubtedly a shamefully wronged woman. Whether that excuses what she and her followers did in their turn to the women of Colchester, St Albans and London, for example, such as skewering them on spears stuck up their vaginas, is another matter. But there!' With a little nod in Jurnet's direction: 'Maybe I'm wrong to say it in the presence of the law, but there's nothing like a distance of getting on for two millennia, is there, to blur the distinction between right and wrong, between just retribution and inhuman thuggery?'

Miriam shivered again; looked at her host uncertainly. 'I'm not sure I care for archaeology, if you don't mind. It makes the earth seem altogether too hollow, covering up God knows what underneath.'

'Exactly!' Paul Abbott looked tremendously pleased. 'Fragile as glass. Why we call it *terra firma* heaven only knows. What's firm about it? Every day the wind blows it about, the rain washes it away, the worms work all the hours there are – change, always change! Only down below, blind but aware, waiting patiently for me and my mates to fetch it forth into the light of day, lies the unassailable truth!'

On the table in the prefab two skulls lay among the coffee mugs.

'Thought you ought to see the evidence whilst you're here.' Paul Abbott added boiling water to the instant coffee. 'They – oh, and a couple of little wooden figurines we've already sent off to Angleby – are what the villain left behind. The question is, what was the metal which activated his infernal machine?'

Jurnet took the proffered mug; sipped and looked at the two heads which, in the way of skulls, returned his gaze with cheerful incuriosity.

'What was it, then – some kind of grave?'

'In a manner of speaking. A couple of shaft burials. Just the heads. The Ancient Brits don't seem to have set much store by the rest of the skeleton – but the head! Ah, that was the centre of the soul, the very essence of being. Not bad, eh, for that time and place, to have such a well-defined perception of a controlling brain? The two figurines – impressive little things in their way – were broken, otherwise I'm sure our thief would have taken them as well. He couldn't know they were that way on purpose, surrogate sacrifices to appease the gods. Imbeciles that we were, by the time we thought about fingerprints we'd already gone into our usual cleaning and conservation drill.'

'Not to worry.' Jurnet put down his mug, having, he reckoned, drunk enough of the Ancient British liquid it contained to fulfil the dictates of good manners. 'I take it you've been in touch with the local police?'

'I haven't, as a matter of fact. Not that I haven't the greatest respect for the village bobby, even if there have been a couple of small misunderstandings with some of our young 'uns after closing time down at the Hero. It's just that, having worked on rural sites before, I was afraid that even to launch the subject on to the village air would be enough to put the rumour about that there were some rich pickings to be had up here, only waiting for some enterprising spirit to come along and liberate them.'

'Know what you mean.' Jurnet nodded understandingly. The copper surfacing despite himself, despite his awareness of Miriam's gaze, level and tinged with a faintly ironic amusement, above the rim of her coffee mug: 'Still, one does, after all, have a duty to report a crime.'

'Oh dear, does one?' Paul Abbott's brow cleared. 'Well, I have, haven't I? Reported it to you.'

'So you have,' the other conceded. 'Just the same, I should have a word with the local chap. It doesn't follow that the bloke we're looking for necessarily comes from round here – treasure-hunting's by way of being a national pastime these days – but at least the village PC will have the local knowledge, know the likely lads: for starters, which of them has a metal-detector. It's always a popular gadget down by the sea where there's a good beach like there is here.'

Paul Abbott crossed the room to a corner where a bulky object shrouded in a stained piece of sheeting leaned against a wall.

'Ta-ra!' he clowned, whisking the cover away. 'I'm only thankful that metal is all they detect.'

Jurnet and Miriam looked at the piece of stone which stood revealed.

'It looks like a tombstone,' said Miriam at last. 'Part of one, anyhow.'

'That is precisely what it is.'

'But you said – '

'I said that the Iceni didn't go in for graves – right? – and, by extension, tombstones. Quite true. Yet we found this Roman-type stone immediately adjacent to the grove, to the Druid Holy of Holies. So what do you make of that?' Too eager to wait upon an answer: 'Read the engraving, for Christ's sake!'

Looking surprised at the man's vehemence, Miriam spelled it out. 'P–R–A–S–U–T–, then it's broken off. What is it – part of a name?'

'Part of a very particular name,' the archaeologist corrected her. 'If I'm right – and I'm bloody sure I am – what you are looking at is the tombstone of Prasutagus, Boudica's hubby, no less – the Romanized client-king whose death started all the trouble. This was the heartland of the Iceni, an obviously important shrine, and I can only surmise that the tombstone was a case of Boudica keeping up with the Jonesii, so to speak. Until, that is, she and the Romans fell out over the old man's will.'

'Would the Druids', Miriam wanted to know, 'have allowed him to be buried on their property in that alien Roman way?'

'As I said, they were politicians. They knew when to temper the wind to the shorn lamb. Besides which – ' the archaeologist's eyes brightened with glee at the 2,000-year-old deception – 'a tombstone, I said. Nothing more. There wasn't a sign of any bones. Who says the Druids actually buried the old fool under this imposing marker?' Abbott touched the incised letters with reverent fingers. 'Incredible workmanship. The depth they could go down to without loss of definition! And you see this beading round the edge? Very Roman, that. Geometrical. Celtic work is quite different.' Warming to his theme: 'You could almost have predicted the inevitable failure of Boudica's revolt from the Iceni style of decoration alone – very free and unregimented, in no way the style of a people programmed to face up to Roman discipline on the battlefield, to legionaries trained to stand their ground with a mob of howling dervishes bearing down on them, not moving a muscle until the geezers were within reach of their swords.'

Disapprovingly (back from her travels still the feminist, Jurnet noted; pleased even at this, at anything which predicated a Miriam unchanged from the one he knew and loved) Miriam said: 'It's easy to see whose side you're on.'

The archaeologist laughed and came down a peg or two.

'When you know me better – as I hope you may – you will know me for the free, untrammelled spirit I am, Iceni to the core! If I seem a bit above myself, it's only the effect of finding old Prazzy's calling-card; its craftsmanship, its cool recognition of the finality of death.' His chubby fingers stroked the stone lovingly. 'Credit where credit is due,' he proclaimed. 'In art as in war the Romans liked to know where they were.'

'Don't we all?' said Jurnet, wondering where he was with Miriam. 'And is it Boudica's tombstone you're hoping to turn up any minute now – his and hers?'

'Alas, no! The poor soul took poison after the final defeat, in the Midlands a long way from home.'

Miriam asked: 'Does anybody know what happened to her two daughters?'

'Silence. We should probably be thankful for it.' Abbott looked positively grief-stricken. You might have thought – Jurnet noted with a surge of liking for the plump little man – that it had all happened in the last few days, something Police Headquarters had unaccountably missed out on. 'All we know about those unhappy girls goes back to the time just before it all started. To when, after Daddy's death, the Roman officials who turned up to take possession of the kingdom in the Emperor's name took the girls to be part of their perks, along with the other goodies. To the Ancient Brits, for all we know, they may well have been the Princess Di and the Fergie of their day. To the Romans they were mere bits of barbarian skirt.' The man smiled, a little wanly. 'One thing, alas, archaeology teaches us – that there never was any such thing as a Golden Age, and it's no good deluding oneself that there ever was. Go forward or backwards in time, it makes no difference. You still find the old familiar bastards waiting to greet you.'

2

They decided that they did not, after all, fancy going to a restaurant for lunch – neither to the Norfolk Hero nor the renowned Swiss establishment a few miles down the coast. Both seemed crass, somehow, opposed to the memory of that black stripe – time's revenge – etched indelibly into the guts of the countryside. As they drove the small remaining distance down to the village Miriam put her hand on Jurnet's knee.

'We could buy some things,' she suggested. 'Have a picnic on the beach. There's bound to be a shop in the village.'

'Didn't Abbott mention something about a Co-op? Where the bimbo with the boobs worked?'

'We'll see.'

At the junction with the highway which, to left and right, followed the Norfolk coastline, a gated road immediately opposite led into a different country. Straight as a die between rows of poplars whose leaves glittered now green, now silver, as the warm breeze tumbled them, it crossed a vast tableland of marshy meadow where cows sat or moved about thoughtfully, heads down, as if pondering matters of moment. A lark sang out of a sky which was at the same time impossibly high and low enough, one could have sworn, to be within reach of an upstretched arm. In the distance a low ridge covered with Corsican pines cut off all view of the sea.

Whilst Jurnet awaited his moment for moving out of the side turning, a Volvo Estate drew in from the highway on to the tarmacked apron in front of the gate, long enough for driver and passengers to goggle at the tariff affixed to a noticeboard at the side before reversing with an outraged screech of brakes at the nerve of some people.

'Five pounds just to go on the beach!' Miriam exclaimed in her turn. 'That's a bit steep, isn't it?'

'Lord Lanthrop's an artful old codger. Says he needs the money to help pay for the upkeep of the road. He says no one's called on to shell out unless they want to – there's no shortage of beaches along this stretch of the coast which you can go on for free.' Jurnet turned the car right, towards the village. 'Wait till you see it. You'll think it's worth every last penny.'

The village shop had two worn steps leading up to the door and a bell that went *ping!* as they went in, out of the glare into a low-ceilinged gloom spiced with the odours of bread and apples, both slightly fermented; of paraffin and bundles of firewood.

A row was in progress.

'I tole you – I don't want no vanilla!' The speaker was a lanky youth, over six foot, Jurnet wouldn't have been surprised, but without the breadth of shoulder to go with the height. 'I can't stand vanilla! How many times I gotta ask fer raspberry ripple? You ought ter know me by now!'

'Oh, I know you all right, Timmy Chance!' The shopkeeper, a woman in her sixties with an old-fashioned look – hair parted in the middle and drawn back into a bun, short-sleeved handknit jumper, white pinafore, strong arms, one of them disfigured with enormous vaccination marks – sounded near the end of her patience. She favoured Jurnet and Miriam with a quick look, long enough to register them as foreigners who could be kept waiting. 'And how many times I got to tell you that asking's not the same thing as getting? Not my fault the man didn't have none on his van this week.'

'Why didn' he?' the boy demanded. His voice was high-pitched, the vowels blurred.

'Reckon he didn't know he had a customer like you to deal with, or he'd 'a known better!'

His eyes adjusted to the poor light, Jurnet looked at the boy more closely and with compassion. Neatly dressed, in jeans and a white T-shirt with a picture of Batman hanging in folds across his narrow chest, he still looked a scarecrow, a creature put together out of odds and ends that did not add up to a matched set. There was something not quite right about the way his arms joined on to his body, like a puppet strung together by apprentice hands that still had a lot to learn.

The boy fished in the front pocket of his jeans and brought out a £20 note which he slammed down on the wooden counter with conscious pride.

'In't my money good enough fer you?' he exclaimed. 'Plenty more where that came from.'

'You could put a million on 'em under my nose and still it won't buy you a raspberry ripple when I han't got none to sell. Put it away, you daft ha'porth, and let me get on serving this lady and gentleman you're keeping waiting.' When the boy pulled out another note, a £10 one this time: 'You don't stop pestering me, bor, I'm going to phone the ice-cream company that I'm stopping stocking raspberry ripple for good 'n all. Then let's see what you have to say!'

The boy's rejoinder was cut short by a further *ping!* from the doorbell. A woman, in her early thirties at a guess, came into the shop, her advent greeted by the storekeeper with a welcoming expression of relief.

'Mrs Milburn – thank goodness! I've got your order all made up – only p'raps you can get it into the head of this gowk here, I'm sure I can't, that I'm not hiding his blessed raspberry ripple under the counter; that the van jest didn't leave any off this week.'

Mrs Milburn was a slender woman whose face, elegantly boned, bore the traces of recent suffering. She did not, however, appear noticeably unhappy and her voice, when she spoke to the boy, was full of a merry cajolery.

'Stop badgering Mrs Cobbold, Timmy! It isn't her fault. Why not go along to the Co-op and see if they've got any there?'

'If I han't got none', Mrs Cobbold interposed with some satisfaction, 'the Co-op won't have none either. It's the one van does all the district, all the way to Sheringham.'

'They may still have some left over from last time,' Mrs Milburn pointed out reasonably. 'They can't all have customers like Timmy, crazy for raspberry ripple and won't take anything else under any circumstances. I tell you what – ' she turned to the boy. 'Put the order in the car for me and I'll give you a lift down there, or into Sheringham if they're out too – '

The boy had turned away from the counter as the bell sounded and, in such light as came through the door and the cluttered shop window, Jurnet was able to get a better look at him, at features which possessed not so much a patent unloveliness as a failed beauty. It was as if a hand poised on the point of turning out something fine and memorable had accidentally slipped, or a mould been removed before the wax had completely hardened, blurring contours, thickening the jawline, protruding the pale blue eyes behind thick pebble glasses which magnified them enormously.

His long face sullen, Timmy countered: 'What if they don't have none there either?'

'Then', Mrs Milburn said good-humouredly, 'we'll try Cromer – Angleby, London, Paris, Mars!' She laughed, looking suddenly years younger. 'Nowhere's too far to go for a raspberry ripple. There must be some left somewhere in the solar system.'

The boy did not seem unduly impressed with the offer.

'I like *her* cones,' he objected, jerking his head in the store-keeper's direction. 'They don't have cones like hers down at the Co-op.'

The other's expression of tender concern did not waver.

'I'm sure Mrs Cobbold will sell us one of her special cones without the ice-cream if you ask her nicely – won't you, Mrs Cobbold?'

'Have it on the house,' said Mrs Cobbold. 'Worth it to get him out of my hair.' Reaching towards the pile stacked like miniature clowns' hats at the end of the counter: 'Better take a few extra, case some get broken on the way to Mars.'

'Isn't that kind?' Mrs Milburn commented brightly, taking the proffered largesse. 'Say thank you to Mrs Cobbold, Timmy, for being so kind.'

After a moment of sulking, Timmy came out with an un-gracious 'Ta' which Mrs Cobbold did not bother to acknowledge. She brought a carton filled with groceries from behind the counter and plunked it at the boy's feet.

'Here you are, then! An' don't forget to pick up your money, or I won't answer for it later!'

When the two had gone, the boy staggering cackhandedly under the weight of the heavy box, Miriam stated their business.

'I don't stock no delicatessen.' The shopkeeper frowned as if she found the suggestion that she might indelicate. Then, soft-ened, as so many – those that were beyond the age of envy, anyhow – by the sight of her customer's glowing beauty, she added: 'I got some nice crusty rolls, though, fresh in this morn-ing. I could make you a couple of sandwiches.'

'Would you? That would be lovely!'

'Cheese? Or I got a nice piece of ham on the bone.'

Miriam turned to her companion, not so much as a smile showing; only a familiar imp of mischief dancing deep in her dark eyes.

'Which will you have, Ben?'

Which would he have! Jurnet heroically repressed the first stirrings of anger. All very well for her, Jewish born and bred, to break the ancient and immutable laws of *kashrut* if she had a mind to. Sin was one of the perks of the initiate; whereas he, working his painful passage to Judaism, had an Old Testament God looking over his shoulder twenty-four hours a day to see what he was up to and marking him accordingly. '*Judaism isn't only a pretty face,*' Rabbi Schnellman had warned when apprised of the detective's intention to convert, since Miriam refused to marry him unless he did. Never a truer word spoken! What kind of religion was it that took account of every morsel of food that passed your lips? Yet again – was it possible that he was getting the hang of it at last? – what a splendid one, too, in its cock-eyed way, the way *everything* mattered, nothing too small to come within its compass, not even a slice of cured pork – cured of what, for Christ's sake?

Was it another one of Miriam's tests?

'Cheese for me.'

Miriam said to Mrs Cobbold: 'We'll have two of each, please!' She giggled, her cheeks growing rosy beneath their golden tan. Could it be that, like Eve with the apple, she was planning some sexy temptation down on the beach, offering herself and a ham roll in one spectacular package, today's special?

Never, thought Jurnet, feeling the stirrings of desire within him, would the Garden of Eden be lost in a better cause.

Pulling himself together for the shop lady's benefit, Jurnet said the first thing that came into his head.

'Bit backward, is he, then?'

'Backward – who?' Mrs Cobbold paused in her buttering of rolls. 'Oh, you mean young Timmy! Wouldn't say that, not really. He's no Einstein, tha's certain, but he's certainly not backward in coming forward. I reckon he knows a thing or two in his own time, his own way. They do say it's wonderful what he's done in the garden up at Fastolfes.' She wiped her hands on a cloth, found some film to wrap the rolls in, and a carrier bag.

'You'll have to go to the Hero if you're wanting something stronger, but there's some Coke in the fridge – '

'Yes, please!' Miriam said. 'Could we have four cans? And four of those lovely-looking apples you've got by the door.'

The woman moved about her store unhurriedly, a pleasure to see, thought Jurnet, who entertained romantic notions about the country; though why, in that case, he had ever chosen to become a city copper, ever taken up with a quicksilver Jewish girl who alternately drove him mad with happiness and thwarted desire, he could not have begun to say. Packing the carrier bag, the shopkeeper reverted to her theme.

'Timmy Chance! Can you beat that for a name? About time he had one – a real proper chance in life. Him and his raspberry ripple!' She shook her head, half pleased for the boy's sake, half disapproving. 'That Mrs Milburn – going to Mars. I mean to say! She'll spoil him, but there! Good luck to him, I say!'

They waited at the gate until a man carrying a watering-can came from behind a little mock-Gothic lodge at one side.

'Coolin' off me marrows,' he explained, as one advancing an excuse of which nobody could reasonably complain. 'The weather this year, it's a full-time job, I don't have to tell you, not if you want to end up with something worth putting in fer the show.' Placing the can on the ground he handed over a ticket in return for the entrance fee. 'When I see you drive up I thought as I'd give you a bit o' time, in case you weren't serious. Marvellous how many come honking to be let in, an' by the time I've picked up me punch and me roll of tickets they've thought better of it. Can't say as I blame them.'

Jurnet said: 'They'll have missed a wonderful beach.'

'Oh ah.' The man swung the gate open, came back to the car. 'Good fer A-rabs,' he said, making it plain that, Lord Lanthrop or no Lord Lanthrop, he was his own man. 'Yesterday we had a camel train come over the dunes. I'm not havin' you on.'

The detective returned imperturbably: 'Nothing about Norfolk surprises me.'

The man laughed and picked up his watering-can.

'Toilet-paper commercial, actually. Have a nice day.'

There were three cars parked on the grass where the road ended, close by a wicket which opened on to a duckboarded path through the pines: a Rolls, a Porsche and a personalized Land Rover, cars that looked as if an admission fee of anything less than a fiver would be an affront to their dignity. When the two emerged from the aromatic shade of the trees on to the beach they could see the cars' owners and their respective retinues in the distance, three separate parties yet – in view of the sands stretching to infinity – ridiculously close together as if, when it came down to it, a little afraid of all that expensive emptiness.

Where the duckboard ended, the sand was as fine as sugar, welling up warm between Miriam's toes. Jurnet waited whilst she took off her sandals and put them in the pockets of her skirt.

Now that they had arrived he looked at her anxiously, wondering whether, after all, he had done well in making Lanthrop their destination, or whether he had just made one more of the spectacular cock-ups which seemed to bedevil their relationship. First archaeology, the thin crust of earth hiding baleful secrets, and now this God-almighty void of sky and sand to cut you further down to size. There were people, he knew, who said that Lanthrop beach was altogether too much of a good thing. By the time you had got yourself down to the water you were too bloody tired to go swimming, let alone face ploughing your way back.

Miriam compounded his unease by inquiring, albeit laughingly: 'What time does the next bus down to the sea go? No – ' cutting short his apology – 'don't say anything. It's marvellous.'

Unable to believe his good fortune, Jurnet became unaccustomedly fussy.

'If the sun's too hot for you we could picnic back under the trees – '

'No.' Miriam shook her head. She glanced back at the pines which, growing squat out of the sand, seemed to be leaning on their lowest branches as upon arboreal elbows, watching to see what the man and the woman would get up to. 'Too dark. Too dangerous.' She pointed out over the beach towards some low dunes which reared themselves like a circle of basking seals half-way between the pines and the water. In the centre of the circle, detached from its attendants, a loftier dune stood out against the sky.

'There,' Miriam said. 'That's our place.'

It was an island made for lovers. Scrambling up its side, the sand

25

sliding away from beneath their feet, they came to the top to discover that some mysterious force at work within the dune had left a summit which was, in effect, a gigantic egg-cup – a narrow rim of compacted sand sheltering a bowl where thrift and vetch and other small plants that thrived on salt air had spread a carpet springy as a mattress, and as inviting.

Nevertheless, the two sat and ate their rolls and their apples, drank their Cokes, with perfect propriety, keeping the real goodies for afters. The only out-of-the-way thing that happened was that Miriam opened her roll, took out the ham and tossed it away, over the rim of the depression and back into the world where observant Jews did not eat pig. Immediately, two blackheaded gulls who obviously had no such inhibition programmed into their genes by the Master of the Universe, came planing in from nowhere, scooped up the meat with triumphant cries and departed as swiftly and utterly as they had come.

Miriam shook out her bronze hair, threw back her head and laughed. A witch, Jurnet thought, his heart turning over with love. Even the birds of the air came to her bidding.

'Don't worry,' she said, biting into the crusty bread reft of its filling. 'I haven't suddenly become religious. Theologically speaking, the roll's just as *tref*, once it's had ham in it.'

'Then why did you do it?'

'It's too hot for meat. A belated sacrifice to the Druids. I don't know.'

Jurnet stood up, climbed a little way up the side of the bowl, far enough up to see the sea, a deceptively meek expanse sprinkled with glitter under the high summer sun like something gift-wrapped for Christmas. Distance lends enchantment, the detective thought, unimpressed. He had never trusted the sea further than he could see it – not as far as that.

Even so, it was less distant than the woman beside him, so near and yet so far, on another planet. His throat dry with tension he turned back to her and said: 'I don't know whether you've spoken to Rabbi Schnellman since you got back. In case you haven't, I have to tell you that I'm as far from being a Jew as I was on the day you flew out to Israel. That is to say, I've learned enough by now to put on a pretty good pretence. But that isn't what you want, is it?'

'No.'

'I know how you feel about marrying out. And about one day

going to live in Israel for good. I understand. I want you to know that.' Because finally it had to be said, even at the risk of losing her for ever, he said it: 'I don't want to come between you and your heart's desire.'

Miriam carefully folded the papers in which the rolls had been wrapped and returned them to the carrier bag together with the empty drink cans. Then calmly, without making a production of it, she pulled her white shirt over her head, unhooked her skirt and laid it neatly aside, removed her bra and panties before lying down on the flowery carpet, her legs spread wide in invitation. With the slightly exasperated affection of one instructing a rather backward child, she looked up at Jurnet and said: '*You* are my heart's desire. How many times do I have to tell you?'

They came together with a serious passion shot through with a glee that, in the end, had them rolling about the sward like puppies at play. Their laughter mingled with the gulls' cries, the thud of the distant breakers and the far-carrying whine of a Rolls or a Porsche child proclaiming that it was bored. An army jet, which crawled across the sky trailing a thin white line that slowly fluffed itself into swansdown, had them waving shamelessly to the pilot, the crew, to anybody else who might be up there, looking down.

When Jurnet finally attempted to stand, Miriam caught him by the ankle and brought him down again. The frail rim of the egg-cup fractured with the impact of their bodies and the two poured out of their secret place with the sand pouring down the side of the dune, all the way to the bottom, where they lay breathless and still embraced until Miriam, flinging her hair out of her eyes, felt it snag on something; whereupon she glanced carelessly over a naked shoulder and screamed.

Disturbed by the mini-avalanche, an arm stuck out of the sand; a brown, leathery arm that did not look human but could not be anything else. An arm ending in a hand that was flexed in a beckoning claw and had a nibbed look, one or two of the finger joints skeletal or missing. A hand that did not make clear whether it was signalling for help or merely gesturing 'Hi!' out of sheer good fellowship.

Either way it was dead.

Very.

3

PC Wyatt glowered. It was scarcely a politic face to put on in the presence of one of the big cheeses from Angleby but the hell with it. PC Wyatt was in no mood for *politesse*.

The Superintendent, elegant in spring suiting, seemed taken aback by his failure to charm away the hostility writ large on the broad face that in normal times, Jurnet guessed, was good-humoured and amenable, everything one could wish for in a village bobby. The great man's voice sharpened: what his subordinate privately termed his Queen Mum smile went into notable eclipse. Casting his eye coldly round the modest room which, up to that moment, had served the village's needs in the way of law and order more than adequately, he announced: 'That filing cabinet will need to be moved out. We'll be sending down our own, as well as two extra desks, a copier, some additional chairs and a table for the switchboard.' Looking about for some further focus of his displeasure, he ended: 'And, for goodness' sake, man, take those curtains down. We need all the light we can get.'

Plainly sceptical that any light on any subject was likely to be forthcoming from that quarter, the Superintendent abandoned the fuming Lanthrop constable and stalked across the room to where, with his own fair hands, he removed the net curtains which obscured the window, allowing them, rod and all, to fall to the floor. Jurnet, standing silently by, could not help feeling a little sorry that Mrs Wyatt, the large woman who had let them into the police house, her husband being not yet back from his round, had not been present to witness the little comedy. Superintendent or no Superintendent, she would have had something to say.

Jurnet himself, with his almost obsessive loyalty to Angleby, his own home patch, viewed the Lanthrop constable's ill humour with complete fellow feeling. He understood exactly the PC's reaction of outrage, which only marginally had anything to do with Superintendents who tore down your perfectly OK curtains. In Angleby, at least, a copper had to be prepared for nasty surprises: such things happened in cities. In Lanthrop, a few break-ins, a battered wife or two, a spot of incest, a couple of vandalized phone boxes and that was it, all the rich tapestry of rural life.

But murder – no!

Not that Jurnet was without a certain sympathy also for his superior officer who was now standing looking intently out of the window, his back revealing nothing but the expensiveness of his tailoring. By rights, if PC Wyatt were going to be angry with anybody, it should have been with him, Ben Jurnet, the twit who had to go sliding naked down sandhills that might otherwise have kept their secret until people in some future century, coming upon bones by then picked clean and anonymous long after PC Wyatt had gone to his reward in the police house in the sky, could, with luck, have taken them for just another of the Ancient Brits who littered that particular part of Norfolk like discarded crisp bags.

The recollection of that ecstatic roll downhill and its consequences left Jurnet embarrassed and readier than ever to believe in a God who, whatever His other characteristics, had a fine appreciation of the absurd. That the most transcendent moment of a guy's life should end in a clumsy scrambling into clothes to cover his nakedness, whilst a dead arm sticking out of the sand beckoned as peremptorily for his attention as a dowager hailing a taxicab, must have been good for a resounding belly-laugh up there.

And Miriam, by now safely back in her own pad in Angleby – what on earth could she be thinking? Still no suggestion that she transfer to his place, to the flat where the stairs smelled of slow-simmered underwear and the black plastic bags of rubbish stacked on the forecourt waited for a dustman who never came. Having, with her usual efficiency, elicited from Mrs Wyatt that a bus was shortly due en route to Sheringham, where it connected with a train to Angleby, and having made a statement chiefly remarkable for its discreet omissions, she had announced her intention of catching it. She had refused to let her lover accompany her to the bus stop.

For all his misery at the way their outing had ended, Jurnet could not repress a twinge of satisfaction that at last, in the most practical way possible, she too had been brought into contact with murder at first hand, an experience which, with luck, might bring her to an understanding of what it was that had made him a copper and, what was more to the point, had kept him one against all her urgings, reasoned and unreasonable, that he change his profession.

Some kind of understanding, anyway. It was too much to hope that she would comprehend the sudden change, as violent as plunging from top floor to basement in a runaway lift, from ecstasy to the angry grief which had possessed him; which invariably possessed him with every fresh introduction to a victim of terminal violence. Upright or evil, pillar of society or double-dyed villain – it made no difference. Buffoon that he was, Jurnet mourned them equally.

The police house, high on a bank above the coast road, looked across to the village church and the marsh beyond the low flint wall which enclosed God's acre; to the pines and a line of sea.

'I do believe there's a heron there, down by the dyke!' The Superintendent turned back to the room, a changed man. 'I don't know how you can bear to shut out such a wonderful view!'

'Oh ah,' mumbled PC Wyatt, not to be won over by pretty words.

'And thank goodness the churchwardens have had the sense not to mow the churchyard!' the other went on, enthusiasm unabated. 'All those poppies! I don't know when I last saw so many, and the gravestones just showing above the grasses – '

'That'll be Bill Gifford,' the village constable announced dourly. 'He gets relief off the gate for looking after the church grass, but he's too busy watering his marrows, I reckon.' The man bent over and with almost audible insult picked up the discarded curtains and draped them over a chair, in the process narrowly missing the Superintendent's nose with the protruding rod. He eyed with hatred the prospect that had earned the outlander's praise. Violated, the scowling brows proclaimed. Murder. Nothing ever the same again.

'An' if you want to know the reason she weren't on the Missing Persons list,' the constable went on as if they were, all three, in the middle of an accounting demanded of him personally, 'it's on account she weren't. Missing, that is. When a woman with a brand-new suitcase and done up to the nines stands waiting at the bus stop for the bus to come along, you can't hardly be surprised to find out she's gone off somewhere, any more than you'd call the Over-Sixties club missing once they've piled into the coach for their ten days in sunny Benidorm. Only surprise, being her, she took so long to go.' At the end of this speech, and as if recalled to reality by the sound of his own voice, belligerent and totally lacking in the deference due to those higher up the constabulary ladder, PC Wyatt rearranged his face with an effort and said, 'Sir.'

'That's all right,' returned the Superintendent, in the sincere mode that always made Jurnet want to spit. 'I quite understand how upsetting this must be for you, turning your snug little world upside down. We'll do our best – won't we, Inspector Jurnet? – not to get under your feet any more than we have to. I suppose the woman – what did you say her name was, Chance? – did in fact catch that bus?'

'Chance, sir. Annie Chance.' PC Wyatt – seduced, by the soft airs now prevailing, into a fairly convincing mock-up of a village bobby on the ball – confirmed with commendable promptness. Jurnet regarded his superior officer with a familiar mixture of dislike and admiring affection. A man in a million. Thank heaven there weren't more like him. 'She caught it all right. Mrs Cobbold at the shop saw her get on and the bus move off.'

'That's one thing settled, anyway. I understand there's a teenage boy, her son. Did he know his mother was going away?'

Jurnet put in quickly: 'The lad's a bit retarded, and we're talking about two, three months ago, remember. We'll have to go a bit gently. He hasn't been told yet that she's dead.' With an encouraging smile at the village constable: 'We wouldn't have known it ourselves if it hadn't been for PC Wyatt here. He was able to make a preliminary identification.'

A strangled noise came out of PC Wyatt's throat, followed by a harsh approximation of speech. 'Smoked like a kipper she were. But I'd 'a known her anywhere.'

'Very aptly put, from what Dr Colton's told me,' the Superintendent commented pleasantly. 'He puts it down to the combination of sea salt and the way the sand has been kept heated up over a long consecutive period during the exceptional spring we've been having this year.'

At a further inarticulate discordance from PC Wyatt Jurnet intervened to add: 'The PC says he's pretty sure the woman went to the local dentist. If so, and there are dental records we can get hold of, we shouldn't have to put the kid through the ordeal of having to say it is or it isn't his ma.'

Freckled and sandy, Detective Sergeant Jack Ellers came into the room looking as if he had been out in the sun with his bucket and spade – which, in a manner of speaking, he had.

'Not a sausage,' he announced. 'Unless you could call several mummified starfish, sevenpence in old money, and a carrier bag with four empty Coke tins in it evidence. I sent the lads home – hope that was OK, sir? Short of digging up the whole coastline there didn't seem anything more they could usefully do. As it is, that sandhill will never be the same again.'

'That ring o' dunes – ' PC Wyatt put in with a bleak local pride – 'wonder is it stays there at all. Every gale, every spring tide, shifts 'em about like they was stage scenery.'

'Glad to hear it. I was beginning to be afraid we'd be run in for destroying part of our national heritage. Sorry, though, in a way, to be done with it.' The irrepressible Ellers addressed himself to the Superintendent, secure in his role of court jester. 'Gave me quite a buzz, going through that £5 gate for nothing. You should've seen the look that bloke at the lodge gave me every time he had to stop whatever he was doing, come and open up, and nothing to show for it.'

For the first time since making Jurnet's acquaintance the village constable actually smiled, and the detective laid a mental bet that the keeper of the £5 road – Gifford, didn't he say his name was? – was not the only marrow-grower in Lanthrop with designs on the cup at the village show. It was, in all probability, the man's first smile since Miriam, turning down the suggestion that she be the one to stay keeping the dead arm company, had fled back through the pines to the car as if the wolves were after her, and then scorched down the road between the poplars to report their find to the proper quarter. Poor girl! Jurnet could imagine her feelings as she waited for the Gifford bloke to put down his watering-can and come and open up the gate to let the Rover out; imagine, too, the gatekeeper's sharp-eyed curiosity that two should have gone down to the beach and only one returned. What on earth must he have thought when a dishevelled young woman, in a visible state of agitation, had asked to be directed to the nearest police station?

The fellow, according to Miriam's later report, had made his thought crystal clear.

'Tried to take advantage, did he? Thought meself, when you come through, wha's a nice girl like you doing with a slippery customer like that?'

Bless the bugger for his kind words! As Miriam had told it, they had made her feel better, actually made her laugh.

Obeying Jurnet's injunction to discretion, she had let fall nothing as to the reason for her inquiry. By the time she had returned with PC Wyatt actually in tow the gatekeeper's curiosity had got the better of him and he had asked point-blank for a lift to where the action was, a request turned down by the village policeman with a gusto which had seemed to have in it something personal.

'This Annie Chance – ' the Superintendent inquired with deceptive simplicity – 'how would you describe her?'

PC Wyatt thought about it a long time.

'Unlucky,' he pronounced at last.

'Go on,' the Superintendent urged encouragingly when no further particulars were forthcoming. 'Unlucky in what way?'

'Every way.' After an even more extended pause for reflection: 'Not just her hubby doing a bunk – before my time, that was, but he weren't much cop, from what I hear. Not just her being stuck with that Timmy, having to bring him up on her own. Mainly because she was the kind of woman she was.'

PC Wyatt regarded his visitors from the city with something of defiance in his face, as if refuting an accusation which, though it had not actually been made, hung about in the air just out of earshot.

'We've got a good place here,' he went on, settling into his stride. 'A proper community spirit, people who care for one another. Nobody in Lanthrop kicks the bucket with the milk bottles piling up on the doorstep before anyone thinks to ask is anything up. But Annie Chance now, she wouldn't be helped no way, not by anyone. If she passed you in the street and gave you a good morning you'd wonder whether she weren't sickening for something, that's the kind she was. Folk wanted to be friendly but she wouldn't have none of it.'

'There are people like that.' The Superintendent nodded understandingly. 'She sounds a rather pathetic creature.'

'Pathetic!' PC Wyatt looked astonished that the woman he had called up from the dead at official bidding could be so misinterpreted. 'Nothing pathetic about Annie Chance. You only had to look at her –' The man faltered, either coming to the end of his descriptive powers or perhaps, like Jurnet, waiting in watchful silence, reminded of his most recent view of Annie Chance emerging kippered from the dune, the shining sand falling away and the myriad small crawling things that had enjoyed her unwitting hospitality during the long concealment dropping off reluctantly, the party over.

'Made any enemies in the village, had she?' the Superintendent wanted to know.

An expression of alarm overspread the PC's broad face.

'She got on the bus with her suitcase,' he reminded his superior officer. 'Mrs Cobbold at the shop saw her alive and kicking. Not our fault if someone chooses to bring her back here and dump her dead on the beach.' His features and feelings under control with an effort, he went on: 'She weren't popular in the village and that's a fact, but tha's not the same things as enemies. Too prickly, too proud, though what she had to be proud about heaven only knows. Still and all, you can't love someone as won't be loved, can you?'

The Superintendent's response to this somewhat debatable proposition was: 'What about the child? What kind of relationship did he have with his mother?'

'Eighteen and a six-footer – not a child any longer. She always kept him clean, fed him proper so far as one can tell, got him into a special school where they did the best they could with the brains they had to work with, which were, and are, on the skimpy side, poor kid. She did her duty. The other side of the picture – everyone will tell you the same, it's no secret – she was a sight too free with her hands where Timmy was concerned, only too ready, big as he was, to give him a clout no matter who might be watching. Hardly a week when somebody didn't come up to me, wanting me to do something about it.'

'And did you?'

'Nothing much I could, was there, sir? I spoke to her a couple of times, for all the good it did. No good threatening her with the NSPCC. Once Timmy was out of school and come to man's estate in a manner of speaking, it come under the heading of a domestic dispute – an' I don't have to tell you, sir, we're told to stay out of those if we possibly can, especially in a case where the victim of the alleged assault isn't complaining. Annie was a tough bird but she weren't more than five-four, five-five at the most. Against a six-footer, even a six-foot weed like Timmy, all height, no muscle, she wouldn't have stood a dog's chance if the worm had turned and he'd gone for her, which he never did. The way I figure it – ' PC Wyatt's good-natured face screwed itself up with earnestness – 'you're better off in this country properly daft than being only a few degrees off kilter, so to speak. Tha's where young Timmy falls – betwixt and between, so nobody done anything, to help either him or his ma. I used to say to myself, "One day she'll go too far an' then the fur will fly!"'

The Superintendent asked gently: 'Are you suggesting the boy could have killed her?'

'The opposite!' The Lanthrop constable looked hard at the big bugs from Angleby and – perhaps foolhardily – decided to give them his trust. 'I won't deny there haven't been times, when I seen the lad out with a swollen ear or a face that looked like it'd been through the mangle, that a bit of fur-flying weren't something I was looking forward to. Except I knew it'd never happen.'

'What made you so sure?'

'I met him out on the Green one time. He had an eye you could light the street with. I asked him why he didn't hit her back.' PC Wyatt blushed for this breach of the Police Code but did not look as if he regretted having committed it. 'He looked at me like I'd said something totally barmy. "It's me ma," he answered, like he was teaching me my ABC's. "She got her rights."'

Jurnet said: 'You mentioned before you weren't surprised to hear Annie Chance had taken herself off, only that she had taken so long to do it. What made you say that?'

'Like I said. She weren't happy, one look at her'd tell you that. No friends, stuck in that dump at the back of nowhere, nothing but hard graft and that idiot boy for company, and her still young, a good-looking woman – you wouldn't have known, only having seen – ' A breaking off was followed by a conscious squaring of the shoulders, a police officer on duty. 'Not what you'd call pretty, but there was something about her. Something that made you look twice.' PC Wyatt went bright red before blundering on. 'There'd have been plenty in the village interested, I can tell you as a fact, if it hadn't meant taking on the son along with her.'

'So you thought that, what with one thing and the other, she might well have lit out at any time, looking for a better life and abandoning the boy?'

'I thought it possible,' the other agreed. 'Like I said, she looked after Timmy's physical needs OK, but the way she knocked him about I couldn't see how there could be much love involved. And then, once he was grown an' Mrs Milburn took him on as gardener, meaning at last he was able to make his own way, daft as he was – well, I admit I sometimes wondered to myself, what's keeping you?'

'Did you never see her in the company of somebody, some man with whom, so far as you could judge, she seemed to be on special terms?'

'Never saw her in the company of nobody. But of course, she could easily have picked up a bloke at the Caff, and no one in Lanthrop any the wiser.'

'The Caff?'

'That's its name. Meant to be a joke, I suppose. The Caff, out on the bypass. Does the best fish an' chips in the county. Annie worked for Mrs Milburn mornings – most mornings anyway, far as I know. Evenings and weekends she worked at the Caff – caught the bus at the stop outside the shop regular as clockwork. Respectable enough place – leastways, we've never had any reason to think different. But all those reps and lorry-drivers coming and going, I reckon there'd be plenty of opportunities.'

The Superintendent had been studying the landscape again.

'Two people just came round from the back of the church,' he announced, turning back to the room and cutting across the conversation with practised privilege. 'Where did they come from? Is there a path or a road back there?'

'Footpath, sir.' PC Wyatt moved to the window and pointed. 'Runs from the churchyard over the marsh and comes out in the pines near the end of Lord Lanthrop's duckboard.'

'Ah. And is there – apart, of course, from following the shore-line – any other way down to the beach in addition to it and the £5 road?'

'There's Baynard's Lane.' The village policeman's tone, Jurnet noticed, had become reluctant, defensive. 'Begins down the road a bit, a little before the Green. It's that bunged up with brambles these days you have to look twice to find it. It's Lord Lanthrop's land and he's given up getting the hedges trimmed. The Parish Council's been on to him, but a Lord – you know how it is. They know how to get away with murder.' Unaware that he had said anything out of order: 'I reckon he's not keen to advertise there's a way of getting to the sea which don't cost nothing.' The man added, elaborately casual: 'Comes out at the side of Annie Chance's house, as a matter of fact.'

'Does it indeed?'

Jurnet asked: 'Which way do the locals use?'

'Footpath mostly, far as they use any way at all. His Lordship lets anyone who lives in the parish go on his road for free, but even so there aren't all that many takers. Half the mums are working, they don't have time to take the kids down to the sands to play, an' if they did, it's my observation, the kids today don't want to go. They'd rather sit home and look at a beach on the telly.' After a moment of glum reflection on the changed values of the time, the PC went on: 'Some of the older lads used to go swimming, till two of 'em drowned, couple of years ago. That put them off, good and proper. Lord Lanthrop had any number of notices put up about dangerous currents, but they all got broken and he's given up, I don't blame him.' He added without a smile: 'Fortunately, it's only strangers dip so much as a toe in the water down there these days.'

4

When, at his own insistence, Timmy had gone back to the strip of woodland whence he had been fetched by the bell his employer kept for summoning him back to the house, Jurnet turned to Hannah Milburn and voiced his thanks.

'I don't know how I could have got it over to him without your help.'

Mrs Milburn looked pale but composed.

'*Have* we got it over to him? I'm not sure. We won't know for certain until Wednesday.'

The detective did not disguise his bafflement.

'I'm not with you.'

'His mother used to work for me four mornings a week – Mondays, Tuesdays, Thursdays and Fridays. Wednesday mornings – as well as other times I'm not sure about, but I expect you know all about those – she worked at the Caff on the bypass. Every Wednesday, so far as I've been able to gather, she brought home fish and chips for Timmy's lunch – dinner, I should say: that's what he calls it. It was obviously the gastronomic high spot of the week. The point is – ' the well-bred voice, the kind that, much as he fought against the reaction, recognizing it for the inverted snobbery it was, always brought out the oick in Jurnet, became blurred at the edges, accessible – 'that ever since Annie left and Timmy came to work here full time I've been giving him his meals, naturally. Somebody had to see he ate properly.' With a little laugh that imperfectly concealed immense self-satisfaction: 'He seems to approve of my cooking. At any rate, he never leaves a thing on his plate. Except on Wednesdays. On Wednesdays, the minute it's one o'clock, he's off down the drive, haring back home for the fish-and-chip dinner that never comes. The first time it happened – that would be the week after Annie left –

38

when half-past three came and he still hadn't got back, I drove down to their house to see what could possibly have happened.'

Her blue eyes suspiciously bright, the woman went on: 'I found him sitting at the kitchen table, the cutlery laid out ready, a bib – can you believe it? – tied round his neck, and a large plastic mat in front of him with a picture of Little Bo-Peep and her lamb on it. He said he was waiting for his ma to bring his fish and chips. Getting him to come back with me in the car wasn't easy, I can tell you.'

After a pause heavy with the weight of recollection: 'And that's how it's been every Wednesday since. He talks quite cheerfully of his mother being away; yet once a week, there he is, with his bib on and his Little Bo-Peep mat in front of him, waiting. The only difference since that first time is that he's always back promptly at two-thirty and always refuses the food I take care to have ready for him. He tells me in no uncertain terms that it's time I knew Wednesday was his fish-and-chips day.'

By now – as if the recital had of itself relieved hidden tensions – Hannah Milburn was looking happier; a woman painted in water-colours whom Jurnet could easily have considered beautiful in the English understated way if his taste had not been locked on for ever to the vibrant colours, the dramatic contrasts, the dangers of Miriam. Her reception of the news of her cleaning lady's murder was everything you could have expected of such a woman – dismay, sadness, but nothing fussy: everything under control, a matter of manners.

'Once', she continued, 'I drove over to the Caff and bought some fish and chips myself and had it waiting for him when he returned, but he wouldn't touch it. Said the only good fish-and-chip dinners were the ones his ma brought home. So – ' smoothing down her denim skirt with hands that looked harder and more powerful than, judging from her face, the detective would have expected – 'the question is, will he accept that his mother is dead any more than he accepts that she's gone off, not on some mysterious holiday, but gone for good?'

'What do *you* think? You know the boy better than I do.'

'Not well enough.' Hannah Milburn shook her head. 'Not nearly well enough. Timmy constantly astonishes me.'

'He didn't cry, I noticed. His face hardly changed. Unless – ' Hesitating, he hardly knew why – it wasn't her child, for Christ's

sake – Jurnet finished: 'Unless it's that retarded people sometimes have a limited range of facial expressions.'

'Not Timmy, I assure you!' The maternally defensive tone was
unmistakable. 'I'm glad you used the word "retarded". It means
"held back", doesn't it? A sleeping intelligence, not one that isn't
there at all.'

Hoping to put things right between them, Jurnet observed:
'From the little I've heard about Annie Chance so far it wouldn't
have surprised me to see a great grin of relief. She doesn't appear
to have been everyone's idea of a loving mum.'

'Not relevant,' the woman returned briskly. 'Loving's
something you do, not something that's done to you. Timmy
loved – loves – his mother. My guess is he can't imagine anyone
he loves dying on him and, unlike the rest of us, he has the sense
not to try to imagine it.'

She leaned forward in her chintz-covered chair and poured
coffee for the detective out of the silver pot which, with its
attendant china, waited on the low table in front of her. Acutely
aware of why he was there in the lovely room full of books and
flowers, among furniture which simultaneously conferred grace
and dismissed him as unworthy to be reflected in its honeyed
mahogany, Jurnet accepted the delicately patterned cup and
saucer with an inward guilt. What had that leathery paw poking
out of the sand and demanding justice to do with this genteel
tinkling of teaspoons?

And where the hell had Mrs Hannah Milburn got her cock-
eyed idea of love?

He enquired with circumspection: 'Mrs Chance was here as
usual, I take it, on the Tuesday, the day before she took herself
off? Did she say anything to indicate that this was to be the last
time she'd be working for you? Or was it, to all appearances, a
day like any other?'

'She said nothing at all.' Mrs Milburn put down her own cup
and saucer and stood up, the light from the wide french window
turning her pale hair into spun gold and surprising an unsus-
pected sensuality in her small-breasted body. 'And, since you
ask, it was a day like no other that ever was.'

'In case somebody hasn't told you already,' Hannah Milburn
said, 'eighteen months ago my husband and my five-year-old
daughter Katie were killed in a car crash.' Putting up a hand as if

40

physically to ward off what she feared was coming: 'No com-miserations, please! I only mention it at all to explain why, on that Tuesday you're asking about, I woke up as I had woken up every morning since it happened – breathing, getting through the day quite efficiently, but not really alive. And then, half-way through the morning, I went outside and found Timmy in the pond.'

'Fallen in, you mean? Or having a paddle?'

'Neither. Sitting there in the water, near the edge where it's quite shallow but very muddy on account of the waterlilies, with all his clothes on. I suppose I ought to mention that once he was finished with school Annie had begun bringing him to work with her, and I'd begun giving him little jobs to do in the garden, to keep him out of her way as much as anything whilst she was getting on with the cleaning. I paid him, of course, for what he did – not much, but something – and, foolishly as it turned out, I always gave the money to Annie instead of to him directly. It was very imperceptive of me – but there! Well, on that Tuesday morning he'd been pegging down runners in the strawberry bed and he said it was bloody hot up there, which it was, and he'd got himself into the pond to cool off. He'd broken off one of the waterlilies, *Nymphaea Gladstoniana* – ' Hannah Milburn burst into young laughter – 'Can you imagine naming a waterlily after Mr Gladstone of all people! Enormous white flowers with curved petals – I'd never known them out so early in the year – and he'd set one of them on his head to act as a sun hat. Ordinarily I wouldn't have been a bit pleased to find someone picking the waterlilies, but Timmy looked up at me so full of himself – '

The woman broke off and seemed to be considering several alternative scenarios. She finally settled for: 'I don't know whether you noticed the pond as you came up the drive? It's rather hidden by the way the land drops away from the terrace. Take a look at it when you leave. It's rather beautiful, even though most of the primulas are over now.' As if aware that horticultural notes were not what was called for, Hannah Milburn fell silent. At last she said with a small sound of impatience, 'It's so difficult to explain. After what I said about that Tuesday being special you'll be expecting something spectacular. But things that change your life, I've discovered, don't have to be showy or dramatic. They can be so small that, when you look back at them afterwards, it seems incredible such little things could have such colossal consequences.'

41

After another pause, Jurnet waiting with a quiet polished by long practice, she began again.

'Do you know *The Snow Queen*, one of Hans Andersen's fairy stories? I'd just begun to read it to Katie when –' Another silence, another fresh beginning. 'In it there's a boy called Kay who has a piece of ice in his heart. He's been kidnapped by the Snow Queen and taken to her palace among the snows, where his friend, a little girl named Gerda, finally comes looking for him. At first, because of the ice in his heart, Kay doesn't even recognize her, doesn't remember anything about his former life – but then Gerda starts to cry and her tears melt the ice so that he regains the ability to love, to come alive again.'

Hannah Milburn sat down again. Her face was wet with tears.

'The ice had melted,' she repeated. 'Don't ask me why, but that's what happened when I looked down at Timmy in the pond, laughing up at me, the waterlily hat on his head. He looked beautiful – can you believe that? Timmy! It was as if someone or something, all at once, had completed that unfinished face of his, drawn in the lines whose absence ordinarily makes him look sullen and loutish. And more than his face, suddenly his spirit was there, present and visible – and who had ever thought of Timmy and spirit in the same breath? But there it was, shining out of him.' The woman stopped, put both hands up to cheeks which had become brightly red. 'How I do go on! You'll think me completely cracked.'

'I'll think nothing of the sort.'

She looked at the detective as if it was the first time she had taken proper note of the tall, lean figure with the dark good looks that, to their owner's annoyance, had earned him – back at Headquarters and carefully out of his hearing – the nickname of Valentino.

'Are all policemen as kind as you?' Hannah Milburn smiled briefly: sombre as she added, 'And just then Annie came out to tell me somebody was on the phone, and she saw him. She was furious. Her whole body stiffened. I hate to think what she might have done if I hadn't been there. As it was, I didn't give a lot for Timmy's chances once she got him home.'

Going slowly and carefully as if to make sure nothing was left out: 'I was feeling pretty dazed myself, you understand, trying to take in what had happened, what was still happening to me. Still, I did my best for the boy as Annie got hold of him by one of those spidery arms of his that look as if one strong tug would be enough to yank them off his body for good. I tried to make a joke of it, something about mud baths being good for the complexion, but it definitely wasn't the climate for jokes. By the time Timmy was upright again, muddy water cascading off him and strands of Canadian pondweed festooning his sodden jeans and T-shirt, he looked more like some mythical monster risen out of the primeval slime than a child who had just been having a bit of fun. He looked awful. Beauty, spirit? I must have been dreaming. Yet I knew that, whatever what had happened down by the pond might have meant for him, for me it wasn't something that was going to wear off. The ice had melted and life was no longer a dreary drag from bedtime to bedtime, but something to be lived again the way it deserved.

'I told Annie to take the boy indoors and clean him up while I went upstairs to find some fresh clothes for him to put on, but she would have none of it.

'"He's not coming into the house in that state!" she shouted. The garage hose would have to do, and if he didn't like it he could lump it. I left her stripping off his wet jeans – tearing them off would be nearer the mark – went indoors and upstairs where I took a large bath towel out of the linen cupboard on the landing. Then I went along to Alan's dressing-room to see what I could find.'

'In case you didn't know,' Hannah Milburn said, 'Alan was my husband, and I've just said something absolutely momentous.' Carefully she repeated herself: 'I went along to Alan's dressing-room to see what I could find. I went to his cupboards and his wardrobe that I hadn't opened for eighteen months, though I knew I should have. He'd had lovely clothes, and Oxfam or somebody could have made good use of them. I'd talked myself, almost, into believing that by ignoring their very existence they would in time – either with the help of some friendly moths or simply under the compulsion of my wishing it to happen – self-destruct, so that, when at last I felt strong enough to slide back the doors, I'd find nothing on the other side except some little hillocks of dust that could be got rid of with the vacuum cleaner. If only I'd had the strength I'd have done with Alan's things what I did with Katie's, after the funeral – made a bonfire up in the kitchen garden and burned everything; everything even down to Tiddler, the teddy bear she'd promised to cherish until the end of the world.'

Into the silence Jurnet ventured: 'But then you wouldn't have had any clothes to offer Timmy.'

'Nor I wouldn't!' Mrs Milburn agreed gaily. 'You see how things turn out for the best! And do you know – it was amazing – everything in Alan's cupboards was as fresh as if it had been put away that morning. I took out some jeans and a belt to keep them up – Alan had been about the same height as Timmy, but he was a big man, powerfully built. Without a belt they'd have been round Timmy's ankles in no time. And I found a matelot's shirt with wide blue and white stripes that Alan and I had bought for a lark in a street market in Marseilles. Alan had loved it, and I knew Timmy would too.

'In the hanging section of the closet there was a beige gaberdine blouson, a short jacket, fitted to the hips, which Alan had brought back from a business trip to Paris only a week before his death, and I took that too. That certainly hadn't come from any street market. It had a famous name embroidered on the breast pocket and Alan had only had time to wear it once.'

'Timmy must have been pleased,' Jurnet said.

'Annie certainly wasn't. When I got back she was still hosing him down. It seemed to make her even more angry that he was obviously enjoying himself, making a game of what was meant to be a punishment. Early as it was in the year, it was really hot. The sun was making rainbows in the spray and he was dancing about, having a wonderful time. He was so skinny though, so odd-looking, so inadequate sexually – ' she came out with it forthrightly – 'you couldn't help noticing it. There was hardly anything there. It was pitiful. Not that Annie seemed to see anything about him to be sorry about. She swivelled the nozzle on the hose so that the water hit him hard. He cried out, "Ow!" and Annie shouted, "I'll ow you!" I could have killed her – oh!' Putting a hand to her mouth. 'I shouldn't have said that!'

'Don't let it worry you.'

'She took the clothes from me grudgingly and said she'd bring them back with her when she came on Thursday. When I said I didn't want them back, that Timmy was welcome to keep them, she didn't seem at all pleased or grateful: not that I wanted gratitude. "You're never going to waste clothes like that on the likes of him!" That's what she said. She seemed especially taken aback by the French jacket, which she didn't want Timmy even to try on, only he pulled it away from her and shrugged himself into it, and then went prancing about in circles on the forecourt, very proud of himself.

'And do you know?' Hannah Milburn laughed, the young laugh again. 'He really did look splendid. Alan's clothes were much too big for him, of course, but in a funny kind of way they seemed to confer on him some of Alan's own bulk and breadth. Though even that – ' The woman broke off and regarded the detective with an amused questioning.

'How on earth do you policemen ever know if people are leading you up the garden path or not – I don't mean about things they deliberately want to cover up, but quite innocently? I mean, when Annie and Timmy were going home at last, down the drive, they met Paul Abbott coming up. He's in charge of the dig down in the paddock and he was the one who had made the phone call Annie had come outside to tell me about in the first place. Of course we had both forgotten all about it, and Paul – he's a good friend but he worries too much – ' Mrs Milburn interposed with a dismissive good humour which made Jurnet turn a mental thumbs-down on the archaeologist's chances in that direction – 'he'd come up to the house to make sure nothing was the matter. He told me he'd passed Timmy and Annie on the way and that Timmy had looked like a clown in clothes that were miles too big for him. So there you are – a clown and splendid! Which of the two of us was right?'

'Both,' Jurnet returned without having to think twice about it. 'Eye of the beholder. Which brings me on to – Taking into account what you've told me, how did you yourself, personally, view Annie Chance?'

'That was another funny thing. After Paul had said he thought Timmy looked like a clown he went on to say that Annie was looking very handsome.'

'How was that funny? You didn't agree?'

Hannah Milburn knit her brows.

'I honestly don't know. If anybody had asked me out of the blue about Annie Chance's looks I suppose I would have said without thinking that she was plain, the way her cheekbones stood out, very prominent – but I don't know.' The woman looked at Jurnet, explanatory but not apologetic. 'A class thing, I suppose you could call it. Deplorable, but there it is. I don't suppose I ever took a really close look at her. What interested me was that she was a good worker, she didn't break things and above all she didn't, like some of the other women I've had in from the village, go in for chat. When she first came to work here – ' making the past sound infinitely remote – 'I wasn't the idle butterfly you see now. As well as being a wife and mother I had built up quite a connection as a freelance translator and it was good to have someone about the house with whom you weren't expected to sit down over gossipy cups of tea. I was sorry for her, I knew there was a backward son and I sensed that she was fit for something better than being a charwoman – but all in a distant way, I have to say. That was how the world was.'

'And after the world changed?' Jurnet prompted gently. 'After the accident, what then? Did that change the way you saw Annie Chance?'

Hannah Milburn said: 'It changed everything, so I suppose it must have. I still couldn't have told you if she was plain or handsome. I hated the way she used to hit Timmy, though I never said anything. I told myself that was how it was with the working classes. They bashed each other: it was part of their culture. What a snob you must think me! And I have to say Timmy seemed to adore his mother despite, as it seemed to me, being forever poised to flinch away from a clout on the ear or a smack on the hand.'

Jurnet watched as the woman narrowed her eyes in concentration upon a far-off object, one difficult to bring into focus.

'Stubborn or stoical? I don't know which of the two words would best describe her – I suppose it would depend on whether or not you wanted to be kind – but it was that which made her look plain, I think: her utter lack of softness, her refusal to respond to softness in others. She, as they say, kept herself to herself. I remember being very surprised when once, out of the blue, she came out with the fact that she'd been not quite sixteen when she became pregnant with Timmy. Surprised on two counts – first that it meant she was still only in her thirties and I'd taken her for much older, and secondly because it was completely out of character for her to give away any smallest detail of her personal life. I must confess, until I saw where she lived, which wasn't until after she'd gone, I used to think to myself sometimes: "Surely you can manage to put a smile on, once in a while!" After

I'd seen it – actually seen for myself the contrast between Fastolfes and the place she'd called home – I felt ashamed.'

'I've seen it too,' Jurnet said.

'Cor!' Jack Ellers had exclaimed, at his first sight of Annie Chance's home sweet home. 'Remind me to book up for my hols!'

Her house was built a little apart from the rest of the village, one of a pair of what, from the look of them, could once have been coastguard cottages, its mirror image deserted and derelict. Taking PC Wyatt's advice to avoid Baynard's Lane if they hoped to reach their destination with some paintwork still left on the car, the two police officers had driven there by way of a village green that was flanked by a smithy, a barn and assorted sheds, all tastefully converted into antique shops stocked with goods with which Jurnet, himself a candidate for conversion, felt an instant shaming rapport. There were old bread troughs converted into log baskets, oil lamps converted to electricity, copper warming pans converted to doo-dads to hang on the wall, all of them presided over by olde English craftsmen and craftswomen whose traditional skill at converting dollars, Deutsch marks and yen into tax-avoidable profit was something to marvel at.

After the sham of it and the deadly artifice of the village street into which they turned, its nattiness of brick-and-flint cottages proclaiming themselves as weekend toys, it was almost a relief to veer left at the end of the metalled road on to a dusty track which ended in an area that was part marsh, part scrub, and part unofficial refuse tip, its single architectural feature some stacks of crumbling bricks covered with flapping polythene and presumably marking the spot where the Council had planned to build some houses and then – bully for them – thought better of it. Incredible that, a bare half-mile along the coast, Lord Lanthrop's road marched between poplars to the most beautiful beach in East Anglia.

To the beach and to the sea. The sea, at least, was one thing the two locations shared in common, though even in this there were differences. On Lord Lanthrop's beach the sea murmured, deferential, knowing its place. At Annie Chance's – either because the sands were narrower at that point or because there were no insulating pines – it growled, bad-tempered like the murdered woman who, still young and passionate, had been doomed to

47

live there listening to its incessant complaining, with only a backward boy and the village's disapproval for company.

'At least', commented Sergeant Ellers, picking up his superior officer's mood with the deftness and delicacy which made them such a good team, 'she ended up in a better class of place.'

'She hasn't ended up anywhere as yet,' Jurnet objected, his mind on the stainless-steel drawer which, pending the inquest, was giving house-room to Annie Chance's kippered body. 'Lanthrop churchyard it'll be finally, I suppose. Ironic, when all she wanted was to kiss the place goodbye.'

Gathering seed-heads on their trouser legs, the two pushed through a tangle of weed that might once have been a garden and – as PC Wyatt had prophesied – found the back door unlocked.

'Whenever I mentioned it to her,' the constable had reported, 'which I did, off and on, she always said leaving it open was simpler than tying a key round Timmy's neck and relying on him not to lose it, and there was nothing in the house worth taking anyway.' PC Wyatt had added awkwardly: 'I told her it weren't only that. A woman on her own, you couldn't count on Timmy ... someone might get in. She give me one of her looks an' said: "Chance'd be a fine thing."'

It was, thought Jurnet, the most depressing place he had ever been in – not because there was indeed nothing worth taking and little enough of that, but because it was so god-awful clean. That anyone should have seen fit to throw away the time and the energy needed to render those splintered floors so bone-white, to wash the walls till they flaked like acid rain, turn the mean windowpanes into twinkling crystal, was not only an insult to human intelligence but to the God who had surely put man on earth for some higher purpose, otherwise why bother.

'PC Wyatt says she was always mad about having things just so, but nothing like this. He says it's Timmy's doing. The lad's afraid when his ma gets back she'll dot him one for letting the place go to the dogs while she's been away.'

'The poor sod!'

One thing was for sure: there was nothing in the house which by any stretch of the imagination could be called evidence. Their total haul of the few drawers in the place consisted of several receipted coal bills folded away neatly in the kitchen table. Apart from them, the only paper in the place consisted of a small pile of *The Times* brought home, at a guess, from Fastolfes for more practical purposes than reading. In the living-room someone had filled in the grate with a fan of pleated newspaper, its edges folded with military precision. Jurnet bent over to look at the date. 25 June: Timmy's work. By then his ma had been gone for weeks.

There were a few clothes in the boy's bedroom, none in his mother's; nothing of any kind except for a pile of impoverished-looking bedclothes lying neatly folded on the striped ticking which covered the mattress. But out at the back, among the grasses, they found a blackened patch not yet quite grown over, where Annie Chance must have disposed of as much of her past life as was not needed on voyage. They found a charred bra strap and a half-burned snapshot of a man who might, conceivably, have been Timmy's father.

Jurnet looked down at the black patch and was reminded of that other blackness up on the hill in Mrs Milburn's paddock where the Romans had got their own back on the Druids. The flame was all: once you put a match to them there wasn't much to choose between sacred oaks and discarded bras. Both, in the context, equalled anger, therefore they equalled each other. There was a name for a proposition like that if only he could remember it from the night-school course in logic he had once embarked upon with high hopes and abandoned in despair upon discovering how little its classroom dialectic corresponded with the real world.

He doubted whether Annie Chance would have remembered either.

5

'So – ' Jurnet summed up – 'Timmy and his mother left for home, and that was the last you ever saw of Annie Chance?'

'The last I *saw* of her,' replied Mrs Milburn. 'Not the last I heard – that is, assuming you want to hear the rest of it.' She looked at the detective with an air of amused apology. 'It's Annie you're interested in, and here I keep getting myself into the act. Sorry!'

'I want to hear everything you want to tell me.'

'*Want* to tell?' Head a little to one side, Hannah Milburn studied her visitor's face with a friendly curiosity. 'It must be the work you do that gives you such insights into what people are really feeling – to realize that, for all the awfulness, I welcome the opportunity actually to speak about that wonderful day.'

'Wonderful because it was the day you came to terms with your bereavement?'

'You've got it wrong, after all.' The other shook her head in disappointment. 'Wonderful because it was the day I came to terms with the impossibility of ever coming to terms with it. The relief of knowing the ill was incurable and that from now on I could give up my pathetic attempts at self-doctoring – I can't tell you! The recognition that everything could be endured once you had accepted that it was unendurable – '

Jurnet said: 'I can understand that.'

'Can you?' Again the close, friendly scrutiny, then: 'I do believe you can. Well – that afternoon, after Paul had gone, I went down to the beach for the first time since the day after the cremation. It was an even bigger test than going to Alan's wardrobe and taking out his clothes. I went to Katie's favourite places and survived to tell the tale. I hadn't taken the car and I came back by the footpath, into the churchyard and then out on to the road. And there, the first thing I saw was Alan, my husband, coming

50

towards me.' With a laugh at the detective's startled expression: 'I blinked a couple of times and then I saw that it was only Timmy, wearing the blue-and-white-striped shirt and Alan's jeans. He was in the most tremendous spirits. It was as if his new clothes had given him not only a new confidence but new powers of co-ordination. He was hardly jerking at all.

'Naturally, I complimented him on how nice he was looking, and he told me that Mr Bailey – he's our village woodman, coalman, and general jack of all trades – had given his ma a lift into Angleby in his van. She'd gone in to buy herself a new frock.

'I said, "Then you'll both look the last word, won't you?" which for some reason Timmy seemed to find hilarious. He burst into great guffaws and shouted, "She'll never get no frock!" He seemed to think it a tremendous joke.'

'Didn't you ask him what was so funny?'

'I didn't, as a matter of fact. He often burst out laughing for no apparent reason. I offered to buy him an ice-cream and he said that was what he had come out for, to buy one for himself.'

'Raspberry ripple,' Jurnet interposed with a smile.

'How on earth – ' The large blue eyes opened even wider in sudden recollection. 'You were in the shop with that lovely girl. Is she your wife?'

'Not yet.' Jurnet felt his face warm with pleasure. He loved to hear Miriam praised. 'And did you have to go all the way to Mars to find Timmy the flavour he wanted?'

'Fortunately they still had some left at the Co-op!' The liveliness went out of Hannah Milburn's voice. 'That day, though, he insisted that, instead of my buying him an ice-cream, he'd buy one for me, for a change. And he put his hand into the pocket of his jeans and brought out a £20 note. Remember, this was before he was getting his own pay.'

'Been at his mother's purse, had he, when her back was turned?'

'I'm afraid so. For a moment I thought, "Poor Annie! Getting into Angleby, finding the dress she wanted, and then, when she opened her handbag – nothing there." But then I thought, "Poor Timmy!", dreading what she would do to him once she got back home again.'

'Didn't you try to get the money away from him?'

'I couldn't. It would have been too humiliating. We went into the shop together and he asked Mrs Cobbold for two raspberry ripple cones with such pride, I can't tell you. He told her he was buying one for me as well and she was very nice about it – she's one of the few people in the village who treats Timmy as if he's no different from everybody else – until she saw the note. Then – you could hardly blame her – she said she couldn't change that for just two 35p cones and he ought to know better than to ask. I could tell by the way she looked at me that she expected me to come up with the 70p, which I didn't really want to do, for fear of hurting Timmy's feelings.

'Whilst I was still hesitating, Timmy picked up the £20 note, stuffed it back in his pocket, and pulled out instead a small roll of fivers. He peeled off the top one and slapped it down on the counter.' Hannah Milburn could not help smiling at the memory, despite herself. '"How about that, then?" he said to Mrs Cobbold. "That do instead?"

'Mrs Cobbold said that he was still a bother, but she took the £5 note and gave Timmy the change. I could see she was curious, though. "Wha's happened to you, Timmy Chance?" she asked. "Your ship come in or something?"

'I put in quickly that Timmy was my gardener now, earning his own money, and I think she accepted that – in fact was pleased to hear it. She's a good-hearted woman. "I always tell his ma as how he's good for something," she said to me, "if only she'd hold her hand back long enough to find out what it is."'

Hannah Milburn sat looking down at her hands. When she raised her eyes once more, Jurnet found himself taken aback by the intensity of her gaze.

'I can't tell you how devastated I am by the news that Annie has been found dead. At the same time, if I am to be honest with you – and I have no intention of being anything else – I have to say that my horror is shot through with a horrid glee that now I shan't have to return Timmy, ever.' She ended, in no way contrite: 'You must think me absolutely despicable.'

Carefully non-committal, Jurnet observed: 'Feeling's a complicated thing. What happened after Timmy bought the ice-creams?'

'I couldn't wait to get him out of the shop, away from Mrs Cobbold's curiosity. Even then, I steeled myself to wait until he'd finished his all up. Then I asked what made him so sure his mother wouldn't be able to get her frock. He looked at me as if I wasn't as bright as he'd previously given me credit for, and answered that frocks cost money. "I'd 'a thought you knew that!" he said, and pulled the notes, all of them, out of his pocket again. He wanted to give them to me to buy a dress for myself instead. I answered that it was very sweet of him, but then I said point-blank that it wasn't his money to give away, was it? It was his mother's.'

'What did he have to say to that?'

Hannah Milburn's expression grew sad.

'He got angry. His face took on that awful lumpen look. He said he'd asked his mother for money for an ice-cream and all she'd given him was 10p. *10p!* He practically screamed it at me. When he'd demanded where in the world you could get an ice-cream for 10p Annie apparently had just shrugged her shoulders and said, "That's your business." He said that just then Mr Bailey drove up in his van to give her a lift and she went into her bedroom to put on some lipstick. Timmy didn't actually say so, but it's my guess that was the moment, with her out of the room, that he went to her handbag and took the money.

'I told him he'd have to give it back and say he was sorry, but he only got angrier than ever. He kept jumping about and shouting that he wasn't sorry, he was bloody glad. After I'd managed to calm him down I promised that if he would put the money out somewhere when he got home, on a table where his mother would be sure to see it the moment she came through the door, I would see that in future he'd get his own envelope with his own pay inside it, delivered into his own hands. I wouldn't put it in with his mother's any more.'

'And did that do the trick?'

Hannah Milburn went to the window again: stood wrapped in sunshine. She did not answer Jurnet's question directly.

'I want you to understand, Inspector, that in spite of what I've said about Annie Chance, I don't presume to judge her. I suppose, if you wanted to be cruel, you could say that since she went away I've been using her son, six foot and dim-witted as he is, as some kind of substitute for my lost, quicksilver Katie. Ridiculous, but there it is. On the other hand, I know that taking him over fully grown and with his intelligence, such as it is, fully developed can't be at all the same thing as having to bring up such a child, the heartache and the sheer hard labour of it. Even with the means to pay for trained help I don't think I could have done it, but Annie Chance did, with everything stacked against her, and I honour her for it.'

'Do you think, then, that in spite of everything, she loved the boy?'

'I couldn't say. It couldn't have been easy.'

'No.' Jurnet considered. 'What happened about the money?'

Again the answer was not direct.

Hannah Milburn said: 'I ought to have taken it away from him. I should at least have gone home with him, made sure it was put away somewhere safe, but I didn't do either. I told myself I had no business interfering.' With a shake of the head in self-rebuke: 'What I really wanted was to distance myself from the violence that was bound to happen once Annie got back from Angleby. Since she's been gone I've often wondered whether I wasn't the one who, by my selfish concern for my own comfort, tipped the scales – to go or not to go: made her feel she couldn't stand life in Lanthrop a minute longer.'

'No need to feel like that. She'd probably been planning her getaway for weeks, if not longer.'

'Do you think so?' The woman favoured the detective with a rueful smile. 'The truth is, I only feel like that half the time. The other half, I know I could never have been so cruel as to make Timmy hand over the money. I couldn't have put into words the fact that I didn't trust him.'

'Did you ever find out what actually happened?'

'Oh, I found out all right! I couldn't sleep that night. It was so hot, the first really hot weather of the year. I pushed one of the casements open wide and leaned out, glad of the air. Sometimes, when it's high tide, you can hear the sea even up here, but that night, apart from a vixen somewhere in the wood, there wasn't a sound.

'I stood at the window in my nightgown, enjoying the spicy freshness of the night. Despite the dark, despite the quiet, everything, I remember, seemed extraordinarily alive, my senses alert. It was as if I really had been born again that day and had to come to terms all over again with all the familiar things. Another animal noise had started up, a small noise close at hand. I couldn't think what it might be until a deeper shadow moved on the shadowy grass below the window and a voice whimpered, "Missus!"'

'Timmy had on the bottom part of his pyjamas, that was all,

54

except for some old trainers with no laces in them. When I'd got him into the kitchen, into the light, I could see that he looked awful. A trail of crusted blood had leaked from his nostrils all the way down to his chin, and there were dreadful welts across his back. I was wrong about the whimper, though. He was in tremendous spirits. He kept shouting, "I got out, didn' I? She lock the bloody door but I got out! I went down the drainpipe and got out!"'

In Hannah Milburn's face Jurnet could read the reflection of the appalled sympathy and also the perplexity which must have commingled on that warm spring night.

'I couldn't decide what was the right thing to do – whether to get on to Dr Stonor or call PC Wyatt, or what. In the end I did nothing. I'm sure if Timmy had been in any real distress I wouldn't have hesitated, but as it was, it seemed ridiculous with him capering about the kitchen like Peter Pan cock-a-doodling.

'"She's a right ole devil!" he kept repeating admiringly. His eyes looked huge behind his glasses. "I bet you never saw such a right ole devil as my ma once she gets going!"'

Jurnet said: 'Am I to deduce from what you say that he never put back the money after all?'

'It was the first thing I asked, of course, as soon as I'd finished attending to his scratches and bruises and sponging away the dried blood from under his nose. It was like trying to doctor a slippery eel, but I got him cleaned up at last and sitting down at the kitchen table with a glass of orange squash. Seeing the state he was in, I knew what the answer would be. Though even so – ' with an unexpected chuckle – 'I have to admit I was still taken by surprise.'

'How was that? What had he done with the notes?'

'Torn them into pieces and put them down the loo!' In a voice unsteady with laughter: 'The only thing he complained about was that he'd been forced to put his hand in the water to make them go down. It wasn't healthy, he said. You could get illnesses from putting your hand in lav water.' Regaining control: 'He seemed to expect praise for having persevered, and as for his ma, she had no cause, he said, to carry on the way she had. It wasn't as if she didn't get her bloody frock.'

'How was that, if Timmy had taken the money?'

'Mr Bailey to the rescue, it seems. He paid for it. When I said that was very kind of Mr Bailey but his mother would only have to

55

pay him back so of course she still had reason to be angry, he looked at me as if I was the one who was thick, and said: ''Not in money she won't. A couple of bonks in the back of that van of his an' she'll be quids in. So what she want to take on like that for?'' He sounded quite unconcerned and as if it were the most natural thing in the world.'

'Well, well! Another useful sidelight on Annie Chance.' Jurnet added: 'I expect she had a few choice words to say when you ran the young feller home.'

'I told you – I never saw her again. And as to running Timmy back home while she was still in that lethal mood, I couldn't bring myself to do it – to say nothing of what she'd have had to say to me for interfering in what, after all, was none of my business. We've a room off the kitchen which used to be the housekeeper's, when we had one, ages ago, and I put Timmy to bed there.' As if in admission of some prank of which she was privately proud, the woman said: 'I raided Alan's clothes closets again without a thought, and brought down some beautiful Sulka pyjamas for Timmy to put on. When I said I'd drive him down to the village first thing in the morning so his mother wouldn't worry, he burst out laughing. He seemed to find the idea that people actually worried about other people hilarious; and anyway on Wednesdays, he told me, Caff days, his ma caught the early bus, before he was even awake. I said that in that case I would phone the Caff to let his mother know he was all right.

'''Please yourself,'' he said, plainly taking me for barmy.' Hannah Milburn looked at the detective, her eyes moist. 'I know I'm being sentimental,' she apologized, 'but it was so sad, so incredible, that in a village, which are supposed to be such friendly places, he could be so isolated, so alone.'

'And did you phone the Caff as you said you would?'

'I did. I asked for Annie, told them it was urgent and personal. After a long wait she came to the phone – I got the impression unwillingly – and said she wasn't allowed to receive calls from outside and I could just as well have left a message. I said I thought she would want to know that Timmy was all right. There was a long pause. I don't think she'd even gone into his room, didn't know he wasn't there. Then she said, ''Ta very much, I'm sure,'' and rang off.' Smiling, well-bred. Mrs Milburn added: 'Time I did the same. End of story.'

'The beginning, so far as I'm concerned. Only hope everyone else I have to talk to is as co-operative as you have been.'

'As I've said, I had particular reason to remember. For others, it was probably a day like any other. Do you think you'll be able to find the murderer after all this time?'

'Trail gone cold, you mean?' Jurnet shook his head. 'Trails never go cold. Down in your paddock Mr Abbott's still hot on the trail of who killed the Druids back in the Dark Ages. Hot or cold, we'll have a good try.'

'I'm sure you will.' Both had assumed the accepted stance of leave-taking, that polite reluctance to disengage which signalled the end.

Jurnet said: 'I'll give Timmy a little while to digest the knowledge that his mother is dead, before coming back for a proper talk with him.' He scanned the woman's face and decided that the goodwill pictured there was more than mere politeness. 'Then there's the media. To date, all they know is that a woman has been found dead on Lanthrop beach. By tomorrow morning latest they'll have a name and a crime to go to work on and Timmy will be number one on their visiting list. The boy will need your help.'

'I'll do my best,' Mrs Milburn promised. 'He knows the housekeeper's room is his to use as much or as little as he pleases. I suppose he sleeps here, on the average, three nights a week. There's never been any question of his giving up his own home, and he pays the rent regular as clockwork. Apart from anything else, it's had to be kept spick and span pending Annie's possible return.' With a sigh: 'Now that we know she isn't coming back I'll have to have a talk with him.' Colouring, she added with a certain fastidious distaste which was not allowed to subvert her given pledge to honesty: 'You will undoubtedly discover that there's been talk in the village. There are complications when it comes to harbouring maternal feelings for a child who happens to be six feet tall and over the age of consent.'

'When isn't there talk in a village?'

Hannah Milburn said: 'I also want you to know that I haven't tried to change Timmy in any way – no absurd dreams of making him over into something he isn't, never could be.' With a little grimace of self-disparagement: 'I haven't even tried to improve his table manners and that's taken some self-restraint, I can tell you!'

The two shook hands and went to the door together. Outside on the step, in the heat of the garden after the cool within, Hannah Milburn said: 'I remember once Katie telling Annie all about having been down to the beach and Annie saying she hated the place: the pine trees gave her the willies.' Screwing up her eyes against the sun: 'Katie came running over to me and whispered so Annie wouldn't hear: "Mummy, what are willies?"'

Jurnet said: 'As it happens, she wasn't found among the pines. She was out on the beach, among the dunes. The one that's bigger than the rest.'

The change in Mrs Milburn's expression was remarkable. She aged before the detective's eyes. He asked: 'Is anything wrong?'

The woman breathed deeply, regained her composure.

'It's just that that particular sandhill was Katie's favourite. We called it Katie's Castle, pretended it had bedrooms and bathrooms and I don't know what else – '

'I'm sorry – '

Hannah Milburn moved her hand in front of her face, as if pushing away a fly that had buzzed too close.

'It's me. I have to stop being silly.'

6

On the driveway a lorry loaded with logs was parked in front of
an outbuilding apparently used as a woodshed, the width of the
vehicle in the narrow way leaving no room for Jurnet to edge the
Rover past without its nearside wheels invading the grass verge.
A board mounted above the driver's cabin announced to the
world that Oz Bailey & Co could be relied upon for coals,
seasoned timber, removals and funerals, prompt service, esti-
mates submitted without obligation. The man, presumably the
driver of the vehicle, who was leaning on the metal fencing
watching with absorbed attention the activities down in the paddock, made no effort to turn at the car's approach.

Jurnet sounded his horn and, when this elicited no response,
shouted out of the car window: 'Move her over a bit so I can get
through!'

Negligently, over his shoulder, the man suggested: 'Take her
up on to the grass, bor.'

'And smash Mrs Milburn's bluebells? Move her over, will
you?'

Without haste, the man abandoned his vantage point and
sauntered across to the Rover. It was comical really, if Jurnet had
been in any mood to appreciate it, for between the two of them –
Oz Bailey, the village jack of all trades and Benjamin Jurnet,
Detective-Inspector, Angleby CID, the resemblance was amazingly marked. The man was shorter and of stockier build, but the
dark hair was the same, the same dark eyes, the same bold
Mediterranean cast of feature which added up to a cross Jurnet
would never have chosen to bear, had he had any say in the
matter. As it was, however, apart from a stab of involuntary
pleasure at the recognition that he was not after all the only bloke
in Norfolk who looked like a refugee from a pizza parlour, the

detective found little to please him in either the woodman's looks or his manners.

'Get a move on, will you? I haven't got all day.'

The man said: 'Where's that bleeding boy then? He were supposed to gi' me a hand.'

'Up in the wood, I think.'

'Shit!'

'Mrs Milburn has a bell she rings for him.'

'No call to bother Mrs Milburn.' Turning away from the Rover, the man cupped his hands round his mouth and bellowed, 'Timmy! Where yer got to, you loony bastard?' with no other effect than to reduce the song of a nearby blackbird to a frenetic gobbledegook. Disgustedly: 'None so deaf as them what don't want to hear.'

'The bell will bring him at the double,' Jurnet insisted, sure in his own mind that the reason Oz Bailey did not wish to bother Mrs Milburn was because there was green wood in the load, hidden underneath the ash and the seasoned oak which showed so honourably on the uppermost layer.

'Boy's a shit. Any other century, they'd keep him under lock and key.' Thrusting his head closer to Jurnet than the detective could have wished, Oz Bailey challenged: 'You're not from round here.'

'Not a crime, is it?' the other returned mildly. It was, he decided, not the moment to reveal his name, his function, his intention to seek a few well-chosen words with the chivalrous bonker who had saved Annie Chance from returning from Angleby frockless. 'I noticed you looking at the dig.'

'You seen the gals they got down there?' Mr Bailey grinned, his teeth white in his dark face, the features suddenly alive with a raffish charm such as Jurnet could well imagine tempting Timmy's ma into the back of his van even without the bait of money. 'Job lot if ever I seen one! Reckon they dug them up along of the rest of the junk.'

'Junk? That all they've turned up, then?'

'So I've heard.' Was the man changing the subject suspiciously fast? 'Tell you something else tha's been dug up, though, you've likely not heard about. Down on the beach. Bill Gifford, what looks after the gate, tole me. A dead body on the dunes, washed up on the spring tides, I reckon. What some folks won't do to get on to that beach free! His Lordship won't like it.'

'Don't suppose the dead body was all that pleased either. Was it a man or a woman?'

'Jest a body, Bill Gifford say. Reckon they stuffed it in a bag afore that Nosy Parker could get a sight of it. Ask the old biddy down at the shop if you can't wait to read it in the papers.'

'Why? How would she know?'

'Don't ask me – except that she bloody knows bloody everything that goes on here.'

'Including that you're just about to move that bloody truck and let me bloody get by.'

In the paddock Paul Abbott was supervising his workers with the fussy tenderness of a mother hen preparing her chicks for the big world. From the way the youngsters listened to their mentor's discourse, lips parted, eyes fixed on his eyes, nodding their heads in complete understanding before, so far as the detective was able to judge, returning to the same slapdash mucking about they had been engaged in prior to his appearance on the scene, Jurnet concluded that the Druids had little to worry about. Their secrets were safe with such innocents.

It gave him quite a pang, in the prefab over another mug of the dig's dire brew, to feel obliged, in the line of duty, to wipe the happiness off that chubby, good-natured face. The rosy cheeks paled with horror at the news that Annie Chance had been found done to death in a dune on Lanthrop beach.

'Hannah!' the archaeologist cried. Not Annie, the detective noted: not Timmy, nor even God, who might be expected to be implicated in some way.

Interesting.

'It's OK,' Jurnet urged, as the man appeared to be on the point of a hasty departure for Fastolfes. 'I've just come from Mrs Milburn and she's fine. A shock, of course, but she took it very well. Not the type to give in to the vapours.'

'No.' Uncertainly, his purpose subverted by the other's calm assurance, Paul Abbott lingered on the threshold, first rumpling the sandy hair at the nape of his neck and then spending what seemed unnecessary moments checking the assorted felt-tipped pens which protruded from the breast pocket of his crumpled safari shirt. 'The trouble with Hannah', he proffered eventually, coming back to his seat and fortifying himself with a deep draught of the abominable brew, 'is that she looks so cool, so marvellously self-controlled, but underneath – I know her, you see – ' He ended the sentence with an earnestness which was touching in its utter absence of self-aggrandizement. 'All this time, more than a year after the accident, she's still walking a knife-edge, hanging on to a precipice by her fingertips, whatever metaphor you care to use. Something like this could easily tip her over.'

'She was fine,' Jurnet repeated. 'Invaluable when it came to breaking the news to young Timmy.'

'Timmy? Oh ah!' The tone was humorous, the two syllables a parody of the Norfolk mode. The mask of jealousy which took over the archaeologist's face, overspreading its cheerful rotundities, was something else again; there and gone so swiftly that its startled beholder had some difficulty convincing himself that he had actually witnessed the momentary transformation. Paul Abbott observed, sunny-countenanced as ever: 'It's odd, isn't it, the way it isn't the done thing to let on you don't actually care for a mental defective? It gets you off on the wrong foot in any kind of company. Any so-called normal guy, you're under no compulsion to check out his IQ before making up your mind about him, but take against the village idiot and it immediately puts you beyond the pale as a stony-hearted bastard lacking compassion.'

'I suppose the poor buggers start off with so many strikes against them already, it's felt only fair to even up the odds a bit. What they call positive discrimination.'

'Is that what they call it? I suppose Hannah will take him over completely now.' The archaeologist's hair came in for some more rumpling, the felt-tipped pens were taken out of their pocket this time and carefully scrutinized before being returned to their nesting place. 'Honestly,' the man said, 'I don't know how she can stand him, he's so bloody rude – times when he seems to be deliberately trying to see how much he can get away with. Times when I have to ask myself, is she looking for a substitute for Katie or a punishment for her death?'

'Hardly that, surely? Mrs Milburn had nothing to do with the accident.'

'Try telling *her* that.' Paul Abbott went on: 'We slept together, you know. Past tense, please note, mentioned in all humility and purely by way of establishing my claim to having some understanding of what makes her tick. She needed someone. Almost anyone would have done, and I happened to be on the spot. I can't tell you the happiness – ' The man cut himself short and began again. 'Of course, once she had Timmy, I became surplus to requirements.'

Jurnet said with deliberate brutality: 'I did hear there's been some talk in the village – '

'I didn't mean that!' the other interrupted in alarm. 'Don't misunderstand me! Good God!' Calming down: 'I can't believe you give any credence to that garbage – '

'I'm a collector. I collect everything, garbage included. First I collect it, then I sort it over like any other rag-picker.' The detective turned an openly speculative eye on the plump little fellow across the table. 'Mrs Milburn told me that you said Annie Chance was good-looking.'

'Did she say I said that? Then I must have. Besides, she was, very, in a gaunt, unforgiving way. I've seen faces like hers in Anatolian mosaics. How sinister you make it sound!' The archaeologist regarded the detective with an interest that had in it something childlike. 'Am I a suspect? I thought it was assumed she went off with some bloke, and I've been here all the time. Ask anyone, they'll tell you. Oh dear!' he ended comically. 'Worser and worser! I'm talking too much, aren't I?'

'Not for me,' Jurnet answered. 'I'm merely trying to build up the background. Before I can begin to move about in it I need to know what it was like, Annie Chance's world – '

'World! Too cosmic a word, surely, for the miserable toehold which was that poor soul's stake in reality.' Paul Abbott surveyed his visitor with a humorous sympathy. 'The trouble with you policemen, Inspector, is that you're in too much of a hurry. I quite understand the pressures – you've probably no choice in the matter – but oh! how much you lose by not having the option, as we archaeologists do, of passing everything you find through the sieve of time. If only you could wait a couple of thousand years or so, until the bones are picked clean and all passion is spent – '

'And no comeback, eh, if you get it wrong?' Jurnet said: 'You haven't had the pleasure of meeting my Superintendent.'

The Caff was moderately full of unsmiling long-distance lorry-drivers who looked as if they had been everywhere, seen everything, drained the plastic tomatoes to the last drop of ketchup and much good it had done them. Seated at formica-topped tables they devoured their food with an air of dogged endurance, shoulders bowed beneath the onslaught emanating from loud-speakers placed in the angles between walls and ceiling. No wonder they called it rock, Jurnet reflected, bracing himself as he stepped over the threshold into the rain of aural missiles. Boulder, meteorite, would be better names for it.

Detective-Sergeant Ellers was the only one in the room smiling.

'I thought we were going to eat together,' Jurnet objected, sitting down and looking across the table to a plate where a solitary chip yet lingered.

'So we are, boyo,' returned the little Welshman, forking up the last survivor and then leaning back contentedly to let his belt out a notch. 'Just ready for seconds.'

'Must be good if it compares with Rosie's.' The Sergeant's wife was a notable cook, an invitation to dine *chez* Ellers a treat to brag about in advance and to drool over in recollection.

'Fried! Rosie'd kill me if she knew I was eating fried. Ignore the fluorescent orange it's wrapped up in. It tastes great.' Jack Ellers got to his feet. 'Want me to get the both?'

'I'll come too. I want to have a word with the chef.'

Behind the counter at the far end of the room a man in white overalls and a cook's cap was frying fish and chips in an elaborate apparatus that took up the whole wall and that looked – ı slight aroma of hot oil being the only giveaway – as if it might equally be a state-of-the-art computer. From time to time, with serious gestures, the man opened one or other compartment of the contraption to check how its contents were coming along. As the two police officers approached he elevated a wire basket of golden chips from somewhere underneath the counter and set them to drain with the solemnity of a priest officiating at a sacred rite.

'Beautiful!' commented Jurnet, intentionally loud enough for the fish fryer to hear. 'They look good enough to eat.'

The man, small and dark, with a gold tooth prominent in his upper jaw and a gold ear-ring dangling from his left earlobe, turned a gratified smile on the new arrivals. You could see that he loved his work.

'You gotta know how.'

'I'm sure.'

'So what'll it be?'

'Got some haddock, have you? Haddock, and some of those chips – a double portion. Same for you, Jack?'

'Same for me. Rosie'll roast me alive. On second thoughts, single portion of chips, though.' Satisfied that he had exhibited a virtuous restraint in the face of temptation, the Sergeant did not seem unduly cast down by the prospect of the coming holocaust.

'Got any skate, Ali?' A woman's voice, harsh and authoritative, called from the body of the Caff.

Filling the detectives' order Ali scowled as he shouted back: 'We got plenty skate!' Exasperation evident in the heavy brows meeting over the bridge of his nose, he took out a pencil and pad. 'One bill or two?' he demanded of Jurnet; and, awaiting the answer, '*We got any skate!* I arst you!'

'Put it all on one – and a word, Ali, if your manageress doesn't object.'

'My manageress can go fuck herself. On'y chance she'll get, tha's for sure.' His feelings relieved, Ali studied the faces of his customers more closely. The friendliness faded somewhat. 'Police,' he pronounced, in the tone of one who knew whereof he spoke. 'What you want?'

'Nothing personal,' Jurnet returned soothingly. 'Detective-Inspector Ben Jurnet, Angleby CID. All I wanted was to know whether you remembered Annie Chance who used to work here.'

'Annie Chance!' The other repeated the name and burst out laughing, revealing what looked like a life's savings bedded down among his molars. 'Mrs Buckle – the manageress – she's the one you ought to ask about Annie Chance!'

'How's that, then?'

'Ask her what happened at Annie's farewell do, the day she put in her notice jest like that, wouldn't even wait to go till after dinner, an' see what happens!'

'You're making my blood run cold. What's she likely to do to me – douse me in ketchup?'

'Got it in one. 'Cept it were the other way round.' The man brought his mirth under control. 'The Buckle give Annie a right ole dressing-down, wouldn't make up her pay to the day, tole her to go whistle for it. So Annie picked up one of them plastic tomatoes an' give it a real good squeeze, several real good squeezes – over her hair, up her nose, down her bleeding cleavage. Jes' bin filled up fresh they were too, ready for the day. You should'a seen!' Ali wiped his eyes on his apron and, his sallow features realigned in the melancholy that seemed more natural to them, inquired with what was undoubtedly genuine feeling: 'Annie OK, is she? She's not in any trouble?'

'Not any more,' said Jurnet.

'All I know', said Ali the fish fryer, 'is what I saw that morning when I come back with the fish. Annie was in the car-park putting a suitcase in the back of a car. You could tell the case was heavy by the way she heaved it up – not jest enough for a dirty weekend but all her winter underwear by the size of it. I thought, "Hello darlin', what you up to?" But of course I said nothing, none of my business; not that Annie would have told me if I'd asked, she weren't chatty that way. Anyway, she was so busy getting the case into the boot I don't think she even saw me. Then she bangs the lid down and goes into the Caff while I'm still busy unloading.'

Jurnet asked: 'Was there anyone there with her?'

'The sugar daddy, you mean?' The other shook his head. 'No. It were jest parked there, empty. When I got inside, out of curiosity I took a look round to see if I could spot the lucky feller but there weren't nobody I could see Annie paying special attention to. Mornings, it's all waitress service an' the girls are rushed off their feet. Bacon 'n eggs –' the fish fryer broke off to mouth the words disdainfully, as if the very saying of them rendered that orifice ritually unclean – 'pork sausages an' fried bread. Harry's the one comes in to do that muck.' He ended: 'By the time I went outside again to bring in a sack of crumbs I'd left in the pick-up, the car was gone.'

'You don't by any chance remember, when Annie eventually left, if she took any of your fish and chips out with her?'

'Funny you should ask that,' was the reply. 'Ordinary Wednesdays she took two orders cod, chips on the side, vinegar an' salt, no ketchup – 25p a portion. It's a perk all the waitresses get, if they want it. Well, after she'd had her little fracass an' was on her way to the staff-room to pick up her things, I beckoned her over and asked did she want her cod as usual. I didn't see why she shouldn't have it that one last time if she wanted to, if only to do the Buckle in the eye. She said no, ta; but a minute later she was back with her bag sayin' on second thoughts she *would* like some

fish to take out, on'y not cod, halibut. Halibut!' the fish fryer
repeated, looking bright-eyed from one police officer to the other,
allowing time for the significance of the menu change to soak in.

'Halibut?'

'Call yourself Sherlock Holmes! Halibut, dummy, what we lay
on strictly for the aristocracy, four times the price of anything else
on the menu – five times some days, it's all according. Annie
weren't buying no halibut to take home to Timmy, that was
certain!' Ali smiled reminiscently. 'I give her a bit of a twinkle an'
asked if she'd like me to tie it up with a pink ribbon, an' she tole
me not to be cheeky – not telling me off, conversational. Then she
opened her bag and asked "How much?" an' when I give her a
wink an' said, "Two at 25p – 50p same as usual,' she give me such
a look! "You're a prince, Ali" – tha's what she called me. "I won't
ferget you," she said. An' I won't ferget her neither.'

'That car – you didn't happen to notice what make, I suppose,
or anything special about it?'

'She hadn't got herself a millionaire in an XJS, if that's what you
mean. Ford Sierra maybe, or a Vauxhall or a Honda. Ordinary
sort of car, nothing to write home about. Blue – or maybe black.
Could have done with a wash. Hey – what's all this in aid of? That
loony kid of hers – is that it? Still crying for his mummy?'

'You know young Timmy, then?'

'I know Annie was an angel to put up with him long as she did.
Look – ' Ali spoke with delicate precision. He looked not at all
apprehensive, only concerned to set the record straight; the
record and his own reputation. 'Jes' because that barmy pisspot's
ready to bare his arse to anyone with the price of a raspberry
ripple in his pocket don't mean I'd touch him myself with a
bargepole.'

Jurnet went a long time without saying anything. The fish fryer
looked at the handsome Mediterranean features across the counter with a glint of amusement.

'You coppers lead such sheltered lives. It's a wicked world,
mister.'

'Yes.' Then: 'Annie's dead, Ali. Somebody killed her.'

A fish slice clattered to the floor. The fish fryer shut his eyes and
began to intone something in a language the detectives did not
understand: a prayer for the dead, maybe. Mrs Buckle the
manageress came over to the counter to see what was holding up
service. Her high stiletto heels wobbled as she walked.

Ali opened his eyes. He picked up the two plates he had heaped with haddock and chips to the detectives' order and emptied them into the bin.

'Cold as a polar bear's bum,' he announced. 'I give you fresh. Better keep in these guys' good books,' he advised a Mrs Buckle who appeared to be in the act of blowing herself up like a frog at the wanton waste of good food. 'Someone's murdered Annie Chance an' they reckon it's probably you!'

7

'Ah, the sweet simplicities of rural life!'

The Superintendent, wonder of wonders, was in a good mood. He had actually laughed aloud at Sergeant Ellers' account of the plastic tomato incident and, when apprised of the existence of the dig in the paddock at Fastolfes, permitted himself a few lines of recitation, delivered with that special affection reserved for poems learnt in childhood and never forgotten to the end of time.

> '"When the British warrior queen
> Bleeding from the Roman rods,
> Sought with an indignant mien
> Counsel of her country's gods – "'

Even the revelation that, if Ali the fish fryer was to be believed, buggery in the village of Lanthrop was as common as raspberry ripple ice-cream in the Co-op freezer had scarcely dented his *bonhomie*.

Jurnet, hot and unfresh at the end of a day which had shown him no clear lead, only a vanishing perspective of Annie Chance retreating into ever deeper shadow, couldn't believe his luck. In somebody who habitually confronted every new murder with what could only be called a murderous rage, one that encompassed not only its perpetrator, whoever that might turn out to be, but equally everyone from the highest to the lowliest copper assigned to the case, this departure from the norm was astonishing.

'The Chief's been down for a chat,' the Superintendent said, leaving it uncertain, to judge by his tone, whether the descent had been from the Chief Constable's office on the top floor, from Mount Sinai, or from altitudes even loftier. 'Did you know that Mrs Milburn was his god-daughter?'

69

Detective-Inspector Jurnet did not know.

'Turns out her father's family and the Chief's are friends from way back. Malory – Sir Luke Malory, perhaps I ought to say: he was in the Diplomatic, got his K on retirement – was, it appears, something of a childhood hero of the Chief's – '

The man's a bloody snob, thought Jurnet. Well, what's wrong with a little harmless snobbery, he amended indulgently.

'Yes, well – ' As if reassured by the invisible telex winging across the void, the Superintendent settled back in his chair and rearranged the gold pen that, like the mace in a more exalted chamber, invariably remained in place on the wide desk in front of him so long as its owner was in occupancy. 'He told me all about the husband and the little girl being killed – dreadful thing, that – and the way Mrs Milburn's pulled herself together, made herself responsible for the murdered woman's child. He told me she'd been on the phone to him – '

Jurnet was feeling too bushed to play games. The fact that he recognized quite well that the prime cause of his exhaustion was Mrs Brenda Bailey did nothing to alleviate the condition.

Mrs Brenda Bailey had turned out to be a large woman who exuded power from every leathery pore. Even to view her in repose was enough to bring on a sensation of fatigue in the beholder. To be obliged to withstand the lady in full cry, the lungs of brass resonating, the bosom rising and falling like a wind-jammer in a force nine gale, was – Jurnet learned too late – something not to be attempted at the day's end but rather in the dewy dawn before resolution faltered and hope withered on the vine.

'Wha's the bugger bin up to now?' she had greeted the two detectives even before Sergeant Ellers, negotiating a goose and a hissing gander, a small flock of manic chickens plus the assorted heaps of pipes and breeze block and scrap metal which gave the area of beaten earth in front of the Bailey *ménage* something of the appearance of an outdoor exhibition of modern sculpture, had well brought the car to a halt. As with Ali at the Caff, Mrs Bailey knew without being told that her visitors were from the police. Was it something peculiar to Lanthrop, Jurnet wondered dispiritedly, or had the years that he and his mate had expended in the service of law and order at last taken their toll, sieved them out unmistakably from the rest of the human race, the way a jockey's bow legs did, or a monk's tonsure?

He got out of the car and said, 'Good afternoon,' larding the words with a Latin charm for which, as ever when he summoned it to his assistance, he despised himself. It was almost a relief to discover that its use on this occasion cut no ice whatever. Nevertheless he persisted winsomely, 'I was hoping for a word with Mr Bailey.'

'Then you'll be disappointed!' Jaws snapping: 'Mr Bailey isn't here, and if he was he in't the talkative kind. You can tell me an' I'll pass it on, if I think it's something worth passing.'

'You'll think it's that all right.' Jurnet let his gaze wander to the gleaming hearse which stood parked on the tarmac cheek by jowl with a battered white van and a black Vauxhall saloon. 'It could even mean business. You never know.'

'Christ!' bellowed Mrs Bailey, focusing properly on Jurnet for the first time. 'You're the spitting image!' The detective's resemblance to her nearest and dearest did not appear to make the visitation any more welcome. 'Somebody must've slipped, eh, to make two out o' that mould. I take care of the funerals,' she continued, not bothering to change the tone of disbelieving mockery. 'You can give me the particulars.'

Jurnet said: 'I happened to run into your husband up at Fastolfes. He was delivering some logs.'

Mrs Bailey pounced. 'Nothing wrong with that wood!'

'Nobody said there was. Only that we passed the time of day together and Mr Bailey told me about a body being found on Lord Lanthrop's beach. Washed up by the tide, he thought. I thought he'd be interested to know that it wasn't the body of a stranger after all. It was Mrs Annie Chance, and she'd been murdered.'

'Jesus!'

Mrs Bailey went pale, then red, then settled for a green-tinged purple that went well with her home-bleached hair. She looked neither surprised nor upset. Anger was what had set off the chromatic display.

'An' what makes you think my Oz would care a tinker's fart, one way or the other, what happened to that bloody slag?'

'As I say, just passing the time of day,' emphasized Jurnet, virtuously concerned to do nothing to spark off domestic mayhem. 'What d'you reckon, then, would be the best time to get hold of him?'

'All depends,' replied Mrs Bailey. 'All depends how many tarts he's got down for killing today. He in't so handy as he was, poor bugger, ever since he got his thumb stuck you know where.'

Jurnet knew when he was beaten. In a voice that did not completely disguise an awed admiration, he said: 'I'll try again soon.'

As the police officers turned to go, careful of the skittering hens underfoot, even more careful of the hissing gander, its blue eyes bright with evil intent, Brenda Bailey said sharply: 'If this is about the money, I know all about that. Anyone knows Oz, knows he's a soft touch, the bloody fool. Pay it back six pound a week was what she promised, and Oz believed her. She uses some of it to buy herself a suitcase an' Oz believes her! A babe in arms would have known she was getting ready to push off.'

Jurnet said: 'She didn't get far, if that's any satisfaction.'

'If you think I'm going to throw me apron over me head an' have a good cry over Annie Chance, you've got another think coming,' declared Mrs Bailey, her anger replenishing itself from some well-stocked private source. 'Forty-seven pound gone up the spout! I wanted to ask that Timmy – he's earning good money now, they say, up at Fastolfes – only Oz wouldn't have it.'

A close shave for Oz, thought Jurnet, his eye on the white van where, if her son was to be believed, Annie Chance had repaid her loan with commendable promptitude. The revelation that Oz's wishes might carry weight with his wife was astonishing until the woman added: 'He were right, for once. Mrs Milburn's a good customer, no point in putting her back up. Ever since her husband and kid got killed on the bypass that boy can do no wrong, though – ' with a leer whose unabashed bawdiness precluded any misunderstanding – 'what he's doing it *with* is more'n I can figure out, but tha's her business. Put it down to experience, Oz says. Some experience!'

Jurnet, in a voice suitably lowered: 'I suppose at least you had the Milburn funerals?'

'Who said? Mrs Milburn were in such a state, Mr Milburn's brother come down from London and took over the arrangements. We weren't fancy enough, I reckon. We're only the agents, we got no facilities. All we see to is the coffins and the transport. Dibdin's in Lynn take care of the rest. We didn't even get asked fer an estimate.'

'Too bad.'

'Wouldn't a' bin all that much in it.' Mrs Bailey accepted with surprising philosophy. 'Cremation. They had 'em both cremated. Stands to reason no one's going to splash out on best oak wi' satin linings and brass handles for a corpse what'll be thrown on the fire like an ole boot the minute the preacher's shut his book up.' She finished: 'An' if young Timmy turns up expecting Bailey's to get his ma buried on the cheap for old sake's sake, it'll cost him forty-seven pound on the nail, I promise you, afore I so much as let Oz measure her up!'

Back at the police house, Sergeant Bowles, who had been brought down from Angleby to man the incident room, was making funny faces. A large, comfortable man not far from his pension, a widower happy to take on any duty that would keep him away from his empty home, he was making funny faces at Wayne, PC Wyatt's youngest. Young Wayne seemed gratifyingly pleased with the performance, and as for Oz Bailey, who was sitting on a chair holding the baby, he was in stitches. All in all, thought Jurnet, arriving with the wounds of his previous encounter still fresh upon him, it was the very model of what a busy incident room ought to be in the wake of a savage murder, full of purpose and efficiency, staffed by square-jawed, steely-eyed coppers dedicated to the getting of their man.

Sergeant Bowles pushed his eyes up at the corners, put out his tongue and wagged his ears. It was too much for young Wayne who, in one of those devilish volte-faces the infant young keep up the sleeves of their baby-gros, began to howl like a banshee; whereupon his mother bounced into the room, cast a look of hatred at Jurnet who, as the latest arrival, must be the cause of her darling's misery, swept the child up in her arms and departed, leaving Oz Bailey the only occupant of the room unshaken.

Leaning back at his ease, the woodman explained: 'Saw you out in the yard chatting up my missus. Thought before I went home meself I'd better come along an' find out what fairy stories you bin telling her while my back was turned.'

Knowing what the answer was bound to be, still Jurnet asked: 'How did you know to come here?'

Sure enough: 'You want bees, you go to the hive – ' the man smiled, depressing Jurnet's spirits yet further. What was it that labelled him so ineradicably for what he was?

The detective looked at Sergeant Bowles whose face, with no infant to amuse, had resumed its large, placid contours. Comforted by its calm acceptance of whatever life had to offer, Jurnet inquired: 'You tell him anything?'

'Nothing at all, sir.' The Sergeant looked a little put out at the suggestion. 'All I said was I didn't think you'd be long.' The good man looked from his superior officer to the visitor and back again. His mouth opened, then closed before he could say anything he might be sorry for. Jurnet knew, as well as if he had spoken, that he had just noticed the resemblance.

'Tole me what?' demanded Oz Bailey, looking amused. He always bloody looks amused, thought Jurnet. *Here's something to take that bloody grin off your face.*

Instantly contrite for the inexcusable uprush of hostility, he began with a gentleness that had Jack Ellers eyeing him with some surprise: 'We may have some bad news for you. That body you were talking about up at Fastolfes – we know who it is.'

'Oh ah?'

'It was Annie Chance. She'd been done in.'

The amused look that had so irked the detective faded slowly like the Cheshire Cat's smile, so much a matter of habit that it took time for the man's dark features to readjust to an altered reality. Except that there was no readjustment: more a disintegration. Oz Bailey threw back his head and with harsh and unbiddable noise lamented the murder of Annie Chance.

Sergeant Bowles, that kindly man, came forward with a small flask magically materialized from somewhere about his person and stocked, it seemed, against just such an emergency: but Jurnet waved him back. Embarrassment writ large on their faces, the three police officers waited for the man to have his cry out, though 'cry' was scarcely the word for the mewing that filled the little room. The gulls that quartered Lanthrop beach would have recognized the noise as an echo of their own. Annie Chance, awaiting resurrection in her dune, had had months to get used to it as they screamed overhead, all unaware of the tasty morsel buried in the sand.

When at last the man had quieted down, the gulls sent about their business, Jurnet said: 'I want you to know I never told your wife that Annie in fact didn't owe you anything.'

'You could've told her I owed Annie Chance more 'n I could ever pay.' Unashamed, Oz Bailey heaved a cathartic sigh and put himself together again, even the habitual glimmer of amusement rearming the corners of his mouth. 'You ever gone to bed with a woman, bor, not jest a little outing for your prick to make sure it's still in working order, but a come tha's worth every minute of yer entire life so far, as well as every minute still to come?' Throwing out an arm in exasperation: 'I don't have the eddication. I don't have the words.'

'You only need one,' Jurnet corrected. 'It's called love.'

'That what it is?' Oz Bailey tried the word on for size, mouthing it silently. 'I dunno,' he pronounced at last. 'You seen my Brenda. Believe it or not, I love that mauther something terrible, even if doing it with her, I tell you, is like climbing a mountain an' finding too late you've left your crampons home; and when you finally get to the top feeling you should break out a flag, like that Hilary and Sherpa Tensing did on Everest, an' shout out that you did it fer England. But Annie, now – ' The man got up, went to the window and looked towards the sea. His voice had grown controlled, elegiac. 'That afternoon in Angleby, the minute she turned up back at the van carrying that suitcase, I knew it was all over. The minute. An' although it felt like bloody dying, I actually wished her luck! That's how I felt about Annie Chance.'

'Did she let you into her plans at all?'

'We went for a cuppa. She said as how she'd met this bloke at the Caff. A rep, she said, didn't say what he travelled in, or where. A quiet type, she said, quite a gent. I got the impression this weren't his territory, he were jest passing through. She said he used to come out of his way on account of how good the fish and chips was at the Caff. Must'a bin a gent, mustn't he?' The man turned back to the room as if interested to study the effect of what he had to say on his listeners. 'I arst Annie what he were like in bed, an' you know what? She blushed, she actually blushed, and said that she couldn't tell. Believe it or not, his intentions were honourable and – ' with a grotesquely mimicked gentility – 'he didn't think it was right to anticipate the marriage vows. I could've bust a gut laughing if I wasn't ready to throw up as it was, tryin' to imagine what Lanthrop was going to be like without her.'

'You drove her back home,' Jurnet prompted. 'Before she went indoors she went into the back of the van with you and discharged her indebtedness – '

'Christ!' Oz exclaimed, mocking. *'Discharged her indebtedness!*

Quite the gent yourself, aren't you? We went into the van and had a ripe ole fuck.' After a moment, he added: 'Timmy, I suppose? Not much that little darlin' misses, bless his heart.'

'Did she tell you when she planned to leave?'

'She didn't tell me nothing.' Face darkening: 'I wouldn't'a known she was gone on'y I had some bundles of firewood to drop off at the shop and Ma Cobbold let on she'd seen her waiting at the bus stop with a suitcase. She said as how she thought I'd be interested, the ole cow. You get the runs in Lanthrop, she knows it afore you ate the stuff what caused it. Soon as I unloaded her order I took off for the Caff.'

'You still hoped to get her to change her mind?'

'Annie change her mind – don't talk daft! I wanted to get a look at her fancy man – what had he got that I hadn't? – and some cracked idea about getting his car number. I won't say as I didn't also have some romantic notion about breaking the geezer's gentlemanly neck – or breaking Annie's. You can take your pick.'

Jurnet demanded: 'You actually saw the guy?'

'Like shit I did. All that was in the car-park was some juggernauts an' a few vans. An' when I got inside the manageress was doing her nut – seems Annie had plastered her with ketchup as a going-away present, she still had her hair full of the stuff, the waitresses were stuffing their dishcloths into their mouths to stop themselves having hysterics, an' that Arabian periwinkle what fries the fish told me she'd left a good twenty minutes before. Life's funny, when you come to think about it,' the man pondered, seeming to find little consolation in the exercise. 'I get there twenty minutes earlier and it could've bin the genteel little rep what finished up on the beach, not my Annie.'

'What makes you say "*little* rep?" You said you hadn't seen him.'

'Nor I hadn't. It were jest something in the way Annie spoke. No Sylvester Stallone, tha's for sure.'

'I see. What did you do when you found out you were too late?'

'What was there left to do? Went home to Brenda an' climbed bloody Everest.'

'He told me she'd been on the phone to him – '

What was the Superintendent on about? Jurnet forced his tired mind to wonder what all the unusual benevolence was in aid of.

Could it possibly be that the Chief, in his god-daughter's interests, was intimating that the investigation into the death of Annie Chance be, not actually dropped of course, but, after a suitable interval and a colorable pretence of activity, allowed to fizzle out like an expired sparkler, to come to rest in a file marked with a cautionary *'No further action to be taken'*? The monstrosity of the thought that the Chief Constable might stoop so low – even worse, that the Superintendent might consent to be his tool – brought Jurnet wide awake in a sweat of anger to discover that Mrs Milburn's purpose in telephoning her godfather had been to congratulate him on the sympathy and finesse which one Detective-Inspector Ben Jurnet, Angleby CID, had exhibited in breaking the news of the murder not only to her but, more importantly, to the murdered woman's handicapped son.

According to the Superintendent, conveying the substance of the Chief's remarks, it appeared that the traumatic events of the previous year had, quite without cause, left the lady with a somewhat jaundiced opinion of the police; but the way the detective despatched to Fastolfes had handled Timmy Chance had been beyond praise.

Jurnet, who could not recall his handling of the boy as anything but the usual shambles of trial and error, accepted the compliment with outward modesty and inward jubilation; rightly or wrongly taking the praise as, in essence, emanating not from Hannah Milburn nor the Chief Constable, but from the one man whose frugally doled out encomiums meant more to him than the hosannas of the rest of Force put together. Just the same, when the Superintendent, having picked up his gold pen and returned it to his jacket pocket, almost immediately took it out again, while the elegantly etched contours of his face settled into a familiar dissatisfaction, the detective could have laughed aloud. The Super was back to his usual bloody-mindedness and all was right with the world.

'I've directed Sid Hale and Dave Batterby to liaise with you first thing in the morning – '

Jurnet and Jack Ellers exchanged glances which were not lost on their superior officer. Sid Hale, with the mournful face of a basset hound, a hardworking copper whose reports were often garnished with brilliant insights and a deadpan graveyard humour, was a welcome addition to any team: but Dave Batterby, the bugger who had made it abundantly clear to everyone from

77

the Chief Constable down that he regarded Angleby CID as no more than a staging post in his preordained progress to the highest echelon at New Scotland Yard! – Jurnet gritted his teeth. Did he really have to be lumbered with him?

The Superintendent said demurely: 'My thought is that the two of them, but Batterby especially, should concentrate on the Caff end of the case – that is, on running the mysterious rep to earth. Whilst inquiries in Lanthrop must of course continue, pending further information *he* has to be the key figure in unravelling the full story. True, the fellow has a long start on the rest of us, but that should merely whet Detective-Inspector Batterby's appetite for the chase – '

'Yes, sir.'

'Dr Colton now,' the Superintendent resumed, homing in on a different target. 'He is, as usual, still busy preparing his final report, together, no doubt, with three copies, each on different coloured paper. In the meantime he is willing, albeit with reservations, to commit himself to the proposition that the woman is indeed dead, that she was killed with a blunt instrument which shattered her jaw and caused fatal damage to her throat, and that the remains are the nearest thing he has seen to a mummy since the year he spent as a student out in Egypt digging Tutankhamun or one of his close relatives out of the Valley of the Kings. Unfortunately – ' with a frown which left unclear who exactly was to be blamed for such an oversight – 'unlike the Ancient Egyptians who, so I understand, were all properly eviscerated before interment, their organs retained in jars designed for that purpose, Annie Chance was buried intact, leaving nature to do the work more properly left to trained technicians. As a result, she has ended up virtually hollow, her insides consumed by the assorted carnivores which it appears, lurk in their millions in the sands of East Anglia, alert for just such an opportunity. What Dr Colton has been unable to state with certainty is whether or not the woman was killed *in situ*. Was the sand dune the scene of the crime or was the body merely brought to Lanthrop beach for disposal?

'Either way,' said the Superintendent, his voice ice-cold with its old familiar loathing of the evil of murder, 'not a pretty picture.'

Miriam's Renault Espace was parked on the forecourt of the block of flats, its perky redness shocking against the terminal depression of its surroundings. Nearby, the long-defunct Morris Minor which Mr O'Driscoll on the ground floor was cannibalizing for some unknown purpose, since he possessed no living specimen of the marque nor indeed of any other make of car for which its rusting bits and pieces might conceivably come in useful, creaked in a passing breeze. It was Jurnet's belief that whenever Mr O'Driscoll felt an overwhelming urge to knock Mrs O'Driscoll about, he hastened outdoors and thumped the Morris Minor in her place. Certainly, mornings when Mrs O'Driscoll appeared coiffed in a kerchief coyly arranged so as to conceal a bruised cheek or a black eye were invariably those which followed evenings when rain or some other inclemency of weather had kept her husband within doors.

Jurnet edged the Rover into the inadequate space left by the bulging black plastic bags which, as ever, awaited a notional dustcart, a notional dustman who, like Godot, never showed up – or, if he did, arrived only to make an exchange, discharging precisely as many bags as he took away. The detective shut off the car engine and sat for a moment staring at the red car, weak with the joy of what its presence portended, strong with the love which presently took him with rejuvenated step over the cracked concrete to the front entrance, past the Nappi-San of the O'Driscolls, beside whose door was garaged a pram in only slightly better shape than the Morris Minor outside, but destined to block the hallway until Mrs O'Driscoll achieved her menopause; up the stairs past the joss sticks of Miss Whistler, the late-blooming spinster on the first floor; up again through the pervasive odours of cabbage and slow-simmered underwear to where his love awaited him.

No question tonight, he made a silent vow, of Miriam having to complain – as she had, loudly and bitterly, in the old days – that he brought his murders home with him. He had her back, he had learned his lesson. Tonight, he promised himself, the nearest they might get to violent death was a little intelligent chat about Boadicea or Boudica or whatever the old girl's name was.

As Jurnet bent forward to insert his key in the lock, the door opened, and there was Miriam, radiant.

'I heard your footsteps on the stairs,' she said, coming out on to the landing to meet him. 'Have you caught the murderer yet?'

Jurnet stared, then burst out laughing. Arm in arm the three of them – he and Miriam and the ghost of Annie Chance – went into the flat together.

8

Timmy was planting out wallflowers along either side of the path which meandered across a lawn bordered with yew hedges clipped to a military precision. As he set them out he sang to them, a song without words which to Jurnet, watching and listening at an unobserved distance, seemed a form of magic, with such uncanny accuracy did its blurry tones capture the sounds of a summer garden. Drone of insects, bumble of bees, the breeze moving silkily across the grass, they were all there; even the velvet of wallflower petals and the scent of wallflowers on a hot afternoon, all programmed into the plants for next spring's consummation. The delicacy with which the boy handled the seedlings in his flabby, ill-coordinated fingers was almost as surprising as the face bent over them, intent and quite beautiful.

The boy looked up, caught sight of the detective and stopped singing. His face resumed its accustomed contours of loutish opacity, though his hands, separating out a fresh bundle of the wallflowers by touch as much as sight, moved as sensitively as before.

'Going to be another scorcher.' Jurnet approached, selecting his genial tone from among his repertoire. Producing a roll of mints: 'Thought you might like these to suck. Keep your throat from getting dry.'

'Oh ah.' The other made no attempt to take the proffered gift. Jurnet returned it to his shirt pocket. 'What you want then?' Timmy demanded. 'Can't you see I'm busy?'

Jurnet, determindedly cheerful, urged: 'Won't hurt to take a breather.'

'What *you* know? I got to get this lot watered in.' The boy's eyes narrowed in suspicion. 'You're the geezer spoke to me already.'

'That's right. About your ma. You were very brave. There were just one or two other things – '

'Wha's brave about me?' Timmy sat back on his heels and looked up at the detective in no particularly friendly fashion. 'T'weren't me as got killed. Ma's the one.' He finished boastfully: 'I reckon you got ter be brave, getting murdered.'

'I'm sure she was very brave.'

'What *you* know?' the boy said again, without aggressiveness however, rather an amused scorn. 'You an' the vicar. He's another one. Come round after you was here – reckon I'm gettin' real popular!' The boy picked up one of the little plants and stroked its long leaves, from base to tip. 'Vicar says as how I'll meet her in heaven. I'm in the middle of whitewashin' the frames an' he got to come round to tell me that! I tell him the bloody cucumbers'll get scorched if I stay nattering wi' him, but will he stop? I'll meet ma in heaven, he says, as if it couldn't wait till I finished wi' the whitewash!'

'I'm sure he meant well.' Jurnet, scrupulous about not intruding on somebody else's patch, was nevertheless relieved to have accomplished his main purpose which was to satisfy himself that Timmy Chance had indeed digested the fact of his mother's decease.

'What I arst him', Timmy went on, warming to his theme, 'is, do they or don't they have fish 'n chips in heaven? Do they have fish 'n chips? I arst him outright, yes or no.'

'What did the vicar say?' Jurnet inquired, genuinely interested to learn how the cloth had fielded that one.

'He said – ' Timmy frowned, concentrating on getting it right – 'he said somethin' about all things bein' possible with God. Tha's what he said.' With a disbelieving shake of the head: 'I doubt they'll be as good as them from the Caff.' All angles and gawkiness, the boy got to his feet. 'I wouldn't say no to one of them mints.'

Handing them over, Jurnet said: 'I told you, they're all yours.'

'Keeps yer throat from getting dry,' Timmy volunteered. He tore open the packet and crammed a good half of its contents into his mouth all at once. There was a crunching followed by a white-speckled dribble of saliva down the boy's chin. 'You police, aren't you?' Jurnet nodded. 'Vicar says police'll find out who did fer ma.'

'We'll do our best.'

'I tole him, they don't have t' bother. I tole him I know who did fer her without needing no police to tell me who.'

'You know!'

'There you go,' Timmy noted calmly, as if reporting on the interesting behaviour of an alien species. 'Jumpin' about jest like he did. I tell him as I tell you, God bleeding well did fer her, jest like he do fer everybody.' Squinting in the strong light, the boy looked at the detective. 'Not everybody knows that.'

'That's not quite the same thing, is it?' commented Jurnet, subsiding. 'What did the vicar have to say?'

'Silly ole fart, he say God take everybody to His bosom in His own good time. Tha's what he say – bosom! Can you beat it, an' him a clergyman! God don't have bosom,' declared Timmy. 'On'y girls have bosom.' A pause, then: 'Like that Sandra.'

Like that Sandra. Overshadowed, if that were possible, by more momentous events, Sandra Thorne's breasts had slipped from Jurnet's memory so that to be confronted with them afresh when the front door of Fastolfes had opened in answer to his knock was almost as much cause for wonderment as first time round.

The girl, with a proper respect for the treasures of which she was custodian, allowed time for surprise, admiration and reverence before inquiring, in a voice of excruciating gentility: 'Who shall I say is calling?'

'I thought that young lady worked at the Co-op,' the detective remarked presently to Mrs Milburn, who had welcomed him into her sitting-room with more warmth than he was accustomed to receive from those he visited in the way of business.

'Sandra? She said the check-out counter got all the draughts from the door and it wasn't doing her chest any good.' A gleam of humour brightened the woman's blue eyes: 'I happened to go into the village shop just as she was telling Mrs Cobbold that she'd asked for her cards, and I snapped her up there and then. It's so hard to get domestic help down here, you have to take what you can get. Her mother goes out house-cleaning so she could hardly take offence, especially as I offered to pay her double what she was getting at the Co-op.'

Jurnet looked about the lovely room, bright with flowers, immaculate. 'She seems to be doing fine so far.'

The Chief Constable's god-daughter, Jurnet thought, was

looking pleased with herself, the water-colour delicacy of her features more defined than he had noticed on his first visit. Even her clothes – a red-and-white-striped shirt that hung youthfully loose over scarlet pants – seemed to proclaim a more vibrant personality. Maybe that was what happened when a woman finally found someone else to take over the bloody housework.

On the other hand: 'Nice for Timmy,' remarked Jurnet, 'to have somebody his own age around.'

Hannah Milburn looked at the detective and laughed. Blushed, yet did not look shy with it, only vivid with the heightened red.

'You really are extraordinary,' she announced.

'What have I said?'

'As if you didn't know!' Quieting, the blue eyes intense: 'You make me sound like a pander.'

Jurnet repeated, disingenuously: 'What have I said?'

'I'm not, you know,' said Hannah Milburn as if he hadn't spoken. 'I just want that boy to be happy.'

'I understood she was making a play for one of the students down at the dig.'

'Oh, that! Paul did say something. Sandra flashes her breasts at anything male that moves. It's purely a reflex action. It doesn't mean anything.' With an abrupt movement the woman turned away, went to the french window and looked out. 'Timmy's somewhere up the garden,' she said, her face indecipherable against the outside glare. 'Was it him you came to see or me?'

'Him actually. I wanted to satisfy myself it had sunk in about his mother, and I had a question or two – I hope you don't mind my taking him away from his work for a couple of minutes?'

'Of course not. But as to whether he really does understand that Annie's dead – . As I think I told you last time, you'll have to wait till Wednesday.'

'Has he shown any outward signs of grief yet?'

'He hasn't cried, if that's what you mean.' Hannah Milburn came back from the window, sat down in one of her chintz-covered armchairs and spoke in measured tones. 'Though I can tell you as a matter of fact that crying has no more to do with bereavement than has putting on black for a funeral. You can be bleeding to death inside with a twinkle in your eye. Forgive me,' she said, as if guilty of impropriety. 'Ancient history. Only brought it up to prove that tears don't mean a thing.' She looked at the detective with a lack of artifice so complete it disturbed him.

84

It wasn't natural, he told himself, to hold absolutely nothing in reserve.

She said: 'I'm sorry you disapprove about Sandra. Getting her here under false pretences.'

Overdoing the stolidity, Jurnet protested: 'Not my business, Mrs Milburn, either to approve or disapprove.'

'But you do disapprove, don't you? You think I'm proposing to play God to a poor feeble-minded orphan when all I'm trying to do is a little harmless matchmaking, the kind women have gone in for since the beginning of time, out of sheer respect for the holy state of matrimony.' Abandoning the light touch: 'A little over a year ago, Inspector, I saw my life winding pleasantly and predictably to its end in the far-off golden distance. Since then –' with an unconscious movement of her fingers, a small hand-wringing that Jurnet found infinitely touching – 'I've learned that nothing is certain, love least of all, and I want to make sure, so far as I can, that Timmy is taken care of, whatever happens. I'm going to turn part of the acreage here into a market garden so he'll be independent, and I've already applied for planning permission for a bungalow where he – and his wife eventually – can live. How can that be bad?'

Jurnet said neutrally: 'He sounds like a very lucky young man. However, what I'm in Lanthrop for is to find out who killed his mother.'

'Is that all you're here for?'

'It seems enough for me.'

Mrs Milburn shook her head. The fingers, Jurnet noticed, had ceased their fretting; lay quiescent in her lap.

'I don't think it is, not really. You see, I spoke about you to my godfather, the Chief Constable – I don't know whether he mentioned it – and he said that, policewise, there was only one thing wrong with you. You weren't detached enough, he said. You were forever fighting your latest corpse's corner.'

Jurnet said gruffly: 'They can't do it for themselves, that's certain.'

'There you are!' Hannah Milburn exclaimed delightedly. 'He also said that there was one item of general-issue uniform you categorically refused to put on, however much refusing to wear it interfered with your chances of promotion.'

'Uniform?' Jurnet, CID, plainclothes, repeated uncomprehendingly.

'Blinkers were what he meant, he said. Worn by properly trained police horses and police officers alike to keep them from seeing more than was good for them and landing themselves in the soup.'

Jurnet said, between set lips: 'I need to understand what goes on.'

'My godfather's words exactly! "He needs to understand." He also said: "Fortunately for the Police Force, it isn't catching!"'

Choosing his words carefully, Jurnet said: 'Young fellow like you, I expect you've got plenty of friends in the village.'

Timmy paused in his watering-in of the wallflowers. He looked up frowning.

'Friends?' The word was spoken as in a foreign language, untranslated, untranslatable.

'Pals,' Jurnet elaborated. 'Mates. Blokes you meet to kick a ball around with, get together over a beer or a game of cards – '

'Oh – ' said Timmy. 'Them?' He went back to his task. 'Nah,' he pronounced. 'I don't have none of them.'

Keeping pace with the boy's progress along the narrow path, Jurnet went over to the offensive. 'Not what Ali at the Caff told me,' he insisted. 'He told me you went about with a whole lot of fellows – '

'Oh!' exclaimed Timmy. 'Tha's what it's about! Whyn't you say buggers when you mean buggers? Tha's right – I used to have a lot o' them all right, till ma went an' blew him up. I could 'a blown *her* up, I can tell you, but now I'm earning regular I don't need the money no more, so I'm not bothered.'

'I'm glad you aren't doing it any more, Timmy. For one thing, it isn't good for your health. I can understand your ma was upset to find out what you were up to.'

'I weren't up to nothin'!' Timmy protested, an expression of hurt innocence overspreading his heavy features. 'The buggers did all the upping, I jes' let them get on with it, the silly arseholes. The blow-up weren't nothing to do wi' them anyhow. I tell ma about buggering, she'd have had the money off me 'fore you could say knife.' The customary note of pride came into the boy's voice as he finished: 'She were an ole devil all right! Vicar says as how she's an angel now wi' wings an' a bloody harp, in't it a scream? I tell him, I'll believe it when I see it!'

'If it's true your mother didn't know about the buggers, what was the blow-up about?'

'About the way I come home stinkin', when I bin up there on the common, working. Said as how she couldn't get the stink out of the house in a week. She tole him, jest because you look arter goats don't mean you have to smell like an ole billy yerself. She tole him she was going to get PC Wyatt an' the Cruelty Inspector to come up to the common an' take a look, they'd have something to say, he'd be lucky not to end up in the nick.' Behind the thick glasses the protuberant eyes crinkled at a happy memory. 'Oh, it were a right ole row!'

Patiently, step by step, Jurnet sorted the story out.

'Somebody keeps goats up on the common – right?' The boy nodded. 'What's the name of the bloke who does that?'

'Joey Corvin, what you think? Everyone knows Joey Corvin up on the common.'

'Right. And this Joey Corvin employed you to help him look after his goats? And Joey Corvin used to have buggers up at his place as well as goats – people like Ali from the Caff?'

'Oh – him. Brought me a bag o' chips once, stone cold. "You better give 'em to the goats," I told him. "All they're fit fer." I got to fill up again.' Timmy stood with the empty watering-can clasped against his chest. 'You're police, aren't you?'

'That's right.'

'Fer police you don't know much, do you?'

'That's why I have to ask questions.'

'Oh ah.' The boy turned away in the direction of the standpipe. 'Han't you got nothin' better to do with your time?'

Jurnet sat on the highest dune on Lanthrop beach and thought about Miriam, about Annie Chance, and about little Katie Milburn who had called the great mound of sand her castle. He also wondered what the hell was keeping Jack Ellers.

After its forensic going-over the dune looked different, and Jurnet was glad of it. It left forever inviolate that other one where Miriam had spoken those unforgettable words, '*You* are my heart's desire.' The secret bowl at the top had gone as well as the carpet of low-growing herbage which had cushioned their coming together. Only Annie Chance, mummifying like some Ancient Egyptian, could still have felt at home there.

Jurnet decided that he was never going to feel the same again about sand. How it had ever come to be considered one of the good things of life suddenly astonished him. Catch him spending £5 again for the privilege of parking his backside on the bloody stuff!

He swivelled landward and was cheered to see the chubby figure of DS Ellers toiling barefoot in his direction, his jacket in one hand, his shoes, their laces tied together, dangling from the other. Jurnet came down from his mini-Sinai to meet him. From the look in the little Welshman's eyes, puzzled but indulgent, he could tell that he thought it a daft place to meet, but there! If it kept his mate happy –

'I wanted to refresh my memory,' Jurnet explained.

'Refresh!' Jack Ellers dropped where he stood. 'Two yards of this and I'm knackered.'

Jurnet sat down on the sand beside him. 'Space,' he said vaguely. 'Quiet. It's as good a place as any to get things straight in your mind.'

'Oh ah? Glad to hear it's good for something. Solved the mystery, then, have you?'

Jurnet laughed, feeling better as he always did in his friend's company.

'I'm leaving that to Dave. Wouldn't want to steal his thunder.'

'I'll lay you twenty to one, if he can't turn up that rep – and be honest, what chance has he, months gone by and nobody set eyes on him? – he'll swear it's on account there never was no such animal.'

'I'd be ready to go along with that myself, almost. We've only Ali's story that Annie ever put that suitcase of hers in that car boot – a car he didn't even notice the make of, and him the type you'd expect to take a note not only of the make, not only of the number, but also what kind of dolly's hanging in the window, on the grounds you never know when it might come in useful. And that conversation Bailey says he had with Annie over the teacups – how much reliance can you place on that? We've only his word. All we know for certain is that Annie was planning to blow.' With a frown: 'Assuming we know even that. That suitcase could've been stuffed with things for Oxfam.'

'Hold on!' Jack Ellers' cheerful voice cut across the returning tide of depression. 'She'd hardly have plastered that manageress with ketchup if she'd been fixing on staying on at the Caff till it was time to draw her pension.'

'You're right.' Jurnet's gloom lifted somewhat. 'OK then – ' he accepted. 'Let's agree that she clearly indicated her intention of shaking the dust of Lanthrop from her feet – but whether with or without a mysterious travelling salesman, whose only positive identification is that he's a fish-and-chips buff, is anybody's guess.'

He let a handful of sand dribble slowly through his fingers. The feel of it against his skin was disagreeable, evoking as it did images of deserts, sandstorms, quicksands, deadness. Oh, he had gone off sand, all right.

He pointed out irritably: 'According to Bailey, she didn't even think to ask the bugger what outfit he travelled for.'

'She didn't need to.' Jack Ellers pulled a pair of bright blue socks out of his jacket and began to ease them over his chubby toes. 'She knew, didn't she? He travelled in dreams.'

9

Abandoning their cars, they took the footpath that led off at an angle through the scented pines. Stepping from the glare of the sand into their shadow, Jack Ellers, who had launched with typical vivacity into an account of his call upon Mrs Cobbold at the village store, let his words peter out in silence; it was that kind of place. Only when they emerged on to the open marsh, passing between cows who rose at their coming and with calm, unhurried steps moved further off as if, no offence intended, they preferred their own company, did he resume his report, quietly and without haste, as though the cows had passed on a valuable lesson.

'She says that when she looked out of the shop window and saw Annie standing at the bus stop with her suitcase she felt she had to go outside and say something on account of Timmy. Who was going to look after him if his ma scarpered? She says she asked her point-blank what arrangements she had made about the boy. She says Annie looked at her without batting an eyelid and said that Timmy would be all right – she had sold him to Mrs Milburn. Those were her exact words – sold him. Most people wouldn't take him for a gift, Annie said, but Mrs Milburn had made her an offer she couldn't refuse. Mrs Cobbold says Annie was got up very fine – I'm quoting her again – in a black outfit that showed everything if you knew what she meant, with court shoes to match and a bag that hadn't come off a stall in Wells market.

'"Where you think I got the money for all this lot?" she demanded, bold as brass apparently. Just then the bus drew in, and she got on with her suitcase. "Cheerio, then," she called out, and that was it. Mrs Milburn mention anything to you about paying a lump sum down for the bonny boy?'

Jurnet shook his head. 'More likely Annie was having the old girl on. Kind of woman she was, she wasn't short of a snappy answer. Funny how people turn out the exact opposite of what you'd expect – ' The detective stopped short in his tracks, dark head raised to the summer air as if scenting some intimation of an elusive quarry. A passing black-headed gull let out a screech of derision. 'Take Mrs Milburn, now – delicate as a bit of china by the look of her. Losing hubby and kid at one go, wouldn't have surprised me if she'd gone and put her head in the gas oven, except they don't have gas out here, do they? Maybe that's what saved her. But Annie Chance – from all we've heard, a tough cookie. She's the one of the two I'd have put down as a survivor.'

'You reckoned without that rep or whoever,' the little Welshman observed. The Welshness upswelling: 'Or God.'

God appeared splendidly accommodated in Lanthrop church, the building, like so many in Norfolk, grander than the size of the village would seem to warrant. Only the state of the churchyard, if Bill Gifford's expression was anything to go by, might conceivably cause a frown in heaven.

'People paid good money for them stones,' he complained to the two detectives who had come through the kissing-gate into consecrated ground. He seemed glad of the arrival of an audience. 'I reckon they'd have had something to say if they'd bin told they was to be buried under a load of twitch while they waited for Judgement Day.'

Jack Ellers said: 'It's called conservation.'

'I know what it's called. We got a vicar never stops sayin'.' Unappeased, the man went back to cutting the small area of grass immediately adjacent to the church. The crackety-crack of the old-fashioned hand-mower no more disturbed the peace of the place than did the twitter of the sparrows engaged in an industrious going-over of the cut grass piled on the gravel pathway. 'Wouldn't have got this bit done neither, only people were complaining it was giving 'em hay fever. Last Sunday you couldn't hardly hear the sermon for the sneezing.'

Jurnet stepped on to the mown turf and looked downward to where, in a sunny aperture between buttresses, two bronze plaques set side by side advertised the names respectively of Katherine Milburn and Alan Caradon Milburn. The names, the dates, nothing more.

Gifford said: 'I'll get 'em edged up neat once I've finished with the cutting. On'y cremations we got buried here at St Blaise's, thank goodness. Last week when Joey Corvin's nephew Andy, up on the common, kicked the bucket an' Joey had him cremated, I thought, "Here we go again – another one!" On'y I'm glad to say Joey decided to have the ashes scattered at the crematorium, in the Garden of Remembrance. Good for the roses, did you know that? Bloke I know works over there, says they never have to spray for black spot.' The man stared with dislike at the plaques embedded in the turf. 'Silly, I always think, like there's a garden gnome buried there or a kiddy's teddy bear. No way for a full-size human being to go. No dignity. I'm sure as Mr Milburn won't thank 'em on the last day when the trumpet's sounding like mad an' he's got to put himself together out of a boxful of ash like you might clean out of a grate of a morning. At least with a skeleton you got something to go to work on.'

'That was a tragic thing,' Jurnet remarked, enlarging the opening with which he had been presented. 'Terrible for Mrs Milburn.'

'Terrible.' The man's mood softened. 'She were a dear little thing, that Katie. Pretty as a picture, and bright with it.'

'And Mr Milburn – what was he like?'

'Big feller. Fine figure of a man, as they say. Can't hardly help laughin' when I look at that titchy little plaque and think of the size of him squeezed into that.'

'Pleasant, was he?'

'Pleasant enough.' A certain note of reserve had come into the other's voice. 'Mustn't speak ill of the dead, but a bit too big for his boots, if you want to know. After all, it's Mrs Milburn's people bin at Fastolfes hundreds of years, not his. Goodness knows what rabbit hole he popped out of. He had no call to give himself airs and graces.'

'Bit of a lady's man, was he?'

The gatekeeper stared.

'Not as I've heard,' he stated frostily. Speaking ill of the local goners was obviously not a privilege which extended to outlanders. 'I'm sure him and his missus was always very fond.' The hostility dissolving in the glow of having something juicy to impart: 'Day after the cremation, afore they even had the committal service here at Lanthrop, she went down to the beach and tried to commit suicide.'

'You don't say!'

'She come down to the gate not long after dinner-time, looking pale and upset as were only natural, but quite calm and collected. Asked arter my rheumatism, a real lady. I were jest going to say a few suitable words, condolences an' so on, when she suddenly puts her foot down on the accelerator an' takes off down the road like she got a train to catch. So when she comes back, not all that long after, before opening the gate I come round to the driver's side to say my piece an' then I see she's all wet, water dripping from her hair, down her face and all over the seat, her clothes stuck to her body with the wet an' I don't know what. "What's happened, Mrs Milburn?" I says, as if I couldn't guess, an' she says, her teeth all chattering, as it weren't nothing, she'd been standing at the water's edge and she'd slipped. Well, I mean! I reckon she went in deep intending to do away with herself an' then thought better of it, jest as she ought, her a regular church-goer, active in the Mothers' Union an' so on. O' course I didn't let on what I thought. I jest asked her in for a hot drink but she said she'd get on home, she'd be all right. I'll never ferget the way she looked, long as I live.'

'She must have looked terrible.'

'Terrible! She were laughing fit to bust. I never seen anything like it. Hysterical. At the committal service next day it were jest the same. All through the service she stood there like a stone – never once sat down, let alone kneel. Then, jest at the end, outside, when they was lowering the casket with Mr Milburn's ashes into the ground she was off again, laughing as if she'd never stop. Vicar didn't know which way to look. Pretended it wasn't happening, it was all he could do, and presently she pulled herself together, poor soul.'

'Very sad.'

'Funny how the two of 'em – Mrs Milburn and Annie Chance, mistress an' maid as you might say – shared the same bad luck.'

'Except that – assuming for the moment your guess about Mrs Milburn's intentions is the correct one – Annie Chance never had the option of changing her mind at the last minute, whether to live or die.'

'I don't know about that.' The man took a moment to glance up at the church tower, the solidity of it, foursquare against the sky. 'She was a sinful woman, was Annie, and as the Good Book says, the wages of sin is death – '

As they waited to cross the high road Jack Ellers asked: 'Were you fishing back there to find out if there'd been any jiggery-pokery going on between Annie Chance and Mr Milburn deceased?'

'Was I? I suppose I was.' Jurnet shrugged his shoulders. Always protective of his clients, he did not even try to conceal that Bill Gifford in the churchyard had rubbed him up the wrong way with his references to the murdered woman. 'If the wages of sin really is death', he observed sourly, 'we'd all be for the chop.'

'Who says we aren't?' his subordinate queried cheerily as, fed up with waiting, the two took their lives in their hands to thread a way between the speeding traffic. Continuing, once they were safely on the further side: 'You aren't serious, are you? I know it's hard to get domestic help out in the sticks, but surely not so hard you'd keep on a daily you knew had been having it off with your late lamented?'

'I shouldn't have thought so,' Jurnet conceded. 'Except that there's a Timmy to put into the equation. And now this so-called suicide business. Did Mrs Milburn or didn't she mean to kill herself, and why the hell was she laughing?'

'Gifford said hysterical. Sounds a reasonable deduction in the circumstances.'

'I dunno.' Jurnet looked about him in a discontent not alleviated by the sight of the two cars parked in front of the police house. One of them, with its distinctive stripe and its searchlight mounted on the roof, was unmistakably the chariot in which PC Wyatt patrolled his bailiwick. The other, a Rover like all the cars at the service of Angleby CID personnel, the detective instantly recognized by its gleaming coachwork, the offensive cleanliness of its window glass.

'Hello! The golden boy's arrived.'

'Christ!' Jack Ellers exclaimed, clapping a hand to his nose as they neared the local vehicle, which stood with its boot lid raised to its full extent, presumably to let much-needed air get to the luggage compartment. From the stench which still issued from that cavity, one might deduce that the air had sensibly declined the invitation. 'What's he been carrying there? Silage?'

'Probably the local cheese.'

Up the incline to the house and along the passage to the incident room the smell persisted. In the room itself, if anything, it strengthened again, its nucleus, as it were, centred on the persons of PC Wyatt and DI Hale who, together with a hugely smiling Dave Batterby, constituted the reception committee. Sergeant Bowles, at a guess, had found a reason for migrating to less malodorous climes.

PC Wyatt announced moodily: 'Marlene's going to do her nut.' He stared down unbelievingly at the front of his uniform which was patterned with what looked like drying slime. Across the room, as far from his companions as its dimensions permitted, Dave Batterby, immaculate, triumphant, stood by a window pushed open as far as it would go. Looking as if he could cheerfully murder him, PC Wyatt said: 'I said as how we ought to call out a pick-up. It'll have to come out anyway, so why not then? There's no way it can stay out in the yard once the kids get back from school.'

'Ben. Jack.' His reeking garments in no better condition than the village constable's, Sid Hale, his long face as ever looking saddened by the follies of humankind but never surprised by them, greeted the newcomers with a smile that was marginally less melancholy than the heart-rending rictus he normally pressed into service as an indicator of mirth; reassured, doubtless, by the proofs he carried like stigmata on his own person, that the world was indeed, as he had always supposed it to be, one big pong.

Keeping his distance, Batterby sang out in a voice upon whose surface self-congratulation floated like globules of fat on mutton stew: 'Not a bad beginning, eh, Ben? We're getting there!'

The damnable thing was that the bugger appeared to have something.

'Can't imagine how you lot came to overlook it,' the man went on demurely. 'That lay-by half a mile along the bypass from the Caff – PC Wyatt here must have pulled into it any number of times, and so must you, since you've been down here, if only to take a leak, like I did.'

Jack Ellers wrinkled his nose. 'So that's what it is! I was wondering.'

'Always the joker!' Batterby remarked with only slight rancour. He could afford to be generous. 'Naturally while I was there I kept my eyes peeled – '

'Sheep still there?' queried Jurnet, not to be outdone in the eye-peeling line.

'Still there,' the other assented, smile even broader. 'All but one, that is to say.'

'How's that then?'

'That pond over to the right – if you can rightly call it a pond, the way the water level's down from what it must have been two or three months ago. More a basin of scum. There was a dead sheep in it – on its back, its legs sticking up.'

'Oh ah?' Jurnet had never even noticed that there was a pond.

'There was this green thing sticking up as well. Annie Chance's suitcase.'

Out in the backyard, circling queasily round the unlovely object that lay on the cobbles amid a buzz of flies, Jurnet was lavish in his praise of the eagle-eyed dick who had recognized it for what it was. Green to start off with, and draped in a veil of green putrefaction, it must have been an easy thing to miss. If only Batterby had stopped acting as if he had captured the Hound of the Baskervilles single-handed his colleague's congratulations would have been even more generous.

Not even the eagle-eyed dick suggested that an attempt be made to open the case then and there. In its present state, that would be conduct beyond the call of duty. The buggers back in the lab in Angleby didn't know what a treat they had coming to them.

'It has to be Annie's,' Jurnet confirmed. 'Anything else would be altogether too much of a coincidence. I don't see any need to get Bailey over here or that woman from the shop. It'll only set the whole village talking. Time for that later. We'll let the lab open it up, and then we'll see what we shall see.'

'That rep's name and telephone number, that's what we want.' Batterby sounded as if he would be satisfied with nothing less.

'Plus a signed and witnessed statement that he did Annie in.' But there was kindliness in Jurnet's ribbing. The sight of the ruined suitcase had made him feel well-intentioned towards all dreamers of dreams, himself included. He made an inward vow that if, by some unimaginable balls-up in heaven or New Scotland Yard, he ever found himself called upon to congratulate Dave Batterby upon his appointment as Chief Commissioner, he would put out his hand in unequivocal goodwill and remind the great man of the day when, taking a leak on Lanthrop bypass, he had found a decomposing sheep and a green suitcase and solved two deaths at one go.

High above the village, Lanthrop Common was an ambiguous kind of place. Heather and gorse, no trees save for an arthritic thorn or two, it lay apparently open to view, with no secrets other than the occasional adder sliding off a sunwarmed stone into the bracken. Rabbits sprang up out of nowhere, zigzagging for cover as the Rover edged gingerly along yet another sandy track that, having promised civilization at the end of it, either petered out in a tip where the jettisoned bedsteads, old paint-cans and bottomless buckets had already taken on the look of ancient artefacts, or in a patch of broken concrete which must once, in a past that seemed almost beyond remembering in this place where time had no meaning, have supported a gun pointing out to sea in defence of liberty.

For all its apparent candour, Jurnet had seldom felt more lost than in this landscape where hardly anything that grew was higher than a man and which yet was as full of concealment as any tropical rain forest. A few feet from the sparse passing traffic, and it was as if there had never been a road – no road, no village, no human heartbeat: only the purple, the gold and the rust of the heather, the gorse and the bracken, and above the implacable sky.

'Wyatt said we couldn't miss it – ' this as Ellers, driving, had drawn yet another blank. 'Must have been getting his own back for that suitcase. Hang on!' The sun suddenly glinted on something that moved in the warm breeze. 'Looks like we've arrived!'

The sign, lettered in Gothic capitals and suspended by two chains from a wrought-iron framework, read: '*Toggenburg. Goat Milk. Goat Cheese*' – or would have done had not somebody scrawled 'CLOSED' across it in red paint.

'Looks pretty final,' was Jack Ellers' comment. 'Not like half-day closing or letting the punters know you've just nipped down to the pub, back soon. Thought his name was Corvin, though.'

'Toggenburg's a kind of goat. Knew a bloke kept a couple. Long wavy hair and eyes like Bette Davis – the goat's, not the bloke. Way he went on about them, they could do everything but yodel.'

Sergeant Ellers turned the Rover into another of the humpbacked trackways they had become only too familiar with. Fearful of the car's back axle, they bumped along askew, two wheels on the hump, the nearside ones in the deep groove apparently gouged out by the passage of a tractor in days before sun and drought had baked the impoverished soil to the consistency of brick. This time, however, instead of dwindling to nothing, the track widened, became almost suburban in its primness. Tarmac had been laid, there was an increasing sense of order, the untamed heath thrust well away from the neat bungalow which came presently into view. Painted white, with plaster urns full of geraniums on either side of the front door, it looked, Jurnet thought, the kind of place where even Miriam, who worried about such things, might buy goat milk or goat cheese without harbouring doubts about the hygiene. Behind a green-painted chain-link fence at a little distance from the house a long low wooden building – presumably the goat house – looked similarly well maintained.

Jack Ellers got out of the car and looked about him.

'Not what you'd usually associate with a male brothel.'

'Hold on!' Jurnet, joining him, objected. The recognition that he himself did not really care for gays tended to make him lean over backwards to avert an accusation of prejudice. 'All we know is what I got from Timmy.'

'And that Ali at the Caff – '

'OK – and that Ali. But let's not jump to conclusions, shall we, before we've even rung the bell?'

'Consenting adults in private, eh?' The little Welshman sighed. 'It's a different world, boyo, from what they taught me at Sunday School in the valleys.'

'Right!' the other agreed. 'One we've got to live in, like it or not. If there should be a can of worms that needs opening up here, we'll drop it into PC Wyatt's lap for him to deal with. Give him some salutary insights into what goes on in the beautiful English countryside. All I, personally, want to know from Mr Joey Corvin is what Annie Chance really came up here to complain about. Was it only the goat pong, or had she found out what else Timmy was getting up to, here on the common? If she had, and she threatened the bloke in some way – blackmail, going to the police, whatever – I want to know. And what, if anything, he did about it.'

Jack Ellers offered the opinion, 'Doubt you're going to find out today. Those geraniums could do with a watering. I don't give them much longer in this heat. You'd think there'd at least be a dog barking. Well and truly closed, if you ask me. The bird has flown.'

'If so, it couldn't have been to avoid us. He had no reason to expect we'd be paying a call.'

Whatever the reason, the quiet of the place was extraordinary, considering that the air was loud with insects swerving about their business as if they possessed a built-in awareness that summer would not last for ever. The louder they buzzed, the quieter it became, the more dangerous.

The two detectives nevertheless rang the front-door bell with proper formality, waited a decent interval before pressing their noses to windows that were sparkling clean and gave on to comfortable rooms within, furnished simply but with some taste. In the kitchen, copper pans caught the sunlight.

'Taking a few days off,' Ellers suggested. 'Unless – going by the way he's mucked up that sign good and proper – he's planning to sell up lock, stock and barrel.' The little Welshman came away from the windows and cast an approving eye over the general good order of the place. 'A weeny bit off the beaten track, though, wouldn't you say? Maybe that nephew of his dying made up his mind for him. That would account for no goats. You can say the hell with a few geraniums but you can't just shove off and leave dumb animals to fend for themselves.' He finished: 'Funny Wyatt didn't seem to know anything about it.'

Jurnet said: 'It's my guess PC Wyatt doesn't come up here all that often. The guy's got this never-never idea of what his village ought to be like and he'd rather look the other way so as not to see whatever doesn't fit into the pretty little fairyland he's dreamed up for himself.'

'There's fairies and fairies.' But Ellers' heart wasn't in it. He fished out his handkerchief and flapped it in the air with less than his wonted cheerfulness. 'Bloody flies!'

Jurnet insisted: 'There has to have been more than the smell of goat to account for Annie Chance coming up here on the war-path. She was a countrywoman, she didn't have to be taught what a goat smelled like. And judging by the way this place is kept, Joey Corvin's goats must smell a lot sweeter than most.'

'Maybe it was a trade dispute and she didn't care for the competition. Maybe it wasn't gents only. Unisex, like the hairdresser's.'

'Christ, I don't know!'

99

The large shed at the side of the bungalow housed a tractor, a pick-up loaded with sacks of crushed oats and linseed, and a Honda Accord, long in the tooth but groomed like an executive Rolls. The key of the Honda dangled from the dashboard.

Jurnet pointed. 'He's never gone off and left that. He must be around somewhere. I'll let him know he's got visitors.'

He went back to the Rover, put his hand on the horn and kept it there longer than he had originally intended. The resultant noise did not seem to make all that much impression on the quiet.

The two listened to the silence until Jurnet said tersely: 'Let's look around.'

Next to the goat house a grass paddock surprised the eye with its improbable green. True, the grass was coarse, in places strewn with the well-chewed remains of hazel and willow branches, in other parts looking ill-used by the sharp hoofs of small-footed animals, but the wonder was that grass could be made to grow at all in such an unlikely setting, with the bracken pressed tight against the surrounding fence, the enemy at the gate. A stable-type door in the goat house gave directly on to this grassed area, the bottom half shut, the upper left open to the air: a dark square through which the two detectives, on the further side of the fence, could make out nothing of the interior.

Nothing, that is, except for the frenzy of flies which filled the space with their ecstatic dance. The sun shone on the hovering bodies, struck gold and silver off wings which moved too fast for the eye to follow. No more silence: in its place a vibrating sibilation that rose higher and higher until it was a pain to the ear and a burden to the spirit, yet still the ear strained to encompass it, loath to let it go beyond the bounds of hearing.

The two detectives stood for a moment staring. Then, as one, without a word exchanged, they came away from the fence, ran to the front door of the goat house and burst their way inside.

The smell hit them like a physical blow. The flies, rising as one to repel the disturbers of their peace, swirled up in an angry cloud before apparently deciding that the intruders represented no threat. With renewed appetite they settled back to their feast and their place in the scheme of things.

Behind the wooden half-wall of each individual stall, below hayracks that looked fresh-filled with hay, a goat – some twenty of them in all – lay dead and rotting, throat cut, stomach distended with gas, yet still beautiful; the brown and white coats softly shining, the upturned hoofs bright, the small ears alert as if attentive to what the flies had to say. The eyes were sunken, fly-encrusted, and Jurnet was thinking, absurdly: '*Not like Bette Davis at all,*' when Jack Ellers gave a shout.

'Here!'

Joey Corvin lay in the end stall, dead like the animal against which his lean body was pillowed, throat cut, man and goat dead of the same death. A shepherd's lamb-foot knife, rusted with blood, lay close to his right hand which, outstretched, seemed still to be reaching for it, as if not entirely convinced that the job had been well and truly done. In death the goat farmer did not look as handsome as his goats and smelled a whole lot worse. Maggots crawled on a face that might once have been good-looking in a grim, uncompromising way but now looked blank, a nothingness. Whatever else the man had found in death, it wasn't answers.

Forcing down the bile that rose unbidden in his throat, Jurnet said in a kind of wonder: 'He topped up the hayracks. Those buckets must have been filled to the brim, judging by what's still left in them. And look – there among the straw – '

Whey-faced and sweating, Jack Ellers asked: 'Those greyish flakes, you mean? What are they?'

'Hoof. Shavings of hoof. That bloke I knew used to say that a goat without good feet wasn't worth its keep. Every four or five weeks he'd trim their hoofs. I used to watch him. He had a knife exactly like that one there, and he used to pare each hoof down very, very delicately, never taking off more than a paper-thin layer at one stroke. I tell you, it was a work of art. I never remember the goats objecting. They seemed to know he was doing it for their own good, and after it was done and he'd untied them, they'd come and rub their heads against him as if they were saying thanks – '

Jack Ellers cleared his throat with difficulty.

'What did he think he was doing, for Christ's sake? Getting them ready for the pastures of heaven? Can you understand how a guy could put out fresh hay and water, trim their toenails – blow their noses and clean their teeth, for all we know – and then cut their throats? His own throat was his own bloody business, but what had *they* done? Can you understand it?'

'Yes.'

Jurnet turned away. Followed by his subordinate, he began the long walk along the gangway between the stalls, each with its carcass and its attendant flies snug behind its own low gate: back to untainted air which the two gulped in gratefully, a delicacy whose taste they had all but forgotten.

'Get on to Headquarters,' Jurnet directed. 'Spread the good news. And Wyatt, of course. Tell that Sleeping Beauty to wake up, get himself over here and see what goes on in the real world. Have a word with Sergeant Bowles. Tell him we need to know what that nephew of Joey Corvin's died of.'

10

The green suitcase, its surface the colour and consistency of phlegm, sat on a trestle table in the police lab looking like a health warning to intending travellers: *leave home at your peril!* Laid out with spinsterish care on either side, a number of small piles identifiable with difficulty as consisting of assorted sweaters, blouses, women's underwear, added up to Annie Chance's trousseau. The ruins of a white handbag, Jurnet noticed, had grown an unexpectedly beautiful frosting of lichen.

'"Journeys end in lovers' meeting", I don't think,' quoted Sid Hale. He looked strangely content at this concrete evidence that the worst could not only threaten to happen but actually come to pass. 'Poor little Bo-Peep! Lost not only her sheep but her Marks and Spencer knicks and knacks into the bargain. Amount she took along with her, she certainly intended a long stay.'

'In that at least –' the Superintendent spoke austerely and as if, even in its terminal condition, the display of feminine apparel occasioned him some discomfort – 'she wasn't disappointed.' Turning to the white-coated young man on whose territory Angleby CID was officially encroaching: 'Wasn't there anything except clothing?'

'There was what might have been a couple of letters, or might not. Irretrievable.' The young man bowed his head, taking the fault upon himself. 'Apart from that, there was only this.' He picked up a polythene envelope containing a photograph and proffered it with some nervousness, as if to a dog of whose good intentions he was not entirely convinced. 'It was in the inner pocket of the handbag. There's a waterproof lining, which is why it survived pretty well, all things considered.'

The photograph was of a large, unattractive baby – one, at a guess, at least a year old; certainly of an age to sit up unaided instead of having to be propped up by pillows, its head too heavy, it seemed, for the pitiful neck to support. There were ample indications in addition to attest that the child was not as other children. The wonder was that the mother of such a child had ever thought to take it to a professional photographer for the making of a formal studio portrait; but there it was in fancy script – the firm's name on the buckled cardboard surround: *Cummings & Browder, Cromer*.

Jurnet, receiving the photograph from the Superintendent after the latter had bestowed on it a brief, unwilling glance, studied the mould-mottled image with a surge of compassion. It must have taken courage to have the infant Timmy recorded for posterity despite everything: courage and love. Enduring love, what was more – else why, even as she ran away, had Annie Chance chosen to take Timmy's baby photograph along with her?

'What we need', declared the Superintendent, the creased brows not making it clear whom he was holding responsible for its non-appearance – Jurnet, the white-coated young man or the dead woman herself – 'is a photo of that damned elusive commercial traveller. Or better still, an address, a telephone number. *Irretrievable!*' – appropriating the lab man's word and transforming each separate syllable into stone. 'All this wretched collection tells us is something we knew already – that Annie Chance's flight to a new life was over before it was ever begun. Our only hope is that Batterby will run the fellow to earth,' he finished, not sounding as if he would put good money on it.

'Assuming he's there to be run,' said Jurnet.

His superior officer received this suggestion with an unmistakable gleam of satisfaction, one which had the effect of lighting up the atmosphere in a way the fluorescent strips in the lab ceiling had signally failed to do. Jurnet, charitably putting aside his first thought that it was the prospect of pricking Dave Batterby's insufferable self-esteem which had occasioned this change of mood – the Superintendent must know as well as everybody else at Angleby CID that Dave Batterby's self-esteem was unprickable – decided that the sudden good humour arose from relief that he and his might not, after all, be called upon to sift through the travelling salesmen of the UK in the forlorn hope of isolating the one among them who, some three months ago, had done for a woman on a remote North Norfolk beach; but instead, with luck, might restrict their area of inquiry to a single village whose natives, hypnotized by the power of the law, must sooner or later yield up their innermost secrets to the light of day.

The Superintendent, his face alight with expectation, stood looking at his subordinate like a dog of high breeding waiting for a bone to be, not thrown, but proffered in servile homage at his aristocratic feet.

'When you come down to it,' said Jurnet, putting his thoughts in order, 'we only have Oz Bailey's word for it that there is any such animal. Annie told him – he says.'

'Told him a story about a diffident virgin – ' the Superintendent pointed out, delicately testing the hypothesis. 'Hardly your common or garden image of the travelling salesman. Wouldn't you say there's a ring of truth in its very unexpectedness?'

'Could equally be that Bailey, making up the story, couldn't bear the thought of Annie going to bed with anyone apart from himself.'

'That still doesn't account for what the chef says about seeing the woman putting her suitcase in the car boot.'

'He also says he didn't notice what make of car. Oz Bailey has a black Vauxhall.'

'Interesting.' But the Superintendent's short-lived affability was already dissolving like sugar in hot tea. 'It would be even more interesting to be able to account for the way Annie and her phantom lover could drive off into the sunset, only to have Bailey turn up at the Caff in his van twenty minutes later, alone and ostensibly looking for her. Nowhere near time enough, even for a part-time undertaker, to get down to the beach with the lady, kill and decently inter her, let alone change vehicles and dispose of the suitcase en route. And how did the van and the Vauxhall get home, I wonder, with only one driver between the two of them?' Finishing with deadly kindness: 'You'll have to do better than that, Ben!'

'Broncho-pneumonia, you say? In that case, you needn't waste your good Sergeant's time any further.' Dr Colton sat back in his chair looking troubled. The notorious procrastinator, dotter of every i and crosser of every t, was always, as a consequence, so short of time himself that it caused him physical pain even to hear of another frittering away that precious commodity. 'Twenty-five years old, living in a homosexual environment and the death

105

certificate says "Broncho-pneumonia" – you can take it as said that the young man died of Aids.'

Jurnet said: 'The chap was in hospital for a while, but his uncle – if that's what Joey Corvin was – brought him home to die. It's a notifiable disease, isn't it, so wouldn't the hospital have a duty to report it? Wouldn't his GP be obliged to let the authorities know he was treating a patient who had it? And, if it *was* Aids, wasn't he breaking the law by writing something else on the death certificate?'

'Surprising as you may find it,' was the reply, 'I have to tell you that, as of this moment, Aids is not a notifiable disease, though it is likely to become one before long. In the meantime, if the certifying doctor deposed that the patient had died of broncho-pneumonia, then I am quite sure that broncho-pneumonia is what it was.' Dr Colton, who, quite without personal hubris, held medical men to be a race apart, dedicated and incorruptible, sounded testy. 'The legal requirement is for the immediate – the immediate, note – cause of death to be entered on the certificate. If a patient dies of lung cancer or emphysema we are not required to put down the cigarette-smoking which may well be the prime cause.' A pause, and then: 'On the reverse of the document, however – though not on the reverse of any copies which may be bespoken by members of the public upon payment of a fee – there is a little box wherein the doctor, if he so wishes – and as things stand at present the decision is his alone – may place a tick signifying that he has further information about the death to impart to the proper quarter. Broncho-pneumonia is only one, albeit a frequent, result of that breakdown of the immune system which we call Aids. Tuberculosis, several forms of cancer – ' Colton broke off with a sigh. 'So many young lives – ' More to the man, Jurnet decided, than the desiccated paper-pusher.

'Yes,' the detective said, letting a moment of silence pass in tribute to the wasted lives, all that wasted time. Remembering what Timmy had told him, however, he pressed on. 'Friend who went to see the young man shortly before the end said he hardly recognized him on account of the purple and blue patches standing out on his face, his arms and his hand – '

('Looked like a bloody clown out of the circus,' had been Timmy's laconic description. 'I told him, "You look like a bloody clown out of the circus," an' he said, "Tha's a laugh, that is," an' he started to laugh, on'y it turned to coughing an' crying an' Joey come running in an' tole me to get the hell out of there. Not nice,' the boy had finished, on his dignity. 'Go outa my way, all the way up to the common jes' to ask Andy how he is, took him a bag of humbugs cost me 56p, an' Joey tells me to get the hell.')

'Purple and blue patches!' Dr Colton sounded as if he had been told good news. 'Kaposi sarcoma! That clinches it. Now you can be sure you're on the right track. Kaposi sarcoma used to be a cancer especially favoured by elderly Jews in Eastern Europe. Now it's one of the tumours of choice among young Aids victims. The Russians used to deny there was any Aids in the Soviet Union until they had this sudden, unparalleled increase in Kaposi sarcoma, and the secret was out.' Brows furrowed, the doctor regarded the detective. 'This surely can't have anything to do with the Lanthrop murder?'

'Only indirectly. Annie Chance's boy used to hang out with that bunch up on the hill. I couldn't help wondering if he might not have picked something up there he wouldn't thank them for.'

Colton said sharply: 'You're aware that you can't test for HIV without the patient's permission?'

'I'm aware.'

It was, even in retrospect, galling that Timmy, the idiot boy, had got the better of him. He had flatly refused to have a blood test. 'What I want someone takin' my blood for? I don't like bein' pricked.'

Which was daft if anything was, seeing that Jurnet had found him at the edge of the wood manhandling piles of wilted brambles without protective gloves and bleeding copiously from a dozen scratches which appeared to bother him not at all.

When the detective pointed out this contradiction, Timmy had looked down at his bloodied arms as if seeing them for the first time. 'Tha's different.'

'They put some stuff on you first. You don't even know it's happened.'

'They got no business taking my blood. They got their own blood.'

'Not *all* your blood, Timmy. Less than you've got running down your arms this minute.'

'I'll have to speak to ma. See what she says.' Obviously considering the conversation at an end, the boy loaded a further tangle of thorny detritus on to the wheelbarrow.

'Timmy, your ma is dead.'

'Oh ah.' Timmy bent over, hefted the handles of the wheelbarrow and began to trundle his unwieldy burden into the wood. Jurnet watched for a moment and then started after him. 'Private!' the boy shouted back. 'Trespassers will be prosecuted!'

'Hold on, though! You just brought that lot out. What you taking it back for?'

'I said private!' Not moderating his pace, Timmy flung over his shoulder: 'Who's the gardener here, you or me? You mind your own bloody business!'

'Fair enough – sorry!' Jurnet caught up with the boy, even, despite the rebuff, taking a certain pleasure in this proof that, for all the overwhelming impression of inadequacy, there were glimmerings of spirit, of inner resource. 'Not for me to tell *you*. Only you've got to admit it does seem funny, first fetching it out and then taking it back in again.'

The boy twisted the wheelbarrow over on to its side, precipitating its contents in a convolution which, with the aid of a fork, he proceeded to spread over the freshly cleared ground beneath the trees. In the woodland shade his normally inexpressive face looked triumphant. 'Let 'em try fuckin' on that lot,' he chuckled. 'That'll fuck 'em! That'll funny 'em!'

'Funny who? You mean the students, the archaeology lot? They don't do any harm do they?'

'They got no business!' Timmy frowned fiercely. 'She say to me, "Timmy, that wood could do with a cleaning out," so I clean it out, right?'

'Mrs Milburn, you mean?'

'When I done she come up an' take a look an' she say, "Timmy you done a good job there. We'll have sausages for tea, you done such a good job." What she don't say is how, now the wood's all cleaned up, they'll be up here fuckin' all hours. I tell that Abbott, "Is that what you pay them fer?" an' all he do is laugh and he say, "I don't. They do it for free." What kind of answer is that?' The dull features were suddenly irradiated from within with a mischievous intelligence that was like a candle lit in an empty room and as quickly extinguished. 'All I say is, they try it next time, brambles up their bums what they'll get, 'stead of the usual. See how they like that!'

'You haven't quite finished the job,' Jurnet said, pointing to an untouched area of gorse and bracken tucked away in one corner.

'Tha's where there's an ole badger.' The boy sounded annoyed. 'Family on 'em. You gotta be kind to wild animals, din't no one tell you that?'

'You might try being kind to those kids. Why should *you* care what they get up to? It's no skin off your nose.' With deliberate emphasis the detective added: 'Shouldn't be surprised you come up here yourself with Sandra, when you're in the mood.'

The boy looked at him with contempt.

'I don't fuck Sandra. You got to be spliced to fuck Sandra. Spliced *and* have a bungalow. That Ian don't have no bungalow. She – (this time Jurnet had no difficulty identifying who was intended by the pronoun –) 'won't put up no bungalow fer *him*.'

'I'm delighted to hear you're thinking about getting married.' Jurnet laid the heartiness on thick. 'A sight better than fooling around up at Joey Corvin's.'

'I dunno,' the boy objected. 'They give me money up at Joey's. Sandra don't give me nothing. Women, you got ter give *them* all the time or they don't want ter know.' Looking hurt, Timmy said: 'That in't fair.'

'It's the way of the world. Tell me, Timmy, did Andy up at the goat farm ever give you money?'

'Yer don't think I did it for nothing, do you? I weren't born yesterday.' The boy's voice changed, became even more blurred than usual, a melancholy that was beautiful and disturbing settling upon the unfinished face. 'Is it right what they say about Joey killing off them goats?'

'Afraid so.'

Tears spilled down Timmy's cheeks, clouded the thick glass of his spectacles.

'I was right fond of them goats. They was – ' after a rummage through his limited vocabulary the boy came up with ' – nice.' Clenching his fists: 'When I see Joey I'm goin' to give the bugger a piece of my mind.'

'Joey's dead too, Timmy.'

'Oh ah? Serve him right, then!'

It was no surprise to find Mrs Milburn out in her garden pretending to look for black fly on her rose bushes but in reality lying in wait to intercept him. She must have seen the Rover parked in the driveway.

'Everything all right, Inspector?' she greeted him, not quite calmly enough.

'Apart from a murder, a probable suicide, and a herd of pedigree goats sent to their Maker with their throats cut,' Jurnet answered, 'everything's fine.'

The woman flushed, her porcelain delicacy humanized, made unexpectedly accessible. Fresh from Timmy's company, Jurnet felt a renewal of amazement that a woman still of childbearing age, however greatly bereaved, who looked the way Hannah Milburn looked didn't choose another partner from out of the scrum that must be panting to volunteer, and produce a family Mark 2, rather than choose to make do with a retarded boy.

'I heard about the goats,' she said. 'My husband always said Mr Corvin's *chèvre* was equal to anything you could get on the Continent.' Not far from tears, she finished: 'They were such lovely creatures!'

'Yes,' Jurnet agreed. 'Timmy was just telling me how nice they were.'

'Nice!' she echoed, before, the penny dropping, she flushed an even deeper red. 'I didn't mean – '

'I'm quite sure you didn't.' Jurnet, relenting, reddened a little himself. Who was he to go ticking her off for putting animals before people? The way the world was, who could blame her? In an altogether friendlier tone: 'It's a sad business. Corvin's lover died a couple of weeks ago – young chap name of Andy Burge, maybe you knew him? – and it looks like Corvin didn't want to go on living without him.' In fairness to the dead man: 'The reason he killed the goats could have been he didn't feel they'd get the tender loving care he'd given them from anybody else.'

But, as the detective had intended, Hannah Milburn's attention had been engaged elsewhere.

'His lover? Mr Corvin was a homosexual? I'd no idea. But then – none of my business, was it? From time to time, when I went up to the farm, I did see a young man in the distance. He looked ill, I thought, so far as I could tell.'

'He was, very.'

Perhaps because illness and death were still difficult subjects, she inquired by way of diversion: 'Would you care for a cup of coffee?'

When Jurnet said yes please, she left him alone amongst the waxed furniture, the chintzes and the flower arrangements whilst she went out to the kitchen to give instructions for its preparation. Returning, she dropped into an armchair with the understated elegance which seemed natural to all her movements.

'Poor Mr Corvin! How strange it is! In this tiny village, where we feel we know everyone as well as we know ourselves – better! – how little we really know of each other's lives!'

Jurnet asked: 'You don't happen to know why Annie had a blazing row with Corvin shortly before she left Lanthrop for good?'

The china-blue eyes opened wide.

'She never said anything to me. But then, as I've already told you, we weren't on terms of that sort.'

'I just hoped you might have picked up some hint. Timmy says it was on account of he'd been putting in a few hours' work up on the common from time to time and his mother carried on because he came home smelling of goat. The inference is that she went up there to demand that the boy be provided with protective clothing, but I don't know. If she was planning shortly to abandon Timmy, goat smell and all, it seems strange that she bothered.'

Jurnet broke off as Sandra Thorne's breasts entered the living room followed, after a respectful interval, by their owner and a loaded tray. The sight of the girl, so sublimely ridiculous, made Jurnet's mind up for him. Not even a momentary vision of the Superintendent, mouthing imprecations like someone out of an old-fashioned silent movie, was enough to deter him.

Once the girl had left, he drank deeply of his coffee, put the cup and saucer down on the small table she had set in front of him, and began: 'You could ask me what it has to do with Annie's murder and I wouldn't be able to swear that it has anything to do with it. You could ask me what business is it of mine anyway and I wouldn't be able to answer that one either. Just the same, for reasons that seem valid to me if no one else, I think you ought to know that up there on the common Timmy was getting up to a good deal more than cleaning out the goats.'

Hannah Milburn's blue eyes darkening relayed the information that there was no need to be more explicit.

Jurnet continued nevertheless: 'In case it matters to you – as, in view of your plans for the boy, it must – let me say that nothing I've found out adds up to grounds for questioning Timmy's own sexual orientation.' With a grimace at his own pomposity: 'What I mean is, I don't for a moment think he's gay, nor that anything is gained by going into what I think of Joey Corvin and his so-called nephew except to say that their taking advantage of a feeble-minded boy doesn't do a whole lot to stir the bowels of my compassion over their sad end. However, that's water under the bridge. The important thing now, as I'm sure you will agree, is damage limitation, if indeed damage has been done, and if, in the present state of medical knowledge, there are measures which can usefully be taken to limit it. Not that it's going to be easy. I had a word with Timmy just now, up in your wood: did my best to explain what the danger could be. To no purpose. He refuses point-blank to be HIV tested, and in the present state of the law there's not a thing anyone can do to force him.'

Avoiding the small table with his cup and saucer Jurnet stood up, Hannah Milburn following suit as if by agreement that these were not matters to be discussed over coffee cups or whilst cushioned in flower-patterned upholstery. He finished: 'What I'm hoping is that you'll be able to persuade him.'

The woman was nearly as tall as the detective was himself. Her eyes, very blue, very bright, looked directly into his as she said, with polite regret: 'Of course I shall do nothing of the kind.' Reprovingly: 'And you called him feeble-minded again. I wish you wouldn't do that. How many times do I have to say he is *not* feeble-minded?'

'Let him prove it, then, by doing the sensible thing.' Taking a calculated risk of forfeiting the woman's goodwill once and for all: 'Yesterday was Wednesday. What's the betting Timmy went home to wait for his ma to bring fish and chips home from the Caff for his dinner? And that you went down and found him there, waiting with a bib round his neck and his Little Bo-Peep mat spread out in front of him?'

Hannah Milburn said steadily: 'What if I did find all those things, just as you say? I also found that when I said to him, "Timmy, you know your mother's dead," he gave me a look – such a look I can't tell you – ' At the recollection of that look the woman crossed her arms and hugged herself, taking comfort from the living warmth of her own body – 'and he said, "I know."'

'Well, then – ' The detective did not attempt to disguise his lack of understanding.

'Well, then!' the other repeated, with a well-bred impatience.

'What it means is that he thinks of Annie as both dead and not dead, which is a wonderful gift, not the sign of mental deficiency you seem to take it for. It means that, even after all that has happened, he still hasn't quite lost her. My one fear is that when the inquest's over and he actually sees Annie's coffin being lowered into the earth, that will be the end of it for him – the end of hope, I mean.'

'No percentage in a hope that hasn't a hope in hell of coming true.' Jurnet pressed on. 'Sooner or later Timmy's got to come to terms with the fact that his ma is dead, period. The burial service, the wreaths, the whole shebang, could be the best thing that could happen to the lad. Something to relate to – I've seen it happen. Being a gardener, he can make Annie's the best-looking grave in Lanthrop churchyard.' In a different tone of voice: 'You really will have to get him to have that test.'

'Even if I do –' Mrs Milburn frowned a little at the imperative – 'and he turns out to be HIV positive, there's nothing anyone can do about it.'

'You don't know that. They're researching all the time. Besides which –' Jurnet made no attempt to hide his disappointment – 'aren't you forgetting something? What about young Sandra, or any other young girl he may take up with?'

'I very much doubt whether Timmy is capable of achieving sexual intercourse.'

'You don't know that, I don't know that – only that any girl who may go to bed with him is entitled to the option of staying out of possible harm's way. If I may say so, Mrs Milburn, now that you've started something, you can't stand back and pretend that nothing has changed.'

'I'll think about it,' the woman promised. She came near enough for Jurnet to be aware of the fresh sweet smell of her. 'As for graves,' she remarked in the friendliest way, 'have you, by any chance, been into our churchyard yet – seen where my husband's and my daughter's ashes are buried?'

'Between the buttresses. Under the window.'

'That's right,' she nodded, looking pleased. 'I always think it's such a shame stained-glass looks so depressing from the outside, don't you? Though actually –' screwing up her face in a way that turned the grown woman into a schoolgirl again – 'from inside, that particular window looks even more dire. It's the martyrdom of St Blaise, with men tearing the flesh off his body using the iron

113

combs they used in the old days for carding wool. That's why he's the patron saint of the wool trade, though it seems a funny reason to me. Other men are busy roasting gobbets of his flesh on a gridiron. Gruesome! When I was a child, every time we went to church my mother would warn me not to look at it, she was afraid I'd get nightmares, but all it did was give me the giggles.' She was giggling now at the memory. Catching sight of Jurnet's face, clouded with concern, she regained her calm. 'Sorry about that. Even after all this time, St Blaise always sets me off. I'll think about Timmy and the test,' she said, 'I will, really. You were quite right to come and tell me. I'm not sure yet what I'll do, but I'll do something. I promise.'

'See that the boy gets the test done, that's all I ask.'

'Not all.' Hannah Milburn stood quiet for a moment. Then she said: 'You still want to know about me and Annie, don't you? Everything you say is an asking.'

'Is it?'

'You know it is.' The woman took the detective's hand, in friendship, trustingly. 'If you can spare the time,' she said, 'I'd like you to come down to the beach with me. Later you may want to take me to the police station, that will be for you to decide. I want to tell you about how I committed a murder.'

11

They stood on the sandhill amid the ring of dunes.

Jurnet exclaimed in surprise: 'It's almost back to what it was! I'd made sure we'd done for it, with all that digging.'

Hannah Milburn nodded.

'I've noticed it time and again. When there's been a gale or a high spring tide you could come down and find the top completely flattened, hardly anything left. Come back ten days later and there it is, looking as if nothing had happened. It's as if there is only one possible shape for it to be, and come back it will, no matter what.'

'Magic,' said Jurnet, inwardly rejoicing that the place where Miriam had called him her heart's desire was imperishable.

'Yes. Magic.' Hannah Milburn pointed. 'Do you see that cloud, the large white cumulus with a kind of unicorn's horn, just touching the horizon? Katie used to get quite upset whenever she saw clouds like that. Not its shape, its position in the sky. "Mummy!" she'd come running. "There's a cloud falling into the sea! Can clouds swim, Mummy? Will it drown?"'

The woman seated herself on the rim of the bowl within which a new growth of plants was already weaving a new carpet. Shielding her eyes, she looked up at the detective standing tall against the sky. 'Sometimes', she said with a little laugh, 'I feel like that myself. A drowning cloud.'

Jurnet prompted: 'You said a murder.'

'You'll have to let me tell it in my own way.' There was a silence: then, 'Do you know what happens at a cremation?'

'I've attended one or two, if that's what you mean.'

The other shook her head.

'I mean behind the scenes, after the coffin has slid away and the

Muzak's still churning out aural gunge to take your mind off what's happening to your loved one behind the scenes.'

The detective hesitated. 'The body is burned, of course.'

Another shake of the head.

'Only part of the story. It isn't a simple matter of the corpse going in whole at one end and emerging at the other as talcum powder prettily packaged in a dear little casket. Back there, there are men with long-handled hooks who break the skeletons into pieces the right size for feeding into a kind of giant hopper which turns them into a nice anonymous ash which can't offend anyone. I bet you didn't know that.'

'I didn't know that.'

'Not many people do.' The woman sounded pleased to be in the know. 'Though when you think of all the gadgets that stand about on our worktops nowadays – all the choppers and the blenders – it seems only right and proper, when you come to think about it, for human beings themselves to end up minced.' Dry-eyed, Hannah Milburn announced: 'I can't bear the thought of those hooks tearing at Katie's little bones.'

'The murder,' Jurnet reminded her, not knowing what else to say.

'Ah yes, the murder. You thought Annie Chance was the only murder victim buried in this sandhill, didn't you?'

The detective looked startled.

'I know that she was.'

'You're wrong.' Hannah Milburn shook her head. 'No need to look at me like that, Inspector – so kind, so forbearing. For your information, my daughter Katie is buried here too. I know she is because I did it myself, the day after the cremation. I drove down here with those silly little caskets bumping about on the back seat and I broke the seal and scattered Katie over her castle, in all the places where she used to play her secret games – '

'Caskets, you said.' Jurnet's voice was gentle. 'You buried your husband's ashes at the same time?'

'Not here!' the woman returned sharply. 'I put Alan in the sea, as far in as I could get without going out of my depth. I was practically up to my armpits before I let his ashes go into the wind, into the waves.' Hannah Milburn looked at the detective with something flirtatious in her gaze. 'Don't tell me, asking round the village, you haven't heard all about how the poor soul crazed with grief, tried to kill herself, only she thought better of it at the last moment?'

'There was something – '

'On the way down to the beach I'd shot past Mr Gifford the moment he opened the gate, but coming back he came over to the car window before opening up. Either he was bursting with curiosity as to what I'd been doing down on the shore when I ought, in all decency, to have been lying in a darkened room with a hankie soaked in eau-de-cologne on my forehead, or perhaps he just wanted to say he was sorry, I don't know. When he saw the way I was, drenched, the water dripping from my hair, I couldn't blame him for jumping to conclusions.'

Jurnet said: 'Those plaques in the churchyard – '

'Oh yes, those. The committal service was fixed for next day, you see. That was why I couldn't have put it off for later.'

'Forgive me if I'm being thick,' said Jurnet, 'but why a committal service at all, if that wasn't what you wanted?'

'Alan's mother would have been livid. She likes to call herself a practising Christian, though if God ever sent out end-of-term reports He would write on hers, "Needs to practise harder." She needed to see her son deposited in Lanthrop churchyard, a long-term account, so to speak, in a reputable bank, redeemable upon a date to be announced later. I wasn't strong enough to say no.' Face lifted to the sun, Hannah Milburn inquired: 'Aren't you going to ask how you can have a committal service when there aren't any ashes to commit?'

'I'm sure you found a way.'

'Absolutely right! Early the next morning, very early, I refilled the caskets, using ashes out of the Aga. Ordinarily it never got riddled until Annie came in, but this time I'd done it the night before to make sure the ash would be cold and wouldn't have that sulphury smell you always get from fresh boiler ash. It took a surprisingly long time to decide how much ash was right for Katie and how much for Alan, and by the time I'd finished tipping ashes into the two caskets and tipping them out again because I'd either put in too much or not enough, there was ash everywhere. Everything in the kitchen was coated with it.'

The animation went out of Hannah Milburn's face as she finished: 'I was just wondering what kind of excuse I could make to Annie for the state the place was in when the back door opened and there she was, the open caskets and their contents in full view. With all the people coming up to Fastolfes for something to eat after the service, she'd had the kind thought of coming in early.'

'Must have given you both a surprise.'

'For me, to be honest, the surprise was the kind thought. It was the first time I'd ever known Annie Chance to volunteer to do anything beyond the call of duty.' The blue eyes intent on the past, Hannah Milburn said: 'I suppose I'd had what you could call a stressful day, I'd hardly slept, and suddenly that kindness from a totally unexpected quarter completely unmanned me. I began to cry as I hadn't cried when they came and told me that my husband and my child were dead. My tears fell into the open caskets, turning the dust inside from grey to a rusty brown. I was still in my dressing-gown and nightdress, ashes in my hair, the taste of them in my mouth. Like Job – wasn't it? – I sat among the ashes and wept.'

'How did Annie take it?'

Wonderingly: 'She put her arms round me and I told her everything.'

'A sight more than you've told me!' The detective's abrupt change of manner was not entirely contrived. 'You've told me how you can have a committal service when there aren't any ashes to commit when what I need to know is *why*. What was it all in aid of?'

Hannah Milburn filled both her hands with sand which she studied with absorbed attention before opening her fingers and letting it trickle away to join the rest of Lanthrop beach. Her voice remained calm, untroubled. 'I told you,' she said. 'Murder.'

Hannah Milburn said: 'Do you know what loving is? It's like owning a fragile piece of china – a Ming vase, say, or a piece of old Chelsea; treasuring it, keeping it bedded down in cottonwool for fear of breakage. And then, one day, you decide to undo the wrapping, to check up or just to enjoy the sight of it for once and – nobody knows how it happened – it's all in pieces. And the person you're really angry with is yourself, because if you hadn't insisted on looking at it in the first place, you could have gone on believing that everything in the cottonwool was lovely. You would never have known that it wasn't whole and beautiful any longer.' The woman stood up, shook sand from her skirt. 'You were in the village shop with that beautiful girl. You must know yourself how fragile love is.'

'And how strong.'

'Strong but brittle,' Hannah Milburn amended, unaware of the self-doubt her words had engendered. 'Do you remember what I told you about Timmy sitting in the pond among the waterlilies? And how I went and got some of Alan's clothes for him to put on?'

'I remember.'

'That lovely blouson – anorak, if you like – among them, the one Alan brought back from Paris only the week before he died?' The detective nodded. 'I'm afraid Timmy's gone and lost it already. I've gone through his things, but no luck. He must have put it down somewhere and then gone off without thinking. Ah well!' The woman sighed. 'Perhaps it's all for the best. Perhaps it was meant to be.'

After a silence which prolonged itself, Jurnet asked: 'You were saying about the anorak – ?'

Hannah Milburn roused herself from her reverie. 'I was, wasn't I? I was saying that on the morning of the day I found my Ming vase shattered I was putting some of Alan's things away in his closet and I noticed that the crimson thread of the embroidered signature on the breast pocket was hanging loose. So, like the good little *hausfrau* I used to be, I went and got my workbox, and fished out a needle to repair the damage before it went any further. To do that, I had to put my left hand inside the pocket itself, to make sure I didn't sew through two thicknesses of cloth by mistake – and that was when I became aware of something already there. It was just a narrow strip of paper, the kind you might have expected to have instructions on it about dry-cleaning, or perhaps some workroom code that wouldn't mean a thing to anyone but the makers. It was neither of those. It was a slip of paper with some writing on it, and what the writing said was, *"Let me lie always close to your heart."*'

Jurnet took his time before commenting.

'Could have been one of the machinists having a joke – '

'I thought about that. But in *English*? I thought about it all day long, until Alan came home, late and a little drunk. I don't know whether I've mentioned that he quite often drank more than he should. He said he'd run into a chap he'd been at school with, and one thing had led to another. All said and done, he said, he was glad he'd decided to go up to town by train that day and had only had a short drive home from the station.

'It's strange,' Hannah Milburn said, looking out towards the sea. 'When I look back to that evening, after Alan came home, it's like looking through the wrong end of a telescope, everything farther away even than that horizon. I see myself, doll-sized, holding out that slip of paper to an equally small Alan who takes it from me, takes a ridiculously long time to read the few words written there, and then lifts up his head and says quite off-handedly that yes, as a matter of fact he *had* taken a girl with him to Paris and yes, they *had* bought the Balmain blouson together.' The woman took a deep breath. 'Not any old girl, he said, as if that excused everything, but a dearly loved mistress of long standing – one, however, who had deprived me of nothing, since what was between the two of them was something I'd never had anyway.' She broke off, turned away from the sea and looked directly at the detective. The remarkable eyes had lost some of their blueness. 'I'm sorry,' she said, 'but you *did* ask.'

'I'm still asking.'

'I'm afraid it gets worse and worse – ' The well-bred English apology, the English rose face distorted, though the voice retained its petalled calm. 'I made a scene. I screamed. I threw myself about, even though, even as I was doing it, I could see that Alan's expression was a mixture of boredom and exasperation. *"When the hell am I going to get my dinner?"* I could see him thinking. But it didn't stop me. I went on and on. After a while he went and poured himself a whisky. And then – ' Hannah Milburn plunged her hands into the pockets of her skirt as if afraid of what they might do if left free to follow their own compulsions – 'there's an even tinier figure at the telescope's end. Katie, in pyjamas, woken up by the noise I was making and bewildered by it. How could she not be bewildered? Up till then we had all been, God save us, so very happy together.'

'What happend then?'

'Alan put down his empty glass, scooped her up in his arms, and said something about Mummy feeling off-colour and needing to put her feet up. "Is it a pain in her tum?" Katie asked, and Alan answered, "Shouldn't be surprised."

'As for me, I couldn't speak. I just stood there with a fist clenched against my mouth to keep the horrible sound from breaking out all over again. So that the two of them were out of the room before it even dawned on me what Alan was proposing. "Tell you what, poppet, we'll take a little ride, what do you say?" He said it was a lovely evening, a little ride would make her feel sleepy, to say nothing of taking them both out of the firing-line until Mummy was her old self again. Katie, bless her, wanted to stay and look after me, but Alan said I'd be better on my own. "A little peace and quiet and she'll be feeling fine."

'By the time it registered,' Hannah Milburn said, 'the car was racing down the drive. Useless to scream after it – though I ran out of the house and did just that – that the Jag had no child's seat-belt, that the man was drunk.

'I went back indoors and sat down by the telephone, waiting to hear from the police that the two of them were dead. I knew it would happen and I suppose you could say I wasn't disappointed. Katie went through the windscreen. I hope they were not being kind when they said she was killed instantly. As for Alan, instead of being, like me, condemned to live with the knowledge that I had killed my child, he died the minute the car hit the tree. But then, he was always the lucky one.'

Hannah Milburn said: 'It was still early in the year, the sun shining but the sea very cold, the day I went into it to scatter Alan's ashes. No – ' correcting herself instantly – 'not "scatter". Scattering implies a degree of ceremony. I dumped Alan in the water to make sure that none of him, not a speck, would pollute the land ever again. I went into the sea as one might go out to the dustbin to get rid of rubbish.' A pause, then: 'Yet, in a way, Mr Gifford and the rest of the village were not all that far out.'

'How do you mean?'

'Until I'd got into the water, I promise you, and felt the piercing cold of it, I hadn't given my own death a thought. But once I realized that only a few yards more and there would be no more pain, an end to love, an end to everything, I can't tell you how great was the temptation to go on pushing through the waves towards that blessed oblivion.'

Jurnet asserted with conviction: 'It wasn't in your nature.'

'Was that what it was?' Hannah Milburn looked interested. 'I've often wondered. All I do know is that death was suddenly too easy. After what I'd done I didn't deserve to be let off so lightly. After a crime there has to be punishment. You're a policeman, you must understand that. I made sure the casket was empty and came back to the beach.'

'And all this you told Annie? How did she take it?'

'The way she took everything, without surprise – and also, thank heaven, without any of that cooing sympathy which would have sent me screaming up the wall. Looking back, I often wonder if she hadn't known all along what Alan was up to. She could have overheard telephone conversations, read letters left lying about. She was, after all, the paid help; and she had no obligation to respect Alan's privacy the way I'd always bent over backwards to.' With a crooked smile for that past self dead with all its illusions wrapped about it like a shroud: 'No besotted love, either, to blind her to what was going on under her nose.'

With calculated brutality Jurnet asked: 'Is it possible, Mrs Milburn, that there was a relationship between your husband and Annie Chance?'

The woman, in no way offended, considered.

'Anything's possible, I suppose. Since obviously I didn't begin to know my husband, how can I possibly say whom he may or may not have gone to bed with? Thank goodness it never occurred to me to wonder at the time, because then I'd have had to tell her to go. And then I should never have had Timmy.'

Troubled for the boy, Jurnet said, his tone firm: 'Timmy's a grown man now. Nobody *has* him, or ought to. He has to have himself.'

Hannah Milburn's head came up abruptly, her eyes bright with sudden tears.

'Don't you think I understand that? Even with Katie I understood it – that every day she had to be encouraged to be more and more herself, not a mere incarnation of my selfish dreams. It's the first lesson a mother has to learn, and the hardest.' Relaxing: 'You needn't be afraid of my baleful influence over Timmy, I promise you. All I want is to make him happy. If doing that makes me happy too, that's an unlooked-for bonus.'

'Let's get back to the kitchen, shall we, with your filling up those caskets with Aga ash, and telling Annie everything that had happened. Considering the rather formal terms the two of you seem to have been on with each other – correct me if I'm wrong – surely she must have been taken aback by this sudden flood of marital confidences?'

'You haven't got it wrong, Inspector, and no, Annie didn't

seem in the least taken aback. Her attitude was wonderfully therapeutic. So far as she was concerned, men were like that and she couldn't understand what all the fuss was about. She put on the kettle for a cup of tea and whilst it was getting hot she wiped the caskets clean and resealed them so neatly nobody could guess they'd ever been tampered with.' Her eyes shadowed, Hannah Milburn bent her shoulders, searching the sand for what was left there of her dead child. 'How right she was!' she pronounced, straightening up. 'About fuss, I mean. Do you realize that if I hadn't made any that evening, Katie wouldn't have been woken up by my caterwauling, she'd have been alive today. Though, when I said as much to Annie, all she said was that I was still young enough to have some more children!'

'She said that, did she?' commented Jurnet, glad he had not been the one to bring up the subject.

'She said that.' Hannah Milburn resettled herself on the rim of the dune, spreading her skirt wide over the sand. Once more shielding her eyes against the sun, she looked up at the detective. 'I don't know why I keep thinking of the Book of Job. Have you ever read it?'

'I must have, some time. God tested him, but it all came right in the end – wasn't that it?'

The other nodded. 'God tested him by, among other things, letting Satan kill off his seven sons and his three daughters. And, oh yes – ' the voice sharp with irony – 'it all came right in the end. Job passed the test with As in everything. For doing so well, everything he lost was restored to him. Everything, that is, except for the one thing that mattered!'

Jurnet looked puzzled.

'I thought he not only got everything back, he got it back twice over.'

'It all depends on how you look at it. He lost seven sons and three daughters and he got seven sons and three daughters back. Not the original sons and daughters restored to life, however, but a new lot, ten strangers. Perhaps, in those days, to the men – or at any rate to the man who wrote the book – having children was what mattered, not the individual, unique human beings that are yours and nobody else's. Ten out, ten in, so all's right with the world! But what about Mrs Job? How do you suppose she felt, a woman who'd been forced to stand by whilst her ten children were slaughtered to prove a theological point? Did God ever

123

think to ask *her* opinion?' Making a comically wry face to excuse her vehemence: 'Maybe I'm wrong. Perhaps she found it easy to love the new children and forget the old. But then, of course, unlike me, she was innocent.'

As they walked over the carpet of needles beneath the Corsican pines, in aromatic shade where she looked more than ever an English water-colour, transparent and insubstantial, Hannah Milburn remarked conversationally: 'Whatever you may think, Inspector, I didn't kill Annie. Katie, yes. Guilty with no recommendation to mercy. If you've a law that covers Katie, put me in your deepest dungeon and I shan't complain. But Annie – ' she shook her head as if amused. 'What would have been the point? Certainly not worth losing a good daily just because she once had an affair with a husband who's dead anyway!'

Hannah Milburn laughed outright, laughter that coincided with their emergence from under the trees into the dazzle of summer, the sun and her laughter both of a piece, rumbustious. Jurnet, confused equally by the sudden explosion of light and his companion's transformation from porcelain into a creature of strength and passion, began, 'All I asked – '

'Don't take on so,' she chided gently. 'It isn't important.'

They had taken the path that led to the churchyard. Hannah Milburn went through the kissing-gate, held it open for the detective to follow.

'Oh look!' she said. 'There's a new grave.'

'Corvin's. At least they didn't hang about with the inquest. It was, after all – ' for some reason Jurnet found himself faltering a little – 'quite straightforward.'

'Ah!' Hannah Milburn stood in front of the raw earth piled up like a meat loaf too large to fit into its baking tin. 'What a good thing they don't bury them at crossroads any longer with a stake through their hearts! I'm sure we should have run out of crossroads ages ago.'

'It wasn't a suicide technically. They found "unsound mind".'

'What an insulting way to put it! Why can't they have a verdict, "Died of love"?' Her face soft with compassion, the woman stood looking down at Joey Corvin's last resting-place. 'There isn't a single wreath. What a shame!'

'The only ones who turned up were a couple of second cousins more interested to know if there was a will.'

'You were there, then? I suppose you had to be.'

'That's right,' said Jurnet, not choosing to admit that his attendance had been motivated by a strictly unofficial pity of which – and in this at least the Superintendent would have had to commend him – he was properly ashamed. Beside him PC Wyatt, present to satisfy himself that the bugger was shovelled decently out of Lanthrop daylight and good riddance to bad rubbish, had stood grinding out every amen as if it were a pain in the gut.

'Poor man!' Hannah Milburn exclaimed. 'They might at least have buried him with his goats all round him to keep him company.'

She moved away, Jurnet watching with an involuntary pleasure as she moved gracefully among the long grasses, bending to extricate the poppies that peppered them with red.

Returning, she laid the flowers on the goat-farmer's grave.

'The trouble is, they don't last any time at all.'

'It's the thought that counts.' After a moment's hesitation Jurnet added: 'Timmy was at the funeral too.'

As soon as he had spoken he regretted it.

Hannah Milburn said with an effort: 'You see! He does what he likes. I'm glad he didn't feel he had to tell me first.'

She moved away again, this time with Jurnet following; towards the two plaques embedded in the turf beneath the St Blaise window.

'I have a private arrangement with Mr Gifford,' she explained, as if apologizing for the green velvet which carpeted that particular spot and no other. 'My mother-in-law comes here often, checking up in case I've let a blade of grass get out of place. Just the same, Alan was her son, and I don't want to hurt her.'

'Weren't you afraid Annie Chance might give the game away?'

'Which is why I murdered her, you mean, to make sure of shutting up her mouth for good?' Sober, sad, Hannah Milburn said: 'You still haven't a clue about Annie, you know. She was like one of those black holes they have in the sky, so dense not even light can get out let alone fantastic stories about funerary caskets filled with ash, not ashes. If I had to have a confidante I couldn't have picked on anyone better.'

'Which', ventured Jurnet, feeling his way carefully, 'makes it all the more remarkable that, so far as I can make out, you don't seem really to have cared for the woman.'

'Quite right.' Hannah Milburn's blue eyes held the detective's dark ones unflinchingly. 'I hated her with a deep consuming hatred. How's that for a motive for murder? I hated her not because of Alan, not because of Timmy, but because she pitied me and I will not be pitied!'

'Asking a bit, aren't you? After what happened, a tragedy like that, the whole village must pity you. It's only natural.'

'The whole village puts on the face it thinks proper for the occasion. It's purely a matter of manners. With Annie it was different. She was *really* sorry, and it drove me mad. Either she could not, or else wilfully would not, see that after what I'd done to Katie it was an insult to my intelligence to pity me, it was treating me as if I were myself a child, one for whom everything needed to be made easy.' Hannah Milburn said: 'Call it vanity, if you like, but I honestly think there is something heroic about being in Hell. The utter hopelessness of your situation gives your life a purpose. When you've committed a murder, Inspector, the last thing you want is to be fobbed off with forgiveness.'

12

Either Dave Batterby was on to something, Jurnet decided, or skate and chips turned him on the way others were turned on by hash or crack. Next to him, Sid Hale, his face as extinguished as an unplugged lamp, sat working his way stoically through a fillet of plaice, or it could have been sole: flat fish, it went without saying. By contrast, the self-appointed Chief-Commissioner-in-waiting positively glowed as he signalled to Jurnet and Ellers across the room, his hand moving in time to the vaguely South American rhythms spilling out of the Caff's loudspeakers; a gesture, however, that was more of a regal summoning than an invitation to the dance.

The two wended their way between tables where the long-distance drivers sat stolidly taking on supplies for the next stage of their joyless odyssey.

'I recommend the skate,' was Batterby's greeting, delivered in the tone of one conferring a favour upon underlings. 'They do a very good skate here. Lally was telling me they get theirs off the boat – no middle-man – fresh every morning.'

'Lally?'

'Lally Buckle. Amalia. Great gal.' Batterby twisted in his chair to get a better view of the manageress where she sat at the cash desk adding up bills and taking money. Compelled, it would seem, by his long-distance approval, the woman wriggled, creasing her mini-skirt another inch or two up her thighs, and touched a hand to her ginger perm. Jurnet felt the half-amused annoyance which his colleague's assumptions of omniscience customarily aroused in him submerge in reluctant admiration. 'We've had a couple of illuminating chats,' said Batterby, repositioning his backside. 'Got along like a house on fire. Where you two off to?' he demanded as the pair, in telepathic sync, moved a step in the direction of the Holy of Holies at the far end of the room. 'They have waitress service at this table. Millie'll be along directly. She's just squeezing me some fresh orange. Anything but fresh brings me out in spots.'

Overcome by this further proof of Batterby's success with the ladies of the Caff harem, the two sat down without protest, Sid Hale looking up from his plate to suggest, on his normal sepulchral note: 'What d'you say the three of us go down to the beach this afternoon for a paddle? Our Dave doesn't need us. He's going to stitch up this case all on his ownsome. Like the skate, eh, Dave? Cut out the middle-man.'

'I certainly haven't been wasting my time,' Dave Batterby admitted modestly. To the broad-beamed young woman in red-checked gingham, red apron and with a red bow in her hair who arrived with the glass of orange juice: 'Millie, you're a doll! And now, if you'd be so kind as to bring skate and chips twice for my two friends here, we'll let you put your lovely feet up for a well-deserved rest.'

'How you do go on!' observed Millie. But she blushed with pleasure and her hand shook as she began to write out the order on the little pad that dangled at her notional waist.

'Haddock for me, if you don't mind.' Jurnet made the correction without seeing the need to explain that skate, first cousin to shark, wasn't kosher. It gave him pleasure to forgo skate for Miriam's sake. He felt warmed by an awareness of virtue: not that it was all that much of a sacrifice. If only, he thought, converting the totality of himself to Judaism was as simple as converting his stomach!

Dave Batterby frowned to have his advice set at naught. 'You don't know what you're missing.' With a smile to the waitress for which some extra teeth appeared to have been pressed into service: 'You tell him, Millie!' But by now, unfortunately, Millie had had time to take in Jurnet's dark good looks. She went even redder as she maintained that in her opinion there was nothing to beat a nice bit of haddock.

Jack Ellers spoke up, confirming.

'Make it two haddocks, love.'

It was the kind of thing, Jurnet recognized, not excusing himself on that account, that Dave Batterby did to you: turned normally sweet-natured guys bitchy. Feeling a little guilty after the waitress's somewhat bemused departure, he got up and announced: 'Think I'll pop over and have a word with our friend Ali Baba while the fish is frying.'

'That gold-plated poofter? You can save yourself the walk. Take it from me, I've squeezed the bugger dry.'

'Oh ah? What did he have to say?'

Batterby had his modest look on again.

'Only everything.'

'Meaning – ?'

'Meaning, six foot at a guess, but looks less on account of being round-shouldered; hair a scurfy brown; discoloured teeth, nicotine-stained fingers, walks with a slight limp. Travels in – wait for it! – sausage casings.' Dave Batterby leaned back in his seat to enjoy the effect of his little catalogue.

'Sounds like a lovely fellow,' said Jurnet, sounding, however, less delighted than the other could have wished. 'The missing rep, I presume?'

'The found one, you mean!'

'Picked the chap up, have you? Can't be all that many firms in the sausage-casing line.'

'Give us a chance. I only spoke to Ali last night.' With a self-satisfaction he made no attempt to disguise: 'He told me he'd already spoken to you.'

'That's right. All I got out of him was seeing Annie Chance dumping her case in the car boot. Didn't even notice what make of car, so he said.'

'Honda Accord,' the other supplied on the instant, eyes shining.

'You don't say! I obviously haven't got your knack of drawing people out. Unless – ' Jurnet finished, smiling – 'he fancied you.'

'Don't be ridiculous!' Batterby snapped, unappreciative. 'It's purely a matter of asking the right questions in the right order and the right way.'

'Easier said than done,' Ellers put in. 'You have to be a bloody miracle worker.'

Dave Batterby, his good humour restored, dipped his head in gracious acknowledgment.

'You said it, Jacko – not me!'

At the far end of the room, cosseted in metal and glass, the fruits of the sea fried secretly, with scarcely a bubble to hint at the transmutation taking place beneath the surface of the hot oil. The air, warm and heavy, faintly aromatic, added to the consequence of the place. In that atmosphere you did not need to be told that fish and chips were serious business.

Jurnet stood in properly respectful silence, watching the fish fryer as, back turned with such complete dismissal as to expunge the Caff from existence, he moved between the various components of his craft, turning here a dial, there a knob, poised to spring like a panther towards the spot where next his services might be called for.

The detective leaned against the counter and recited composedly: 'Five-seven but looks taller on account of wearing lifts. Black hair worn in a pony-tail, complexion sallow, duelling scar across forehead and left cheek. Walks pigeon-toed and drives a Ford Sierra.'

At his superior officer's side Sergeant Ellers looked pained.

'You got it wrong, Ben. Should be four-eleven, grossly obese, head shaved, toothless, long beard not been combed in a year, wooden leg, cast in right eye and runs a red Porsche.'

Ali the fish fryer turned round, the dark face that registered annoyance unable quite to smother an underlying glee. There was no mistaking the mischief in the deep-set eyes, long-lashed like a child's. The man shook his head, for no other purpose, it seemed, than to make his ear-ring dance.

'Wha's all that in aid of?' he asked innocently.

'Me and Sergeant Ellers here were just correcting a few minor slips you made in that very helpful description of Annie Chance's rep you gave to Detective-Inspector Batterby.'

'That the shit's name?' Ali peered past the two detectives, out into the body of the Caff as a captain on his bridge might survey the waves flowing endlessly to the horizon. Having located the shit in question, engaged in what, from that distance, looked like playful badinage with Mrs Buckle, his small, soft features stiffened.

Jurnet offered casually: 'You do know wasting police time is an arrestable offence.'

Unalarmed, the fish fryer brought his gaze back home. His gold tooth catching the light, he asked: 'Detective-Inspector Batterby – have I got that right? He told me to call him Dave. An' what kind of offence, then, do you call what *he's* doing?'

'I'm not with you.'

'If there's one thing I can't stand', said Ali, the gold tooth disappearing behind disapproving lips, 'it's humbug. You can give Detective-Inspector Bloody Batterby my compliments an' tell him if he wants to hear truth from me he'll have to speak truth himself first.'

'Now you're talking in riddles.'

'You tell him,' the other insisted. 'He'll know what I'm on about.' He turned away to lift a basket full of fish slices out of a deep tank, leaving it hooked above to drain. When he came back to the counter it was as if some of his contempt had transferred itself to Jurnet. 'Take a proper look at him, why don't you, copper, and then ask him when he's planning to come out of *his* bleeding closet!'

The moment Ali spoke Jurnet knew that he had spoken the truth; that all the things about Dave Batterby which had got up his nose hitherto had suddenly slotted into place like the pieces of a jigsaw puzzle. At the other end of the Caff, he noted with a new understanding of what he was seeing, Batterby and the manageress were elaborating the figures of their flirtatious *pas de deux*. If it went on much longer, he shouldn't be surprised, customers waiting at the desk to pay their bills would return their wallets to a place of safety and make for the hills pronto. Jurnet watched the charade with an altered perception in which pity struggled with the residual disapproval which lay too deep in the heart's core to be washed out like grit from raw spinach. Poor old bugger! The world was going to have to change a lot more before a gay Chief Commissioner ruled at New Scotland Yard.

The fish fryer inquired with apparent irrelevance: 'Not a bird-watcher by any chance, are you, Inspector?'

'What?'

'A birdwatcher. A twitcher. You ought to try it, you could learn something. Norfolk's a good place for twitching – though as it happens, the bird I'm thinking of I saw in the Lake District, in one of them mountain streams they have up there, clear as glass. A dipper, some people say water-ousel – '

'What is this – a natural history lesson?'

'Like I said,' said Ali, ignoring the interruption, 'this bird was in the stream, underwater. Not drowned or dead but flying, honest to God flying under water. I saw it with my own eyes.' The man stopped short, caught up in the wonder. 'An' I said to it – ' he continued eventually – 'I bent over the water and I said to that little bird, "You an' me both!"'

'What are you on about? How can a bird fly under water?'

'The 64,000-dollar question! Fly through air – if you're a bird, no problem. But fly through thick wet water that's pressing the guts out of you as you go – how's that possible? Yet I swear by my mother's grave I saw that dipper do just that.' The tone, already sharp, became metallic. 'Doing what I, what every gay, what your mate Batterby has to do every day of our bleeding lives – fly under water, friend, force a passage through a world tha's a different element, one we're not made for only we have to take it or leave it because it's the only one on offer – '

The man turned away, back to his dials and knobs, the simplicities of fish frying. After a moment Jurnet said: 'I'm sorry – '

'You make me sick,' said Ali the fish fryer, not bothering to turn round. 'I tell you as how gays are bloody heroes what ought to get the VC and all you say is sorry! You ordered haddock; OK, it's done. Millie'll bring it over. Go back to your table, why don't yer, an' ask good old Dave who does he think he's kidding?'

Mrs Milburn's mum was dead right, Jurnet decided, when she warned her little daughter to look the other way. He'd be lucky himself if the window in Lanthrop church which depicted the martyrdom of St Blaise didn't bring him awake at night, screaming. As an advertisement for the Christian life it did not have a lot going for it.

But the colours! The blues and the reds and the golds which celebrated that ancient butchery shafted down from their horrific beginnings in an onslaught of light that engulfed both the hit-and-miss chords of the old fellow at the organ and the voices of the congregation, so that light and music became one and the funeral service for Annie Chance less a requiem than an intoxication. The rainbow splendour did not reach quite as far as Annie herself in her black-covered coffin. Set out in front of the pews, it had the look of a lot put up for auction for which the bidding was on the slow side getting started.

Never mind: Timmy more than made up for the way his mother, even on this day of all days, seemed bent on keeping herself to herself. Dressed in a dark grey suit made to his measure, none of Mr Alan Milburn's left luggage, the boy looked wonderful. Something about the occasion, or the church, or the light which permeated it, seemed to have purged his features of their grosser elements, revealing the angelic lineaments beneath. Or perhaps it was Mrs Milburn's efforts with soap and water, brush and comb, which were responsible for the solemn pride with which he held himself, for the air of a being set apart.

At that moment, fortunately for Jurnet, in danger of being unsuitably carried away, Timmy sneezed. Before Mrs Milburn at his side could spring to the rescue with a Kleenex, he wiped his beautiful new sleeve across his nostrils with a deftness born of long practice. Without being able to explain why, the detective was glad, for Annie's sake.

Lanthrop church was crowded to the doors, the whole village present, including the weekenders and people who, in the ordinary way of things, wouldn't have given Annie Chance, the drab with the idiot boy, the time of day. The archaeology students from the dig were there in force, irreverent in their earth-stained shorts but looking pleased to be given the opportunity, for once, of being in on an Ancient Brit rite whilst it was actually happening.

The overflow in the churchyard had put paid to the poppies and the long grasses. The high voices of children playing hide-and-seek among the tombstones mingled with the chimes of the ice-cream van which had craftily parked itself earlier in the day a little further along the road, too far from the church to give a harassed PC Wyatt grounds for moving it on, but near enough for the transaction of serious business. As media people and amateur photographers clicked away immortalizing the scene, the tinkle of 'Oranges and Lemons' interwove prettily with the knell of the solitary bell donging away in the church tower.

All that was missing outside was a merry-go-round and a coconut shy. All that was missing, both outside and in, was any sense of loss.

In all that congregation, Jurnet wondered, was anybody sorry that Annie Chance was dead?

Timmy? Well how much did he really understand of what was going on? The boy had on a lovely funeral suit, he looked brilliant – but grief-stricken? No. If he had shed a tear earlier there was no sign of it now. On one side of him he had Mrs Milburn in support looking tremendously well-bred in a hat of natural straw and a dress printed with small flowers in muted colours, and on the other Sandra Thorne in black chiffon, her breasts ballooning the delicate fabric as if they might in fact be buttocks which had unaccountably got themselves stuck on in the wrong place. A few feet from where the three sat in the front pew the coffin rested on its trestle, a shape beneath a black cloth upon which someone had placed, slightly askew, a cross made of white carnations.

If indeed, despite all the pomp and ceremony, Annie Chance's son still had no conception of what it was that lay hidden away in that oddly shaped box, what were the chances that its imminent committal to the earth would bring the truth home to him? Not for the first time, the detective mentally kicked himself for not having taken the boy to the mortuary to indentify his ma, see her dead however upsetting the sight must have been. That way, at least, you could have been sure that, come next Wednesday dinner-time, no feeble-minded youth would be salivating at the kitchen table, waiting for the fish and chips that never came.

Correction. Somebody was grieving for Annie Chance. As, the indoor business over, the coffin processed slowly down the aisle, borne on the shoulders of four pallbearers – undertakers' men, judging by the cut of black suits that had the look of having been handed down from employé to employé, down a long line of physiques of varying shapes and sizes, each of which had left an ineradicable imprint on the heavy cloth – Jurnet noticed that one of them was having difficulty keeping his steps aligned to those of his three companions. Teeth gritted, tears rolling down his cheeks, Oz Bailey the woodman stumbled over the ancient flagstones as if even one quarter of the dead weight of his dead love was more than he could bear.

Jurnet glanced across the aisle, to where he could see Mrs Bailey, the redoubtable Brenda, watching her husband's distress with an undisguised anticipation which proclaimed louder than words: *Just wait till I get you home!*

Outside, at the appearance of the coffin at the church door, it abruptly stopped being a holiday. Even the ice-cream chimes had stopped playing. Up in the church tower the bell went on donging as if it was not only the one sound it knew, but as if it was the one sound in the universe. The sun shone, the sky was blue, yet suddenly death was the sole reality. When a baby, symbol of new life, screamed in imperious protest, no one was comforted. New life was as mortal as old.

'"As for man,"' intoned the vicar, '"his days are as grass: as a

134

flower of the field so he flourisheth. For the wind passeth over it and it is gone; and the place thereof shall know it no more."'

Jack Ellers, who had stayed outside during the service, came quietly to Jurnet's side, his chubby face unsmiling.

'See anything – anybody?' his superior officer inquired softly.

'Nothing.'

Gently prodded into position by the ever-vigilant Mrs Milburn, Timmy was put in place by the open grave, Sandra Thorne resolutely guarding her right to stay at his side. Across the raw gash in Lanthrop earth the excavated soil, its top crust already crumbling in the heat, awaited its return to its former place, a healing of the wound. Two of the undertakers' men, one of them an Oz Bailey who had stopped crying but still kept his teeth clenched tightly together, prepared to lower the coffin into the grave, fixing the ropes in place as the vicar began: '"We have entrusted our sister Anne to God's merciful keeping and we commit her body to the ground in sure and certain hope of the resurrection to eternal life – "'

'You thinkin' to put her there,' interrupted Timmy, 'you got another think coming!'

Immediately, the reverential mood broken, a jabber of noise engulfed the scene, the media men moving in closer, hunters to the kill. The vicar, clutching his surplice about him, stammered something inarticulate and looked to Hannah Milburn to save him.

'It's all right, Timmy,' she said, laying her hand on his sleeve and using the tone of voice with which mothers hush their infants to sleep. 'She'll lie at rest there. At rest. All right.'

'Bloody in't all right!' Timmy shrugged off the restraining hand and looked about him belligerently. 'Who was it dug this bloody grave? Who was it had the bloody nerve?'

Red in the face, Bill Gifford, black-gowned and carrying a silver-tipped staff in his persona of verger, pushed forward and said angrily: 'I had the bloody nerve, tha's who! Nothing the matter with it, no more 'n there is wi' any of my graves. What you know about it?'

'You think it's so good,' said Timmy, turning to the speaker, 'you're welcome to it. My ma don't want it, I tell you that!'

Sensing what was coming, Gifford moved to back away from the excavation. Too late. With a shout that could equally have been a cry of rage or a whoop of triumph, Timmy flung out one of his spidery arms and with unexpected strength pushed the man in. Mindless of his new finery and before anybody could stop him, he darted round the hole to the piled-up clods on the further side, gathered up an armful and sent them tumbling down on to the hapless Gifford.

By now the din in the churchyard was frightful. Cameras were whirring, people in the back rows demanding to be told what they were missing. Down in the grave Mr Gifford was making a noise like a belling heifer. The vicar, after a last accusing glare at the heavens, had covered his face with his hands. Only where the coffin rested on the ground, like luggage waiting to be forwarded to its proper destination, was there a small area of calm, of dissociation. Annie Chance, it proclaimed, was in no hurry.

Three of the pallbearers stood gaping. It was Oz Bailey who, with the assistance of Jurnet and Jack Ellers, finally laid hands on one of the ropes intended for the coffin and used it to haul the near-apoplectic Gifford back up into the land of the living.

'Look what you done to my gown!' the man cried, advancing on a Timmy Chance who – the angel look vanished, a foolish grin on his face – stood watching the proceedings with the complacency of one who had had his say. 'Look what you done to my trousers! He'll have to pay for that, won't he, vicar? You tell him he'll have to pay!'

The vicar took his hands away from his face and agreed in a voice that would have agreed to anything. 'He will have to pay.'

'Loonies like you ought to be locked up!' Gifford shouted, unappeased. 'I could've broken my leg! Both on 'em!'

'Pity you didn't!' returned Timmy, unrepentant. 'What right you got ter bury my ma nex' that bugger Joey Corvin? Pity you didn' break your bloody neck!'

At these words Mrs Milburn, who had been looking more than a little distraught, smiled with sudden understanding. She put an arm round the boy's shoulders, gave them an affectionate squeeze.

'Not Mr Gifford's fault, silly! Mr Corvin just happens to have been the last person to be buried in the churchyard. Nobody's died since, so the next grave just happens to be the one for your mother.' In a voice of great tenderness she finished: 'It won't make any difference to *her*, I promise you.'

The boy shrugged off the protective arm: stuck out his lower lip rebelliously.

136

'What you know about it? You bin dead an' under the ground, have you, an' know what dead people got on their minds? I say my ma won't lie nex' ter that ole goat if you pay her! Every time she laid eyes on him, she say, it was all she could do not to spit in his face!' On a note of admiring recollection: 'She did go on!'

Amazingly, it was Sandra Thorne who cut the Gordian knot. Leaning across Timmy, she tugged at Mrs Milburn's skirt to get her attention. Nodding towards the coffin with a genteel tremor which set her nipples jiggling, she suggested: 'Why don't you just have them dig another grave and bury her further along?'

13

'Quite a day,' observed Jack Ellers in the calm of the evening, piloting the Rover towards Angleby and home. Away from the coast the landscape had acquired an ambiguous look. Fires flickered along the lines of stubble, as if, the corn harvested, it was the turn of darker forces to celebrate the turn of the year.

It was too quiet. Something else was missing: the background boom of the sea. From the safety of the hinterland Jurnet speculated quite seriously as to whether everyone who lived within hearing of that interminable racket was not, by definition, stark, staring bonkers.

'Yes,' he agreed. 'Quite a day.'

'Don't know when I've attended a better funeral blow-out.' The chubby Welshman emitted a dainty belch in tribute. 'Even my Rosie – don't tell her I said so, though! – could learn from those little patty things with the savoury fillings. Food of the gods, boyo! Mrs Milburn certainly did the village proud.'

'Not only the village. Looked like everyone out for the day in North Norfolk accepted her invitation to come up to Fastolfes for a memorial cuppa.'

'Plenty for everybody, that was the wonder. Nobody went without that I could see. Must have cost her.'

Jurnet said: 'I don't reckon she did it for the village, nor for Annie either. She did it for the boy.'

'Fallen on his feet, that one! And, after it all, his ma still not buried! What she must be thinking, poor bitch, after all the kerfuffle, to find herself back in the undertaker's fridge like a pot of yoghourt nobody fancied! Way I heard it, Gifford was all set to get on with digging another grave as far as you could humanly get away from Joey Corvin and still be in consecrated ground – I'm sure Mrs Milburn made it worth his while – only the thought of the press and all the other nosy buggers finally decided 'em to leave it till things quietened down a bit.'

'Oh ah,' said Jurnet, neglecting to mention that the suggestion of delay had been his.

'I can't see Mrs Milburn laying on a second do, though. One thing's for sure – ' a second appreciative burp – 'she'll need to teach that peasant of hers a few manners.'

'I doubt she intends teaching him anything. Her line is that she took over Timmy the way he was, the way he is, and it's not her place to make him into something different.'

'Kidding herself if that's what she thinks.' The little Welshman drove for a while in an unaccustomedly thoughtful silence. The burning stubble on either side of the road, so far from dying down, seemed to be gaining strength with the declining sun. Narrow tongues of flame stretched themselves in the breeze which had sprung up with the close of day. There were places where the Rover pierced through a pall of smoke drifting lazily across the car's path. 'I suppose we ought to stop off at the next police house and let the bobby know what's going on up his patch.'

'I suppose.'

It was not a serious suggestion and neither pursued the subject: but the atmosphere lightened. The two had had a day out with death and now, the Rover eating up the miles back to Angleby, life called, and love: Rosie, Miriam. Let the ruddy fields go up in smoke, it wasn't CID business.

Eyes half-closed so that the evening light, filtered through his eyelashes, became the glory of Miriam's hair, Jurnet stretched out his legs contentedly. Pleased with the vision, he was able to return to the subject of Annie Chance and her son with a smile that transformed the natural melancholy of his lean, Italianate face.

'You can't say young Timmy didn't add a welcome spice of drama to a day which was otherwise a dead loss.'

'Let's hope at least it's registered at last that his ma has really and truly gone to her Maker. Shouldn't care to bet on it, even now. Who'd ever think a few IQ points one way or the other could make all that difference? An alien from outer space would be easier to get through to.'

Jurnet nodded. 'Know what you mean. And it's not so much *his* stupidity, is it? You end up convinced you're the one who's thick.'

They were entering the northern suburbs of Angleby when Ellers noted casually: 'All those kids from the dig were there. Considering the way their boss goes for Mrs Milburn – you can see it a mile off – don't you think it odd he didn't show up with them?'

'I noticed Mr Paul Abbott was conspicuous by his absence. Could be he figured that, with all the attention concentrated on the village, it might be a good day out for metal-detectors. Maybe he stayed home to mind the shop. Or maybe not.'

Foolishly jubilant at being himself close to home, getting closer by the minute, the whole world reflecting the image of his love, Jurnet turned on his colleague and friend a look of unalloyed affection.

'We'll have to ask him, won't we?'

The whole world? Well, the whole world less the Superintendent. The sole image reflected back by the Superintendent was that of his exasperated and exasperating self.

The cause of his anger, Jurnet recognized thankfully, moments after entering into the presence, was nothing to do with the fact that no backward boy, no woodman, no fish fryer, no archaeologist, no Uncle Tom Cobbleigh and all had as yet been charged with the murder of Annie Chance. Whatever else you might say of the man, you could never say that, for all his corroding sarcasms, he didn't give you leeway: space and time to slot into the physical and mental topography of the world where the foul deed had been committed, to become yourself part of the tangled skein of innocence and guilt that had to be unravelled if justice were to be done.

Dave Batterby, in an attitude copied from the ads in the Sunday glossies, sat perched on a corner of the great man's desk, one perfectly creased trouser leg, one almost-Gucci casual swaying with young executive *élan* against its finely wrought panelling. That the desk was the Superintendent's personal property – antique, so Jurnet understood, and worth a bomb – was beside the point. Had it been police-issue laminated plywood the *lèse-majesté* would have been no less.

Anyone knowing the Superintendent less well might have wondered why, if he so passionately objected to a subordinate making free with one of his desk corners, he didn't order the offender to get the hell off and be done with it. Jurnet knew that was not the Superintendent's way. An open display of anger was not gentlemanly. More, it was heat as wasted as the flames that roared up a chimney, leaving the hearth cold. If however, by contrast, the coals were thriftily stoked up, some ashes sprinkled on top to slow down combustion – why, then, you could keep the fire going almost indefinitely, all the fiercer within its hidden core.

Jurnet smiled at Batterby with a kindness born of his new knowledge of the man, willing him to get off his arse before the gates of New Scotland Yard clanged shut forever on his dreams of greatness. Unfortunately, the unwonted friendliness only misled its recipient, encouraged him to shift his bulk until two buttocks instead of one rested on the gleaming mahogany. Into the Superintendent's eyes came a light of intense enjoyment. It came to Jurnet with a sense of shock that there was nothing about Dave Batterby the man did not already know.

'I've been waiting for you two to get in.' The Superintendent greeted Jurnet and Ellers with a suavity that indicated that Batterby was not the only one to have fallen out of royal favour. 'What can either of you tell me about a Mr Gifford? A Mr Bill Gifford?'

'He's the bloke on the gate down to Lanthrop beach,' Ellers answered for both. 'The one who let you in and out when you were down there. Also the dogsbody at the church. Digs the graves, mows the grass – '

'Mr Gifford has been on the telephone. Did you know that, in addition to the pursuits you mention, he also grows marrows which for the past two years have carried all before them at the annual Lanthrop and District Horticultural Show?' His countenance darkening: 'More to the point, did you know that – Mr Gifford's words, not mine – whilst you two were busy feeding your faces up at Fastolfes, some villain entered his garden and hacked his marrows to pieces, ruining his chances of winning the cup outright this year? Mr Gifford also informed me that in the course of the afternoon he himself had been pushed violently into an open grave and could easily have broken his leg, though, as he rightly said, that was nothing to what had happened to his marrows.'

Jurnet, equally straight-faced, said: 'He had no call to bother you, sir. He should have called in PC Wyatt.'

141

'Exactly what he says he did! And, if he is to be believed, PC Wyatt's response was to burst out laughing. Not the best way to enhance the public image of the police in the county, would you say?'

The Superintendent leaned back in his chair, looking from one to the other. Pointedly ignoring a Batterby busy trying on expressions of appreciation, humour and concern, in the hope of hitting upon the right one, he demanded: 'What gives, Ben? First murder and now marrowcide! Does the rule of law no longer apply in Lanthrop? What in the name of heaven is going on there?'

Miriam beside him, Jurnet drove to Lanthrop again. No sun this time: a full moon and a star-peppered sky that hung over the quiet land like a marriage canopy. Across the stubble, the abandoned church which, on previous journeys, had aroused Jurnet's pity for its unloved condition, had taken on the lineaments of a castle out of a fairy tale. One touch and, with a crystalline tinkle, it would shatter into a thousand pieces, every last one of them reflecting the moonlight, the starlight, his happiness.

'You are my heart's desire.'

Steering the Rover along the silver ribbon that wound towards the coast, Jurnet found himself thinking of Annie Chance, of Joey Corvin, of Hannah Milburn, her dead husband and her dead child – all of them, one way and another, casualties of love: all of them, collectively, a warning of what could happen to people who let their hearts run away with their heads. Tonight, under the moon, their dire examples went for naught. If anything, their very failure at life only intensified Jurnet's amazement at having, against all the odds, made it.

Reaching for Miriam's hand, he raised it to his lips. 'Hope this doesn't bring back bad memories. I shouldn't have said yes to Abbott without asking you first.'

Miriam shook her head, the bronze of her hair subdued by moonlight but not vanquished by it.

'I told you, I want to go. You can't stay away from a place just because something bad once happened there, or you'd never go anywhere. Besides – ' this time the hand offered itself for kissing without being sought – 'it wasn't all bad that day, was it?'

'Not all.'

'Perhaps he's made some sensational find and that's why he's throwing a party.'

'Doubt it. What he really hopes, the artful bugger, is that I'll be there to use my influence with PC Wyatt if, as he clearly expects, the party gets a bit out of hand. Seems he's hired a disco, and sound carries a long way through clean country air. What he said was most of the kids will be pushing off any day now and he felt he owed them one last orgy before they went their separate ways, back from the eternal truths of the past to the plastic deceptions of the so-called real world. The guy's a poet! When I suggested that if an orgy was really what he had in mind, it wasn't the cleverest thing in the world to ask a police officer along, he admitted that what he was planning, actually, was barbecued bangers, baked potatoes and plonk; that he couldn't even offer the wood any longer as a venue for sinful carryings on since that moron Timmy Chance had turned it into a bed of thorns. He did say that the rest of Boadicea's hubby's tombstone had turned up, but that's hardly sensational.' With a laugh: 'I'll have to learn all over again to stop calling her Boadicea.'

The smell of burning that greeted the pair as they arrived at the dig boded ill for at least the culinary part of the projected festivities. A Paul Abbott in unplanned blackface who greeted them at the gateway into the paddock, the light of an enormous bonfire reflected in his spectacles, explained cheerfully that plans had been updated. The object of the exercise was not, after all, to produce hot bangers but a layer of carbon comparable to the one already laid down by the Romans in their destruction of the Druids' sacred grove; one that 2,000 years hence would provide gainful employment for whole generations of archaeologists as they probed and puzzled and published learned papers speculating as to its cause.

'The spuds are safe, anyway,' their host finished cheerfully, 'and the plonk. Come over to the table and have some. Mind the cables,' he instructed. 'We're running the whole caboodle off our geriatric transformer which has been threatening to blow itself up all season. This could be the day. Such fun!'

Outfaced by the bonfire, the screams of the youngsters circling its crass reds and yellows like Indians on the warpath, the silver of the night had retreated. Swags of fairy lights outlined the boundaries of the excavations. Higher up the field, nearer to the woodland at its end, couples illuminated by floodlights were dancing on a square of dance floor laid down for the occasion; dancing to a disco turned up to a *boom boom* to make the heavens flinch. No chance of the boom of the nearby sea penetrating that barrage.

Jurnet followed Paul Abbott and Miriam to a trestle table loaded with wine bottles modestly labelled for good reason, paper cups, a small mountain of potatoes baked in their jackets and a heap of incinerated fingers which their host insisted were sausages – these last not so much to be eaten as exhibited as evidence of good intent.

'Could be it's because you're burning wood,' Jurnet offered helpfully. 'Charcoal's what you want for barbecues.'

Paul Abbott groaned in his jolly way.

'Don't tell me! We bought three sacks of the stuff, only Pete soaked them by mistake when he was sluicing down the tables and no way could we get it to ignite. So young Timmy came to the rescue with the wood Hannah's been counting on to see her through the winter.'

'Piled on more than was needed, by the look of it.'

'Try stopping him! Did you ever see anyone more obstinate than that witless leprechaun?' Abbott drank deep of the plonk and pushed a hand through his thinning hair. 'What you see burning there, my friend, are the fires of jealousy. The lovely Sandra has transferred her favours back to Ian, her old love, and the discarded swain has been working off his bile stoking up the fire as if he's just spotted the Armada heading in to Lanthrop beach and he's alerting England.'

'Isn't Mrs Milburn here? She seems to know the trick of calming him down.'

'No. Hannah isn't here. Said she didn't think it was her scene, I can't think why, especially as she's the one set up the whole sizzling situation. When Ian marched in out of the blue I was really touched. Lazy, ignorant, big-headed with it, as I often had occasion to point out to him, never make an archaeologist if he lives to be a hundred – just the same he loves us. One of the other kids on the dig must have let him know about the party and he's come all the way from London to participate.' The smile had faded, worry had taken over the plump, good-natured face. 'Can you believe it, it was Hannah who'd got in touch, found out his address and told him about tonight's bash! She'd even sent him

144

the fare money and met him at Sheringham station. What d'you make of that?'

'Haven't you asked her?'

'Only heard it this evening.' The archaeologist took off his glasses, rubbed his heat-reddened eyes and peered hard at Jurnet as if seeing him properly for the first time. 'What you reckon? You're the detective.'

Jurnet, having tasted the plonk, tilted his cup unobtrusively, enough to let the rest of its contents trickle out on to the grass, a libation to the spirits of the place, Druid and Ancient Roman alike. Given the quality of the vintage, he hoped they would not take this small act of homage as an insult.

He protested: 'A detective's the bloke who asks the questions. It's up to others to supply the answers.'

The other laughed.

'Lucky you! We archaeologists can't even agree on the questions.' An unaccustomed frown relocating itself among the freckles: 'Can you understand her? One minute she's building a bungalow as a love-nest for the young couple; next thing you know she's deliberately resurrected the opposition. Why?'

Disguising his private satisfaction at the news, Jurnet suggested: 'Maybe she's come to the conclusion it's not her business to arrange Timmy's life for him. She's told me more than once the last thing she wants is to make over the boy.'

'Exactly what God says, I shouldn't be surprised, before He puts the boot in. Dear darling Hannah!' The archaeologist shook his head. His sooty face widened in a grin that was affectionate but not foolish. 'I only hope she isn't laying up trouble for herself.'

'I haven't seen Mrs Milburn for some time. Last time I spoke to her she told me Timmy's stopped going back home on Wednesdays to get his fish and chips. That has to be progress.'

'I suppose. I gather that since the funeral he more or less accepts that his ma is dead. I say more or less because, according to Mrs Cobbold at the shop, he's forever popping down to the grave to leave her off a Mars Bar or an iced lolly in case she's feeling in need of refreshment six feet under. Pathetic, really – but then, when are we ever going to stop feeling sorry for Timmy, or guilty that we find it so difficult? And just when the boy seems to be on the point of arranging his life satisfactorily – or of having it arranged for him – Hannah goes and kiboshes it. I wish I could understand what she's up to.'

Jurnet began: 'I'm sure Mrs Milburn has the lad's best interests at heart – '

'Not the same thing at all! What Timmy Chance needs is neither a god nor a surrogate mum but a nice uncomplicated fuck – but then, who doesn't? Do try a baked potato. They're out of this world – '

His arms round her waist, hers entwined round his neck, Jurnet and Miriam swayed on the dance floor. Out of the loudspeakers came a sound that was more a summons to arms than to love, but the lovers' bodies moved to a subtler music, one that they did not so much hear beneath the brazen disco beat as feel in their blood, the silver-tipped sea surging through their veins: the waves breaking on Lanthrop beach.

All about them, boys and girls clad – or more accurately, unclad – in what could easily have been the gleanings of Iron Age middens gyrated in ways that obviously gave them enormous pleasure. Absorbed in their rituals, such attention as they had left over for the pair anchored in the middle of the floor like characters out of an old movie, concentrated itself in admiration on Miriam's hair, the floodlights amplifying its red lights into a sun to rival the moon sailing serenely above.

Suddenly, without warning, the apparatus shut itself down, the floodlights went out and Miriam's hair with it. After a first roar of disappointment the kids began to jump about even more energetically than before, as if the electricity supply had not actually failed but instead transferred its current into livelier, more receptive channels. At the other end of the field the cabin lights were out, along with the rest. Only the absurd fairy lights remained, twinkling childishly, and the flames of the bonfire still challenging the sky.

It could have been brilliant, was the general consensus, once your eyes had adjusted themselves to the change of light level, if only it hadn't been for the silence. If only the moon and stars could have provided power enough to run the disco they would have had a lot going for them. As it was, the dancers retreated from the silence as from some impending danger, some drawn towards the bonfire, others seeking corners as yet unoccupied by couples lying embraced on the dewy grass.

Only Jurnet and Miriam remained on the dance floor, swaying to the rhythm of the distant waves.

After a while Jurnet said: 'If that bloody boy hadn't gone out of his way to cover the ground with prickles, I'd pick you up, throw you over my shoulder, and carry you into that wood to a fate worse than death.'

'Male chauvinist Ancient British pig!' Miriam murmured, swaying, eyes closed. 'Why that wood specially? I thought it looked scruffy. Is it magic?'

'Nothing special. You bring your own.'

But, in the speaking of it, the magic had been broken. Gently disengaging herself from her lover's arms, Miriam reminded him: 'We promised Mr Abbott we'd take a look at his tombstone.'

'Can't see the bloody thing in the dark,' Jurnet protested, compliant nevertheless. Hand in hand the two stepped down from the wooden floor. At the other end of the paddock a spray of sparks flung itself heavenward. Jurnet said: 'You saw young Timmy as we came by. How did *you* think he was looking?'

Miriam shivered a little in the warm night.

'I suppose that other time in the shop, I didn't get a really good look at him. I hadn't remembered he looked like that.'

'He's a mental defective, for Christ's sake!'

Aware of Miriam's lovely face turned towards him in surprise, Jurnet felt guilt rising within him. Paul Abbott, with his affectionately chiding strictures on Mrs Milburn, had been misinformed. It was he, Ben Jurnet, the high-minded cop ha ha, who had taken it upon himself to act God and, in so doing, to scupper Timmy's already sufficiently fragile hopes of happiness. What would happen if and when the boy found another girl prepared to take him on? Were even a well-heeled Mrs Milburn's resources enough to buy her off similarly, and the next one, and the next?

The poor wronged kid!

Miriam drew away a little and looked at her lover searchingly.

'Something's suddenly wrong,' she pronounced.

'With me, not you. And not suddenly.'

As if their very preoccupation with Timmy Chance had conjured up his presence, they became conscious of the boy's approach at the same moment; his arms and legs moving in their curiously disjointed way, his face like unrisen dough in the moonlight. If he saw the detective and his companion standing across his path he gave no more indication of it than to swerve jerkily away towards the gate where Sandra Thorne and the young man called Ian were standing together.

The two were not embraced: indeed, stood a little apart as if to accord the girl's breasts the breathing space due to them. Encased in a black tubular-knit chemise which crushed the twin globes into a single hummock the shape and approximate size of an Inuit igloo, they dominated the space between.

Without taking his eyes off them, Ian said, 'Bugger off!'

'Who you tellin' bugger off?' Timmy demanded. 'Who's askin' *you*?' To the girl, in a voice which, whether from emotion or the smoke of the bonfire, sounded even more blurred than usual, he complained: 'You promised you'd teach me dancing.'

'Can't teach you with the disco off, can I?' Sandra Thorne returned snappily.

'Don' see why not. Didn' turn off my feet, did they? Bloody noise, better off without it.'

The young man said again, without animus: 'Bugger off, loopy.'

'I in't loopy,' said Timmy Chance, 'an' she's my girl. Go on,' he said to Sandra, 'tell him you're my girl, an' you're goin' to teach me dancing.'

Sandra Thorne let out a little cry of exasperation. 'Really! Can't a person have a little private conversation with a person without another person barging in and wanting to dance when there isn't even any music? Ian and I haven't seen each other for ages. We got a lot to talk about.'

'No, you han't,' Timmy contradicted. 'Nothing happen in this ole place you can't tell in two shakes.' Addressing himself directly to the young man: 'Nothing happen 'cept Joey Corvin an' his goats, an' they buried ma. Pity you missed that. That was a right ole do. There!' he concluded, pleased with the demonstration: 'Didn' take long to tell that, did it?' Proudly: 'An' somthin' else. Sandra tell you the missus building us a bungalow in the orchard to live in, her an' me?'

'She told me,' Ian answered, not unkindly. 'Except she says Mrs Milburn hasn't even got permission to build yet.'

'She'll get!' the other proclaimed confidently. 'Missus always get what she wants.' His eye caught by a sudden gleam on the black tube, Timmy put out a hand and asked. 'What's that you got on there?'

The girl retreated in some perturbation.

'It's a brooch. Ian brought me a present. Wasn't that kind of him?'

'That – a present?' Timmy hooted. 'Where he get that – out of a cracker?' For the first time in the encounter – Jurnet, watching to one side, noted the change with an involuntary pleasure – the doughy face transformed itself, becoming mischievous and aware. 'Bloody bit o' tin!'

'It's not!' Sandra Thorne sounded really put out. 'It's sterling silver, ever so expensive and it's got my name engraved on it. If you know how to read it, that is!'

'Bloody bit o' tin!' Timmy repeated cheerfully. He appeared quite unaffected by the insinuation of illiteracy. Ian was the one up in arms.

'What do *you* know, brainless?' the young man demanded angrily. '*You* wouldn't know sterling silver if you had it for breakfast!'

'Presents,' said Timmy, with the finality of one pronouncing the last word on the subject, 'presents for ladies ought to be gold.'

'Oh, bugger off, for Christ's sake!'

And to Jurnet's surprise, Timmy did bugger off, lurching away from the gate, his haste taking him over the grass faster than the discordance of his limbs would have seemed to promise. The detective watched as the boy skirted the empty dance floor, stumbled over cables and coupled bodies until – the silver of the night as instantaneously terminated there as the power supply elsewhere – he disappeared into the black of the wood.

14

The tombstone of Prasutagus, sometime King of the Iceni, put together like a kindergarten jigsaw, five pieces only, lay on sacking on the floor of the cabin. The transformer remaining stubbornly unresponsive to the bangs and the curses emanating from the shed next door, Paul Abbott had found an old-fashioned paraffin lamp with which to illuminate his treasure; a tremulous glow that seemed reluctant, Jurnet thought, to resurrect the past and set time going all over again.

Whether it was this quality of the light, the impending shutdown of the dig, or an under-estimation of the kick of the house plonk, Jurnet and Miriam found their normally cheery host sunk in a mood of deep melancholy.

'Have you been enjoying yourselves?' he asked, and when they had both replied yes, very much, as good guests should, he looked at them in an unfriendly way which only became unfriendlier when Miriam, with the best of intentions, added for full measure: 'It's been great fun!'

'Fun!' the man echoed, chewing the word and spitting it out again. 'One bloody grave-marker, a few feet of wood ash, and you say fun!' Crossing over to the five pieces of stone he kicked one of them hard with his sandalled foot, seeming to take a perverse pleasure in the pain the action evidently caused him. 'King!' he sneered. 'Piffling little tribal leader, not worth mucking up Hannah's field for. Druids, Boudica, Early British riff-raff! What's wrong with bloody Boadicea anyway? Who the hell cares how you spell it? Who wants to know?'

Jurnet said off-handedly: 'Read an article in the *Argus*. You must have seen it. It called what you lot are doing out here the most interesting excavation going on in England at present.'

Paul Abbott grunted.

'That was that turd Tring at the Museum, staking his claim on the chance we turned up something really worth having.'

'Are the actual objects all that important?' It was Miriam's turn to be a little ray of sunshine. 'I mean, nobody suggests you can pick up Stonehenge and take it away. Or Avebury, or Hadrian's Wall – '

'Meaning I should get Hannah to put in turnstiles and charge 50p a gawp?' Looking marginally happier, the archaeologist said: 'We gave Alan Milburn an undertaking – one that we have every intention of keeping with his widow – to backfill the site and re-turf it at the end of the day. We've kept the spoil religiously, and the turves are stacked face to face and moistened daily so they won't dry out – something I could be doing with advantage at the moment, eh?' The man straightened his shoulders, turned on the pair a smile of pained sweetness. 'Dear people, my apologies. Apologies to you, to Druids, to Boudica and all her kin, to Iceni great and small, wherever they may be.' Shaking his head as if bemused by aspects of himself not previously encountered: 'Not, believe it or not, a case of "*If I can't turn up another Sutton Hoo Ship Burial and get invited on to all the chat shows I'll thwow up, so there!*" Envy of a different kind. It's all this bloody moon and all those kids having it off out there as if love was something cheap and simple you could get out of a slot machine like bubble-gum.' Paul Abbott looked down at the tombstone and laughed. 'Ten to one it wasn't the geezer's name at all – just the nearest the Romans could get to the local lingo. From now on,' the archaeologist declared, 'I shall call him Profiteroles, unless anybody has any objection.' None forthcoming, he finished: 'Did you ever think that Hannah is one of the very few Christian names that are spelled the same coming or going?'

Jurnet said, 'That's right!'

'But chiefly going.'

With the sudden *whoosh!* of a carousel starting up, the lights came on again. The disco, if anything reinvigorated by its enforced rest, took up from where it had left off, even louder than before, if that were possible. Nearer to the cabin a noise hard to identify grew in volume; a noise with excitement enmeshed in it, and protest, and finally a shriek shot through with unmistakable gentility: 'Watch out, can't you? Be careful!'

'What on earth – '

As Abbott went towards the door it was pushed open from

outside, and an unseen force precipitated Timmy Chance into the room in a flurry of arms and legs that made it surprising to discover there were no more than two of each.

'What you think you're doing?' the boy shouted as Jurnet caught and righted him, set him safely on his feet. 'What the fuck you up to?'

It took a startled moment for the detective to realize that it was not to him that the inquiry was directed. His arms waving like tentacles, his face red and stupid, Timmy stood at the door, barring the way.

'She can come in if she want to,' he hurled at the invisible enemy. 'You sling yer hook!'

The young man called Ian bounced into the cabin, brushing the boy aside with a casual arrogance, a conviction of his own physical superiority, that reactivated all Jurnet's sympathy for the underdog. For the second time he sorted out the flailing limbs; held on to the gawky body with hands that were firm but not ungentle. Murmured an admittedly inadequate, 'Cool it!'

'What's all this?' Paul Abbott demanded. 'This is a party, not the Wars of the Roses. What gives?'

'That's what we're here to find out.' The young man's face, Jurnet noted, was as red as Timmy's, but not with anger. His brown eyes were bright with excitement. 'You'll be interested in this, Paul, I promise you.' Over his shoulder he called through the open doorway: 'You can come in now, love.'

'Who he calling love?' muttered Timmy, tight in the detective's restraining grip.

'I don't think I want to come in, thank you.' Sandra Thorne, outside, sounded affronted. 'It's too rough and there's too many people. I think I'll go home.'

'You can't do that. And there's loads of room, really.' Ian spoke reassuringly. Turning back to the archaeologist: 'This you gotta see!'

'He give her a bit o' tin out of a cracker,' Timmy thrust in hotly. 'He got no business! She in't his girl, she's mine. I give her a present, who's he to say no? You're police – ' he appealed to Jurnet. 'You tell the bugger where he gets off.'

Sandra Thorne came tentatively up the steps to the cabin and entered the room. A bra trimmed with pink lace bulged out of a ragged tear in her tight dress.

'A lovely little silver brooch with my name on it – ' Wasting no time on preliminaries, she launched into an exculpation of her immodest condition. 'He tore it off like a wild animal and threw it in the hedge, would you believe? Goodness knows if I'll ever find it again, all that muck. What my mum will say when she sees me I don't like to think.'

Despite her threnody of complaint, however, there was pride in the girl's face. Men had been fighting over her; very proper. Making no attempt to cover up the tear, she stood, a busty *femme fatale*, calmly assured of her destiny.

Abbott stared at the girl wildly; then seized Timmy by the front of his T-shirt, twisting the fabric to tighten his grip; the foolish face, its mouth open, its goggle eyes magnified by their pebble glasses, brought close to his own. 'So it was you!' he shouted. 'You all the time with the metal-detector!'

'It weren't! I never! Lemme go!'

'You thief! You ruddy vandal!'

Jurnet came forward and said quietly: 'Leave off, will you? You're never going to get the truth out of him that way.'

Sandra Thorne put her hand up to her throat in a simpering gesture. Encircling her neck was a collar made of gold wires twisted into a heavy plait that terminated at either side of her throat in horses' heads modelled with genius and veneration. Their nostrils flaring, their manes streaming, they strained to break loose from the golden threads that held them. Almost, you could feel their hot breath on your skin, hear their snorting effort to be free.

'Epona,' said Paul Abbott. He had quietened down, his voice hushed, sacramental. 'The Great Mare.'

Sandra Thorne's neck was too short to display the torc to its best advantage. To keep her chin from banging on the horses' heads she was obliged to tilt her own head back in some discomfort. Giggling nervously under the archaeologist's fervent scrutiny, she turned to Miriam, one woman to another.

'It's a little on the flashy side, don't you think? You couldn't wear it with everything.'

It wasn't a wood you could properly call a wood, Jurnet thought irritably, the brambles reaching out for his shirt, his crotch, snaking between the laces of his canvas trainers. He could, he felt, have negotiated the Amazonian rain forest with less peril to life and limb.

153

At his side Miriam cried out 'Oh!' as a spray of rose hips caught in her hair. Disentangling the prickly intruder whilst she held the torch and tried nobly not to flinch, he could have kicked himself. What were the two of them doing in this vegetable mantrap? They ought to be back in Angleby, in bed. In bed.

Somewhere on the far side of the wood, a vixen screamed.

'You know you could never have left without knowing what it's all about.'

Miriam's ability to tune in on his thoughts had ceased to surprise him. Still, he contended huffily: 'It could perfectly well have waited till morning. After 2,000 years, another day isn't going to make all that difference.'

'With somebody like Timmy', Miriam pointed out, 'you never know. He could change his mind. If there's anything else there besides that necklace he could take it away and hide it overnight. Or he could cover up the place so well you'd have to dig the whole wood to find it again.'

From the paddock came the distant beat of the disco. Interwoven with the night sounds of the wood it had modulated into something mysterious and threatening.

'The Iceni are coming,' Jurnet jeered, mocking his own unease.

But it was only Paul Abbott, thrashing through the piled debris with a reluctant Timmy in tow.

'For Christ' sake,' pleaded the archaeologist, his face and bare arms, in the torchlight, a patchwork of abraded skin, 'see if you can't knock some sense into this bonehead. He won't show me where it is – he bloody refuses to show me!'

'You got the paddock to dig in,' Timmy Chance maintained. 'You got no business comin' up here.' Appealing to the detective for the second time that evening: 'You're police, you tell him what's the law. Trespassers will be prosecuted, tha's what it says on the board. He can read. Maybe he'll believe it comin' from you – he don't take a balls' bit o' notice of me.'

'I know all about trespassers,' Abbott protested. 'You heard me yourself phone Mrs Milburn.'

'Saw you pick up the phone all right. Never heard her say nothing back.'

'Only because there was a fault on the line and I couldn't get through.' The archaeologist was all but dancing with impatience. 'You saw me send Ian up to the house to tell her. You saw me!'

'That bugger!' said Timmy imperturbably. 'Bugger like that tell Missus, she'll say, "Pull the other one!"'

'She'll do nothing of the sort! Mrs Milburn will be over any minute to give her permission. A formality. We don't have to hang about waiting.'

'You're the one in a hurry,' Timmy Chance observed. 'I don' mind waitin'.'

'It isn't as if she'll say no,' the other began placatingly, trying a softer approach.

'How you know what she'll say?' The boy's face had become sly. 'Even if she says yes, she don't know where, does she? On'y one knows where is me and I in't sayin'.'

Looking shocked by this unexpected turn of events, Paul Abbott exclaimed: 'You'll have to tell Mrs Milburn!'

Timmy responded calmly: 'I'll think about it.' The boy was full, not of his own importance, but of the importance of the knowledge of which he was the chosen vessel. He had taken off his glasses. Illuminated from below, his eyes no longer appeared protuberant; instead, velvety depths, secret and knowledgeable.

Jurnet smiled at the boy with understanding; accorded him his entitled respect.

'Sorry as I am to have to tell you, Timmy, there's one person you'll have to tell even without being asked.'

'Sandra, you mean? 'Tin't none of her business either. She's got her present, tha's all she get. If me ma was to ask I'd tell her where, only she's dead, she won't ask. I might tell Missus, but again I might not – '

With suitable pomp and circumstance Jurnet pronounced: 'Not Sandra, laddie, not your ma, not Mrs Milburn. The Queen.'

'It's called Treasure Trove,' explained Jurnet. 'That's the legal name for any gold and silver things that have been hidden away deliberately and then found again when the original owner's beyond tracing. It's called Treasure Trove and by law it belongs to the Crown. The Queen, that is.'

'You're having me on,' Timmy asserted. 'The Queen never bin to Lanthrop. Ask anybody, they'll tell you the same. Well – ' he amended, 'I s'pose she could've passed through, goin' to Sandringham or driving back to Buckingham Palace, if she fancy to come a different way, but she never been in this here wood. You ask the Missus, she'll know if she been here or not!'

'She doesn't have to have been, not personally. If it's something made either of gold or silver, it's hers.'

'Tha's not fair!' the boy cried. 'She got the Crown jewels. She got her share!'

'It's the law. That's how it is.'

'What kind o' law is that? You're police, whyn't you see to it?' The boy's astonishingly malleable features developed an aspect of antique cunning. 'What if I don't say where? If I don't say, she'll have to put up with the Crown jewels an' lump it!'

Jurnet, whilst smiling to show his sympathy, shook his head. 'Won't wash, sonny. You have a duty to report what you've found to the Coroner and, in due course, to hand it over to him as the Queen's representative. If you don't, you could be guilty of a criminal offence.'

'What'll they do me?' Timmy demanded, unimpressed. 'Put me in Dartmoor? Three meals a day an' all found? What I hear, they don' cut off yer balls any more.'

'They certainly don't do that. Only, what would Mrs Milburn do about the garden with you in prison? You wouldn't want it to go to rack and ruin.' Noting how the boy flinched at the prospect, Jurnet pressed home his advantage. 'And all for nothing. Now it's known there's something buried here they won't stop digging till they find it.'

Paul Abbott shouted: 'Tell him about the money, why don't you. Tell him he'll be paid the value of what's found.'

Jurnet frowned at the intervention. He was obscurely gladdened when Timmy, without waiting to be told, muttered sullenly: 'I don't want no money. I got enough money.'

Out in the darkness the vixen screamed again. Suddenly, out there, beyond the rim of torchlight, time had ceased to register: vixens screaming, wolves baying at the moon, Ancient Britons burying their gold like squirrels burying their nuts and – as with squirrels so often – never coming back for it. Not, like squirrels, because they had forgotten where they had put it, but because they had not lived to remember. *Boom boom* went, not the disco, but the sound of Roman soldiers moving in to the kill.

The wood was full of noises: of life, of death, but chiefly of memory, the measureless past that was, as Paul Abbott had said, the only reality. Jurnet put an arm round Miriam and found she was shivering.

Clad in wellies and Barbour, Mrs Milburn came out of the dark and asked in her well-bred, water-colour voice: 'What is it, Timmy? What's the matter, dear?'

The boy was crying. Grief possessed him, a grief utterly lacking in the *gravitas* proper to suffering. Hannah Milburn enfolded the unlovely gowk in her arms, kissed him with small, delicate kisses.

'There – there – ' When Paul Abbott made as if to speak, she cut him short absent-mindedly, all her attention centred on the boy. 'Later, Paul. If it's about the torc, Ian told me – '

The archaeologist ploughed on regardless. 'What he didn't tell you, I'm quite sure, was something he didn't have the brain to notice – that it was as perfect and unblemished as on the day it was made.'

'Hush – ' said Hannah Milburn, gently rocking Timmy to and fro. 'No,' she agreed, looking out over a bony shoulder. 'He didn't say anything about that. Is there some special significance?'

'It means – ' returned Abbott, the gyrating light from his torch orchestrating an excitement he could no longer contain – 'it means, don't you see, that it isn't just another shaft burial. In a shaft, every object deposited there has first been broken – slighted, killed, whatever you want to call it – the inference being that a thing, no less than a human being, has a life of its own to be sacrificed to the gods. To find a torc like the one tonight, in mint condition, must mean there's a cache somewhere. The Druids would have heard of Boudica's defeat, they'd have known the Romans were coming – it follows! For God's sake, Hannah, speak to him! He must know we're going to find the place sooner or later – '

'We?' the woman queried coolly. 'This is my land, you know. Nobody digs it up without my permission.'

The archaeologist flushed.

'I'm sorry. I didn't mean – ' But Mrs Milburn had turned back to the boy.

'It's a secret.' Timmy raised his head, his tear-stained face. 'Everybody have secrets.' Defiantly: 'I don' see why I can't have secrets like everybody else.'

'No reason at all.' Mrs Milburn spoke encouragingly. Timmy drew the back of his hand across his dripping nose.

'*My* secret!' – relishing the combination of words. 'Somethin' nobody knows but me an' the ole badgers what used to be there, on'y they're gone now and I'm the on'y one. I tell where it is, it won't be a secret any longer. Once that ole bag in the shop hear, every bugger in the village'll know.'

'That's quite true, Timmy,' Hannah Milburn agreed gravely. 'And not only the village. Everyone in England, the British Isles. You'll be famous.'

'You're having me on.'

'No, I'm not,' she assured him. 'It isn't every day people find things that have been buried in the earth for hundreds of years. You'll be in all the papers.'

The boy considered before announcing wistfully: 'I like a secret. Me an' no one else.'

'People have to make choices, Timmy. That's often the way.'

'Will my picture be in the papers as well?'

'It's certain to be.'

'Wi' the Queen? She goin' to nab the bloody lot, least she can do is have her picture taken along o' me.'

'I'm afraid I can't say about that.'

The archaeologist burst in: 'There can't be all that many abandoned badger setts – '

'Be quiet, Paul! It has to be Timmy's decision and nobody else's.'

In the dark wood, in the circle of torchlight, they waited for the boy to speak.

15

'Three more bodies!' exclaimed the Superintendent. 'Well done, Ben! Keep up the good work!'

'Two actually,' countered Jurnet, doing his best not to sound cheeky. 'The third one was a horse. The chap from the British Museum found an iron tyre and he reckons a chariot was buried along with the rest.' Taking a chance after a quick look at the austere countenance which was giving nothing away: 'AD 60, sir. A bit outside our terms of reference, wouldn't you say?'

The joke, thought Jurnet, some of the Superintendent's habit of anger invading his own gut, the bloody ironic joke was that, after a mere couple of days, here he was nearer to solving a 2,000-year-old mystery than to knowing who had killed Annie Chance the day before yesterday, in a manner of speaking. The even bloodier joke was that if only her son had happened upon that badger sett a few months earlier, there could well have been no murder needing investigation. All that gold! If past *ex gratia* rewards were anything to go by, Timmy was going to be a rich man, his mother under no compulsion to catch the bus, lugging a cheap suitcase, en route to a rendezvous with death on Lanthrop beach.

In the light of day, the turves peeled carefully back and laid aside, it had been amazing. By torchlight it had been pitiful almost beyond bearing, curiosity and greed alike eclipsed by an overwhelming impulse to put everything back the way it was. Timmy, his secret exposed, stood bawling and would not be comforted. What we should all be doing, Jurnet had thought, directing his torch downward into the hole the boy had opened up for their inspection.

It was the badgers, at a guess, who had disturbed the large bones scattered round a horse skull whose eye-cavities glittered crystalline, so compelling in their sightless gaze that, to the little group clustered on the edge of the drop, it had seemed, for an incredulous moment, that they were the ones under examination, not the other way round.

'Epona!' Paul Abbott had said, as if invoking a charm to keep them from harm.

Gold shone wherever the torch beams played among the tumbled bones: gold basins, gold bracelets and brooches, gold clasps and intricately patterned gold ornaments that might once have adorned shoulder plaids or wide leather belts. Their quantity would have been astonishing had not all astonishment been pre-empted by the two skeletons which lay with scarcely so much as a finger-joint missing on either side of the hoard, not so much on guard as lost in a dream from which it would have been a supreme discourtesy to awaken them.

How had it happened that the badgers, going about their domestic chores, had not disturbed the sleepers? In daylight, no doubt, the experts who could be counted on to arrive in droves would produce answers that would satisfy themselves, if nobody else. By torchlight Miriam, whispering for fear of awaking the sleeping pair, had announced with complete conviction: 'Her daughters. Boudica's daughters.'

'AD 60,' the Superintendent repeated. 'Two thousand – no, nineteen hundred and thirty-two years ago.' In a voice spiked with no more than its normal, everyday astringency: 'On the same time-scale that makes it – let me see, I think I've got it right – only till 3924 to wait in order to find out who killed our Annie.'

'No time at all,' agreed Jurnet.

On the strength of that iron tyre Timmy's find had gone down to history instantly as the Lanthrop Chariot Burial, one of the great archaeological discoveries of the century. Jurnet, admitted to the paddock after some small difficulty with a security man at the entrance, made his way to the wood across grass still littered with the condoms and potato skins of Paul Abbott's end-of-term party. The discothèque had gone, the detective noted, but not the wooden dance floor where he and Miriam had swayed to the rhythm of the distant sea. Would anyone remember to come and collect it, he wondered, or would it gradually sink down, below the grass, below the worms, to await resurrection at the hands of some future Timmy?

Jurnet listened intently, frowning that he could no longer hear the waves breaking on the shore. Only at night, perhaps: only under the moon. Only with the woman you loved in your arms.

In the wood the British Museum boffin, his mouth purple with blackberry juice, was, in the nicest possible way, pulling rank on the local hobbledehoys. Alistair Tring, the Angleby Museum curator, whose small beaked face was equally purple, though in his case with suppressed rage, nevertheless contrived the smile of policy one might expect to see on the face of a hyena waiting for the King of Beasts to finish his meal, and hopeful of some crumbs from the royal table. Cameramen strung with lenses and light meters, and got up in a state-of-the-art scruffiness which must have taken hours to achieve, circled the excavation, alternately extending and telescoping tripods that resembled sexually aroused robots. One of the photographers, having read on his light meter news which did not please him, turned at Jurnet's approach.

'Move that fucking tree over a couple of feet, will ya?'

A middle-aged man sweating in a pin-striped three-piecer whom the detective recognized as from the Coroner's office, ostensibly present to compile a duplicate list which he was in no way competent to do, was in reality there, Jurnet guessed, to count the spoons and to let it be seen that he was counting them.

Below, in the excavation itself, two young women and a young man in white coats, jeans and trainers, were moving about with incredible delicacy, the young women positioning measuring-rods and using fine brushes to displace powdered bone and time-expired badger faeces from golden bowls that once the Druids in their sacred grove had raised to the horse-goddess Epona; the young man recording on tape everything that was done, everything that was there to be seen. From time to time, one of the finds, its place in the scheme of things recorded for posterity, was wrapped in soft linen and handed up to brown-overalled men who squatted waiting at the edge of the drop equipped with wicker hampers stuffed with straw.

A little apart from the others, two cadaverous individuals who might have been chosen for their special affinity to skeletons, devoted their attention to the skull and bones of the horse, handling the relics with an anxious love, and using their own cameras as if distrusting the histrionics of the crasser breed moving round the perimeter. From time to time the two put their

161

heads together in a low-voiced colloquy before bending afresh to their task as to a secret rite. Their eyes glanced indifferently off the golden goodies being unearthed all around them. Like children reserving the best sweets for last, at the two human skeletons which still rested undisturbed they carefully did not look at all.

Paul Abbott, unshaven and less happy than might have been expected, came over and said: 'I still can't believe I'm awake.'

'What you need', advised Jurnet, 'is a good cry like Timmy.'

'I believe you're right!' Looking more like his usual cheery self, the archaeologist added: 'It's funny – I've been on any number of digs – nothing to compare with this of course, but still – ' Taking in the buzz of activity: 'Maybe it's what astronauts feel when they head out towards the stars – their own obscene intrusiveness, I don't know. Thanks to Timmy, archaeologically speaking my fortune's made, yet all the while I'm rejoicing – and don't misunderstand me, I am, as they say, over the moon – another part of me wants to do exactly the same as that backward boy: seal it all up in earth again and tiptoe away with a finger to my lips, do not disturb.'

'Timmy ought to be feeling more resigned to his fate. This lot must be worth a king's ransom.'

'It would have to be some king! It is, literally, priceless. Just the same, a price will be put upon it. Unless they suddenly change the way it's done, the Treasury will appoint an independent reviewing committee to assess the current market value, and whatever they decide will be paid to our – or should I say to Hannah's – boy. When she reads about it in the papers the boobacious Sandra is going to curse the day that under the influence of the full moon and some mysterious sweetener from Fastolfes, she scarpered with young Ian after the party.'

'They've gone then, have they?'

'They've gone. To Gretna Green, according to Mrs Cobbold down at the store, than whom only God knows more about what goes on hereabouts.' The archaeologist rumpled his hair, took off his glasses, put them on again. 'You'll be telling me to mind my own business – '

Jurnet said: 'If it's about Mrs Milburn, I reckon it *is* your business.'

'Thank you for that.' The man inclined his head with dignity and a kind of despair. 'I mean – what's she playing at? One

162

minute she's going to set them up in a market-gardening business; the next, she's bribing another bloke to play Young Lochinvar and spirit the maiden away. What's behind it?'

Jurnet chose his words carefully. 'Could be, considering Timmy's mental capacity, or lack of it, she's had second thoughts about the advisability of encouraging – '

The other shook his head vigorously. 'Not on. She's always blinding off about how intelligent the boy is, only it's an intelligence you can't measure by IQ tests.'

'Well, then – '

'Well, nothing,' Paul Abbott contradicted. 'That's why I'm speaking to you, the fuzz. For her own sake I hope to God Hannah's wrong and Timmy's what, to everybody but her, he seems to be, a feeble-minded youth with green fingers. Because if she's right and he's more than that – '

'What are you getting at?'

'What, I ask myself, made her suddenly change her mind and, in effect, send Sandra packing at a moment's notice? And the only answer I can come up with is that she'd found out something about the boy she didn't know before. Something that's put a totally different complexion on the whole situation.'

'What sort of something?'

'I think she's found out it was Timmy who killed his mother and she's covering up for him.'

All in all, it seemed only fitting to Jurnet, coasting down to the village conscience-stricken at having, against his better judgement, told Abbott all about the goat farm and Timmy's subsequent refusal to be tested for HIV, that he should round a bend in the road and find the boy directly ahead of him, jerking along in that gait of his which seemed incapable of keeping to a straight line. The handle of some gardening tool protruded from the canvas bag which he wore slung over one shoulder.

Jurnet stopped and leaned out of the car window.

'Fancy a raspberry ripple?'

Timmy shook his head, kept on walking. 'I got somethin' to do.'

Combed and clean in his T-shirt and jeans, the boy still looked untidy, his gangling body out of kilter with the garments which clothed it.

163

'You look as if you could do with a raspberry ripple,' Jurnet persisted. 'I know I could. I'll drop you off wherever you want to go.'

'I got somethin' to do in the churchyard.' Moving away downhill: 'I don't need no lift.'

'Tell you what –' Jurnet, having set the car in motion, brought it alongside once more. 'I'll pop into the store while you're getting on with whatever it is, pick up a couple of cones and bring 'em over for us to have in peace and quiet.'

Without waiting for either a yea or a nay the detective drove down to the village store where he found Mrs Cobbold busy sticking labels which said '*A Present from Lanthrop*' on to a polythened pile of what advertised themselves as 'Shining Lights' – plastic sets consisting of hand mirror, hairbrush and comb encrusted with multicoloured foil that, even in the subdued light of the store, flashed blue and red and emerald.

'Four seventy-five,' she greeted the detective, holding a set up for his inspection. 'You'd think you needed your head examined to pay tuppence for such rubbish, but there it is – four pounds seventy-five and one of our best lines in the tourist season.' The storekeeper laughed her comfortable laugh and pushed the pile on the counter to one side. 'Can't hope to interest *you* in one, that's certain. So what can I do for you?'

Jurnet ordered the raspberry ripple cones and, in the short time at his disposal, contrived to elicit news about Sandra and Gretna Green. Through the shop window he saw Timmy cross the road and enter the churchyard.

'Not that I believe a word of it,' Mrs Cobbold asserted, as she wielded the ice-cream scoop with old-fashioned generosity. 'I don't even know as they do it any more – marry them over the anvil, and all that. I reckon it's jest Mrs Thorne wanting to protect her gal's good name. I tell her not to worry: Sandra's not one to get herself into trouble like some.' The woman had also glimpsed Timmy, jerking his way between the passing cars. 'Tha's the one I'm sorry for.'

'I don't think there was all that much between them.'

'Not that!' The storekeeper spoke with a warm emphasis. 'That Sandra were only in it for what she could get. The lad's well out of that!'

'They say he could be in the way of picking up a bit of money for those things they've dug up, up the road.'

164

'Not that either! Be honest, who could fancy Timmy Chance if he came wrapped up in the Bank of England? There's some people', declared Mrs Cobbold, 'could own the whole world and you'd still be sorry for 'em.' She lifted an empty cone from the waiting pile and pushed it across the counter. 'The way he goes on about how there's never enough cone for the ice-cream! Drives you round the bend!'

Jurnet paid what was owing, picked up the gift and fitted it over one of the filled cones.

'I'll tell him it's from you.'

In the churchyard the poppies were over, the stalks balancing their neat little pots of seed with the aplomb of Chinese acrobats twirling plates on the end of a stick. Annie Chance's grave, all on its own in a corner, looked stand-offish, keeping itself to itself the way Annie always had. To Jurnet's surprise, nothing seemed to have been done to it in the weeks since burial; but perhaps today was the day for getting things moving at last. As the detective approached through the dead grasses, he could see Timmy bent double, doing something carefully with a trowel, a care that degenerated into a hasty tumbling of soil back into place when he became aware that he was no longer alone.

'One raspberry ripple,' Jurnet announced, handing the ice-cream over with a flourish. 'The extra cone comes courtesy of Mrs Cobbold at the store, to whom, I am sure, you will remember to say thank you.'

'The old bag,' mumbled Timmy, taking the offering without grace and demolishing it in gargantuan slurps which appeared to take no account of its coldness.

Jurnet, his own appetite diminished by the performance, allowed his own cone to fall to the ground as if by accident. When the last of Timmy's had gone protesting to its doom he strolled round the grave to join the boy.

A trowel lay on the ground, and next to it a can of Brasso and a piece of rag. Jurnet stared at these last unbelievingly.

'You're never thinking of getting in there to polish the coffin handles?'

'None of your business – '

For a moment Jurnet's heart was wrung with compassion. For a moment: then, glancing down at the soil which Timmy had disturbed and which lay about parched and crumbling, he caught sight of – what was it that lay there, not quite concealed?

Timmy shouted, 'Bugger off!' before subsiding to watch in surly silence as the detective squatted down purposefully and pushed the earth aside.

Brought forth to the light, the sun blazed. Two suns, that is to say: the sun in the sky and the sun on the golden breastplate – if that was what it was – which Jurnet's questing hands had uncovered. Its golden locks incandescent, its mouth twisted in a superb disdain, the golden sun lay on Annie Chance's grave and stared up at its simulacrum in the sky as if it didn't think much of it.

Timmy said sulkily: 'She always like to keep her hair nice.'

'A mirror!' Jurnet turned the golden sun over and brushed away the dirt that adhered to the underside. The sunlight bounced off the hammered metal with an intensity that made him momentarily shut his eyes. 'A looking-glass! Is that what you thought it was?'

'I'm not thick,' said Timmy. 'What you think I thought it was, then? A packet o' cream crackers?'

Jurnet's voice was gentle. 'She's dead, Timmy.'

'I know that! Don't mean she don't like to keep her hair nice.'

'You'll have to give it to Mr Abbott. It'll have to go in with all the other things. Those are the rules. I know!' Holding up a hand at the sight of the stubborn blankness which overspread the boy's face. 'Put that back in the bag like a good fellow and give me a minute. I know just the thing!'

Dodging recklessly across the road, Jurnet ran back to the village shop where he bought a set of 'Shining Lights' from an astonished Mrs Cobbold, plunking a £5 note down on the counter and having to be reminded to pick up his 25p change.

'Don't bother to wrap it.'

Back in the churchyard the toilet set with its bits of coloured foil sparkled in a way to put to shame a mere hunk of ancient gold without so much as an atom of plastic to recommend it. Timmy, enraptured by the play of colours, seized the proffered pack with delight, his fingers exploring the contours of brush, comb and mirror as best they could through the wrapping.

'An' a brush an' a comb! What about that, then?'

The boy picked up the golden sun and held it out to the detective.

'I'll swap you!' he crowed. 'I'll ruddy swap you!'

The exchange made, he took up his trowel and, crooning with glee, dug a hole in the middle of Annie Chance's grave deep enough, by his reckoning, to render his gift available to a dead woman with a mind to keep her hair nice no matter what. Jurnet noted with something like awe that his face had become beautiful.

'Nex' time I come,' Timmy promised, raising his voice enough to be heard six foot down, 'I'll bring yer a bottle of shampoo!'

16

At Police Headquarters, with the passing of the months, they had all but stopped talking about the murder of Annie Chance. Life, as they said, had to go on; which, so far as Police Headquarters was concerned meant, in effect the exact reverse, two other lives in the Angleby area – that of an elderly widow and a child – having more recently been brought to a violent end requiring police attention.

At the Castle Museum Alistair Tring had had his little day, when the artefacts of what the tabloids persisted in calling 'Boadicea's Treasure' were briefly on view prior to their translation to the metropolis. The cost of security for the week's display, whilst crippling to the Museum's budget, was a source of deep satisfaction to the puffin-beaked little curator, confirming his good opinion of himself.

The Superintendent had gone to see the show and returned in a vile temper, as if the sight of the manifest worth of Timmy Chance's discovery had somehow enhanced the infamy both of his mother's end and of Angleby CID's incompetence in failing to produce the miscreant responsible for it. Jurnet's own attendance in the company of Miriam had not been a brilliant success either. Paul Abbott, uncomfortable in a city suit, had been there, wanting to know if the detective had seen Hannah Milburn lately and shaking his head dispiritedly when told he had not.

'Why do you ask?'

Moving away before Jurnet could question him further, 'I don't know what's got into her,' the archaeologist had complained.

The golden hoard – the sun retrieved from Annie's grave included – had been displayed against a blow-up of the opened badger sett complete with horse and girls, the guardian skeletons *in situ*: a presentation given dramatic point by the inclusion of two circlets of gold wire which – so the accompanying card helpfully informed the viewer – were the instruments of the girls' deaths, each of them ritually strangled.

Neither Jurnet nor Miriam had noticed the wires before. Having once seen them, it was difficult to look at anything else. Miriam, grown silent and haunted, had stood in front of the display case so long that one of the security guards had moved closer, until reassured by his recognition of her companion, the groovy git from the CID.

'Hiya, Valentino,' the guard had greeted him, intending only to be chummy. 'World treating you OK?'

'OK.'

Outside, as they crossed the bridge that led back to the city and the unrevenged present, Miriam had demanded: 'Oh why, after all this time, haven't you found out yet who killed Annie Chance?'

Even so, failure that he was, she went to bed with him when they got back to the flat, embracing him with a dark elegiac passion which he found both delightful and dismaying: so that when it was over – lingeringly, a long farewell – it was not a complete surprise to find that she had dragged her suitcase out from under the bed and was taking the hangers out of dresses prior to packing them away.

'Where are we going?' Jurnet inquired without hope.

'Not "we". I'm going up to London. There's a man over from the States with some new acrylic yarns I ought to see.'

'Less than two hours on the Intercity. Less than two hours back.'

'I thought I'd spend a few days with Mother. I've hardly seen her since I got back.'

'Don't stay away too long.'

'I don't know. It depends on you.' She came close, making his heart twang with the imminent loss of her. 'You're too happy, Ben. You're never going to find out who killed Annie Chance while you're as happy as you are.'

'If what you're suggesting is that I can only do my job as long as you're on another continent, I'm asking for my cards tomorrow.'

'Not necessarily another continent. Anywhere that isn't here. You know it's true.' The large dark eyes remained serious. 'I'm a

169

diversion – if you like, a kind of adultery. I come between you and the loyalty you owe to whoever it is that's been murdered. The love.'

'The love! Are you saying I'm in love with Annie Chance?'

'Of course,' she answered, as if it were the most natural thing in the world. 'The way you're in love with them all. The way you have to be.'

He knew it was true. He put out his hand and touched her wonderful hair, memorizing her.

'You're like one of those princesses in the fairy stories, always setting tasks, making conditions. Unfortunately for that scenario I'm no Prince Charming. What if I don't succeed?'

'This isn't a fairy story.'

All the same, at Headquarters next morning, six months to the day since Annie Chance had stuck her dead hand out of the sand, it seemed as close to one as made no difference. Jack Ellers had taken the call. Jurnet, brooding over Dr Colton's report on the injuries sustained by the elderly woman, his latest love, raised his head with no more than desultory interest at the change in the little Welshman's tone and posture.

'The rep!' he cried out to his superior officer, crashing the receiver back on to its cradle. 'Come on! We've got Annie Chance's bloody rep!'

Down by the river, the Apple Tree, as was to be expected from an establishment accorded respectful mention in the Guide Michelin, exuded an air of elegant understatement which proclaimed louder than any advertisement that to eat there cost money. The adrenalin draining away after their dash across the city, siren blaring, Jurnet predicted glumly: 'Probably picked it up at the parish jumble sale. If she isn't having us on.'

'She's not the type, is she?' Ellers brought the car to a standstill outside the restaurant's main entrance. 'She said as how she'd let the air out of his tyres, so he won't be driving off in a hurry.' The little Welshman shook his head in approving wonderment. 'Those quiet ones – they're the ones to watch!'

Reluctant, when it came down to it, to risk having his hopes dashed, Jurnet still lingered. He said, eyeing the chic frontage with a certain spleen – he had more than once thought of taking Miriam there for a meal and been afraid to risk it: it was the kind of place where they put up a menu without prices – 'Can you see any rep affording to eat there?'

'Maybe he travels in oil wells. Want me to come with?'

'No. Wait here. I'll bleep if I need you.'

Inside the restaurant, at a table by a window through which reflections of the passing river dappled the diners with eddies of light and dark, a girl sat drinking coffee with a man in a blouson which had no need of the embroidered signature over the breast to confirm its exalted pedigree. Unfortunately for its wearer, the blouson was not a good fit – or perhaps it would be more accurate to say that its wearer was not a good fit for the blouson, a garment made for a frame of altogether more heroic build than the narrow chest and sloping shoulders to which it was asked to accommodate itself. Even more unfortunately for the general effect, the man was crying, weeping salt tears into his demitasse, his whole persona at such odds with the superb tailoring he had the effrontery to flaunt as to lose him any possible sympathy his posture of grief might otherwise have engendered.

The girl, at least, was all attention. She had taken one of the man's hands into her own across the table top and was chafing it with gentle firmness as against the cold. From the way, seen across the dining-room, her lips moved, she was murmuring 'There, there!' the way a mother might soothe a fractious child.

It was the only thing maternal about her, thought Jurnet, astonished despite that alerting telephone call to find, as he drew near – to the manifest disapproval of the suave gentleman manning the desk immediately inside the door – that the comforter was Hannah Milburn. So far as he could judge in the ambiguous light she looked years younger than in his memory, not a woman putting on an act either, but a girl, the genuine article. Her hair was crimped in a crinkle-crankle hair-do, and her bright pink dress, going by the length of leg visible, was more like a T-shirt which had stretched in the wash.

Close to, the detective saw that Hannah Milburn's face too had changed, the aristocratic bone structure less obstrusive, the mouth unashamedly sensuous, all the passion formerly pent up behind that fastidious façade made explicit. He could have sworn that the blue of her eyes had darkened since their last meeting. The smudges of fatigue beneath them did not destroy the illusion of youth: on the contrary. She looked like a child who had stayed up past its bedtime.

171

She greeted Jurnet's arrival with a pretence of startled pleasure. 'Detective-Inspector Jurnet! What a coincidence!'

At the name and title the man with her abruptly stopped crying.

'You're quick,' he said, his reddened eyes fastened upon the newcomer as upon a deliverer.

'Not the word I'd have chosen myself,' Jurnet returned unsmiling. 'If you are the person I think you may be, we've been expecting you to drop in for a chat ever since the body of Mrs Annie Chance was found on Lanthrop beach six months ago.'

'You *are* quick,' the man insisted. He produced from his sleeve a handkerchief of a startling whiteness and blew his nose on it, the sight of the snowy linen, for some reason, bidding fair to set him off once more. 'Endymion Mobbs,' he introduced himself, stuffing the handkerchief out of sight again and with its disappearance regaining some semblance of calm. 'Mother was a great admirer of John Keats. And yes – ' Endymion Mobbs conceded – 'I knew the police wished me to help them with their inquiries, that's the phrase, isn't it? I heard it on the news at the time and all my instincts were to come forward. I'm a law-abiding citizen. But there was Mother to think about, you see. The shame would have killed her.'

At this last, to Jurnet's astonishment, the man began to laugh as violently as, a moment earlier, he had been weeping. Hannah Milburn leaned forward in her place, full of a lively concern. The nearby diners looked away in embarrassment and talked loudly of this and that. The gent at the desk had, in the interests of decorum, already taken a step in the direction of the window when Jurnet brought his hand down on Endymion Mobbs's shoulder, cutting off the hysteria in full flow.

The man brought out his handkerchief again; wiped his face with it and smiled up at the detective with the sweetness of perfect trust.

'Just the same, Inspector, you *were* quick,' he said.

The Superintendent had taken up his favourite posture, at the window looking down on the Market Place. Soundlessly on the other side of the double glazing the hucksters cried their wares to sceptical Norfolk faces, acquaintances met and parted, shook with remembered mirth. A kindly, humorous world full of

172

kindly, humorous people, give or take the odd murderer or two, the occasional bad apple among the pyramids of shining fruit piled high on the stalls. From inside the bastion of Police Headquarters the Superintendent regarded this failed Eden with that black rage of love which, given the circumstances, was no more and no less than Jurnet, knowing him, had expected.

The Superintendent crossed to his desk, took his seat, implacable. Glowering at his subordinate: 'You realize, of course, that if we had managed to pick him up when the trail was still hot, we might have cleared up this case months ago?'

'Yes, sir,' said Jurnet, adding, with only seeming inconsequence, 'He says that this is the first time he's worn it.'

Endymion Mobbs had complained, disappointed: 'So you weren't all that quick after all! I didn't see how you could possibly be that quick. I stopped the milk and the papers and told everybody we'd be gone for a couple of weeks. I'd have made it three except I knew nobody would ever believe Mother'd stay away that long. All those years, two weeks at Mablethorpe, never a day over – they'd twig at once something was up. Though even then – ' with a childlike pride at having taken every possible contingency into account – 'I reckoned, whatever the neighbours said, the police would be bound to wait a bit longer before they actually broke in. It's a serious thing, breaking in. By then, I reckoned, I could have been in Brazil, like that Great Train robber, and you couldn't touch me.'

'What stopped you?' demanded Jurnet. 'What were you doing here, at the Apple Tree?'

Despite the heat of the interview room, the man had refused to take off his blouson, anorak, whatever you bloody called it. He plucked absentmindedly at the embroidered signature and slowly, as if with gleeful purpose, two more of its letters reduced themselves to a hanging thread. To the watching detective this unravelling of the famous name seemed suddenly insufferable, an attempt to shuffle off responsibility. Three people, possibly four, had died as a direct or indirect result of that chic embodiment of male vanity. If there was any justice in the world it ought to be dragged on a hurdle to Tyburn, hanged, drawn and quartered; at the very least, walled up in concrete where it could do no more mischief.

173

Endymion Mobbs said: 'When I got back home that night, the day Annie stood me up, Mother could see something was wrong. I'd never said a word about her but, looking back, I'm sure Mother had an idea something was up. She always said she could read me like a book. That night, the state I was in, it didn't take much to get the whole story out of me – not just Annie but how I'd been planning to go off with her into the wide blue yonder, never to see Spalding again.'

'Was she angry?'

'Oh, Mother was never that! Quiet but firm. Never angry. She put her arms round me, called me her dear boy. "A thing of beauty is a joy for ever," is what she said, cuddling me in her arms. They're the first words of Keats's *Endymion*, in case you didn't know, and Mother always said they were the first words she uttered when she saw what a beautiful baby the Lord had sent her. And I was.' Endymion Mobbs leaned forward to stress the point. 'Beautiful. I could show you photos. It wasn't till I was twelve or thirteen that I lost my looks, though Mother said it was only a phase I was going through, I'd grow out of it.' As if Jurnet required any instruction in the matter, the man finished, without self-pity: 'I'm still waiting.'

'You still haven't told me what you were doing at the Apple Tree?'

'I stopped at Tourist Information and they said it was the best restaurant in town.'

'I mean, why Angleby at all? It's hardly on the direct line from Spalding to Rio.'

'Oh, that was Annie.' Every time the dead woman's name was mentioned the man's voice trembled on the edge of tears. 'I wanted to say goodbye to Annie before I left England for ever. First I drove to Lanthrop, but you know –' the thin voice renewed its earlier tinge of grievance – 'they've stuck her away in a corner. That's not right. I had to ask a fellow trimming the grass which grave was hers. So I thought, I'll go to Angleby, she was always on about the shopping and all that. I'll go to the best restaurant, have a slap-up meal and drink a toast to the memory of the only woman who ever looked at me twice. And here I am.'

'But why now?' demanded Jurnet, watching mesmerised as a curlicued 'A' took its leave of the blouson. 'Annie's been dead for months. Why after all this time?'

'Time?' Mobbs ran the word over his tongue as if testing its taste, its meaning. 'After that awful day I just couldn't seem to settle back to life with Mother as if nothing had happened. For a couple of weeks I was off work, I felt so bad. I kept telling myself that Annie had let me down, she wasn't worth getting upset about. I had a good job, Mother kept a lovely home, you could eat off the floor. It didn't do a blind bit of good: I couldn't settle. Then I heard on the telly that they'd found her body –' The man's small chin lifted in triumph. 'Can you believe me when I say it was the happiest day of my life? Annie murdered and me over the moon! Can you believe that?'

'You must have had a reason.'

'Don't you see? It meant she hadn't let me down after all! She'd been prevented, she couldn't help it. It wasn't true she was a tramp like Mother was always trying to make out.' With a throbbing intensity the man declared: 'She meant it when she said she loved me.'

The handkerchief was brought out again, crumpled but still whiter than white. Endymion Mobbs looked at it for a moment, then spread it out over his knees. Deliberately and with an air of quiet satisfaction he tore it into four pieces, across and across again.

Looking up from his task he remarked chattily: 'Mother is quite famous in Spalding for the way she does the laundry. Everyone says she's the one ought to be on telly, doing the commercials.' With a brief, dismissive laugh: 'She always says she can read me like a book, yet the day it came out that Annie'd been murdered, you should have seen the state she was in! She thought I'd done it, you see! "I know you couldn't hurt a fly, Endymion," she kept on saying, but I could tell by the way she looked at me, different, that she was trying to convince herself, she wasn't sure any longer. You could say –' Endymion Mobbs spoke as if the possibility had just that moment occurred to him – 'that she was the one who put the whole idea into my mind. I mean, if somebody suddenly makes it plain that they think you capable of things you never suspected you were capable of, well, you begin to think perhaps you are, if you take my meaning.'

During the interval of silence which ensued, the man apparently pondering his own proposition, Sergeant Ellers quiet in his corner leafing through his notes, Jurnet tried in vain to remember the next lines of Keats's *Endymion*, which he had done for GCE and thought the pits.

'All the same,' confided Endymion Mobbs, stroking the blouson with loving hands, 'it would never have come to anything if it hadn't been for this.'

'How d'you mean?'

'Didn't I tell you Annie gave it me? That last day, when she met me in the lay-by as we'd arranged, she said, "I've got a present for you." Even in the days before I heard she'd been killed, when I thought she'd let me down, I'd look at it hanging in the wardrobe and think it can't be – you'd never give a present like that to somebody you were just about to ditch. Even if it *was* something she'd been given where she worked. She'd made no bones about it, and I was just as chuffed as if she'd saved up for a year. More chuffed. It was the honesty, d'you see? The lack of pretence.'

'Honesty?' Jurnet handled the word with the care due to its fragility. 'I wonder was Annie honest enough to tell you she had a son she was leaving behind?'

The man remained unruffled.

'I read about him in the paper. The lad's grown up, isn't he? He's got his own life to lead.' With a simplicity which moved Jurnet despite himself: 'Far as me and Annie were concerned, the world began the day we found each other. Before then, as it says in the Bible, the earth was without form and void.'

Hardening his heart, the detective insisted: 'Even though the boy's a bit soft in the head?'

'Is he? Can't be all that soft, what I've read about him finding all those things used to belong to Boadicea. They say he could end up a millionaire once he collects the reward. When I read about it I thanked God he never found them before Annie said she'd come away with me.' Endymion Mobbs gave a little laugh. 'Look at me, Inspector. Can you see a woman with all that money in her pocket choosing me to run off with?'

'The blouson. The anorak.' Returning his attention to the garment, Jurnet noted that two more letters had gone their way to oblivion. Soon there would be nothing left but a pattern of tiny pricks where the needle had gone in and out 'You seemed to be suggesting, just now, that the anorak had something to do with your subsequent actions – '

'Mother's actions, actually.' His eyes wide with outrage: 'She gave it away to the charity shop! I'd never even worn it – kept it hanging in my wardrobe in a polythene cover I'd bought specially. I'd take it out sometimes to try on, but I'd never worn it out of doors. Mother came in once when I was trying it on in front of the glass and said I looked a laughing-stock. I knew she only said what she did because Annie had given it me, I made allowances. Only she wouldn't let it alone. She'd say things like, "At least you're not making a spectacle of yourself by wearing it out in the street, that's something to be thankful for" and "Some people have more money than sense," meaning Annie for having, as she thought, bought it in the first place. I bit my lips not to answer her back until the evening I got back from a hard day covering the Kettering district and there was the cover hanging empty in the wardrobe and Mother said she'd been having a clear-out and she'd done me a favour, it was taking up valuable space – ' the enormity of what he had to relate made the man stutter – 'so she'd taken it down to the charity shop. Whatever they got for it would help to feed people starving in Africa and it was good riddance to bad rubbish. It was unbelievable! If it hadn't been past seven when I got home, and I knew they'd be shut for the day, I'd have gone down to the shop then and there, and bought it back.'

Looking at the blouson, Jurnet said: 'Evidently you were round there first thing in the morning.'

'I had to wait for them to open. The lady said they hadn't even had time to price it. If it was a mistake, she said, very nicely, I could have it back, it was perfectly all right. But I said no, that wouldn't be fair, and I gave her £50.' Endymion Mobbs laughed merrily. 'You should have seen her face!'

'I can imagine. You were very generous.'

Still laughing, the other shook his head.

'Not generous at all. It wasn't my £50 in the first place. It was Mother's. She doesn't believe in banks, always keeps her money in a canvas bag in the larder, in a crock under the potatoes. I wasn't supposed to know, but I did.'

'What happened when she found out?' the detective asked.

The man settled the blouson on his shoulders with little reassuring pats.

'I came back from the charity shop and there she was when I came into the kitchen, bending over the crock, the potatoes all over the floor, and pretending she hadn't even heard me come in. She likes to make out that she's getting hard of hearing but really, you can take it from me, Mother can hear the grass grow. I never knew anyone who can hear better. It just wasn't possible that she hadn't heard my key in the front door and my footsteps on the linoleum in the hall, but there she was, with her back to me, pretending she hadn't heard a thing.'

'What did you say to her?'

'I didn't say anything. After what she'd done, things between us had got beyond saying. I could tell by the look of her back, though, that she was upset about the money – Mother has a very expressive back, you only have to look at it to know what kind of mood she's in.' Endymion Mobbs sat up straight. A look of pride came over his face. 'I was in a bit of a mood myself, I don't mind telling you. When I saw her bending over I freely admit that my first instinct was to pick up the bread knife from where it was lying on the kitchen table and kill her. She didn't deserve to live, treating Annie's gift like that, treating me like I was nothing. "A thing of beauty is a joy for ever,"' he quoted again, unexpectedly. 'Do you know how it goes on?'

Jurnet looked up startled. 'I was trying to remember. Something about loveliness, is it?'

'"Its loveliness increases; it will never
"Pass into nothingness."

That was how Mother was treating me – as if I was a nothingness.' The sales rep took a deep breath. 'I actually picked up the knife, all ready to use it, but then I looked at Mother's back again and realized just in time that this was exactly what she was provoking me to do. She *wanted* me to kill her.'

'Why should she want that?'

'Isn't it obvious? To shut me out of heaven of course. Annie and me together – that was the one thing she couldn't bear the thought of. Sweet, lovely woman that she is, Annie must be in heaven and murderers go to hell. Mother wanted to keep us apart through all eternity.'

'So what did you do?'

'Put the bread knife back on the table before I got carried away. Oh, it wasn't easy, when what I wanted to do, more than I'd ever wanted to do anything in the whole world, was stick it into her, hard, between her shoulder blades, far as it would go. But I wasn't going to play into her hands.' With an air of self-congratulation the man finished: 'I put the knife back in its place and picked up the bread board instead and hit her over the head with it.'

'Do that hard enough and it could come to much the same thing.'

'You don't know Mother! Once, when she was on the lav, the cast-iron cistern crashed down on her and all it gave her was a slight headache.'

'What did the bread board do?'

'I do exercises,' said Endymion Mobbs with a certain shy boastfulness. 'Morning and evening, never miss. You can feel my muscles if you want to. I gave Mother a good hard hit and she keeled over on the floor, unconscious, but not dead. Not at all dead, snorting like a steam engine, in fact. I tied her up with clothes line – when I was a Scout knots were the only thing I was any good at: you never know when something will turn out useful, do you? – and then I locked her in the larder, taking the rest of the money, naturally. £11,452 it was. I took it up to my room and counted it before leaving. I wanted to know where I stood. I only took a few things with me, apart from the blouson and I wore that. It being a warmer climate in South America, or so I understand, I reckoned with that kind of money I could run to some new clothes as well as the fare to Brazil. Don't look so worried,' the sales rep exhorted kindly, sensing his interrogator's concern. 'The larder's got a window, covered with wire mesh, plenty of ventilation. I took a last look at Mother before I left and she was breathing very nicely. I left a slab of her favourite Dairy Milk unwrapped and ready broken into squares where she could reach it when she came round, even with her hands tied.'

Jurnet pointed out: 'Half a pound of chocolate won't last for ever. An old lady, everybody thinking she's away, she could easily die of hunger and thirst before anyone twigged something was up.'

'Not Mother,' Endymion Mobbs returned with perfect confidence. 'She'll find a way out, she always does. And there's a lot of nourishment in Dairy Milk. All the advertisements say each bar contains the equivalent of a glass and a half of milk – so there you are, food and drink combined.'

Unpersuaded, Jurnet said: 'Let's hope someone has heard her.' Seized by a sudden further worry: 'You didn't gag her, I hope?'

'Of course not,' said the travelling salesman. 'I knew she'd never call out for fear of what the neighbours would say.'

Whilst the word went out to Spalding, Lincolnshire, to check out

179

47 Lensmure Road without delay, the detective returned to Annie Chance and the green suitcase recovered from the pond near the lay-by.

'What was I to do?' Endymion Mobbs sounded aggrieved. 'I'd parked the car with the boot unlocked as she'd told me, and, as per instructions, gone into the Caff for a cup of tea. Annie wanted to make sure nobody saw us together. When I came out, first thing I did was look in the boot and there it was, together with a carrier bag which I found out later had my blouson in it.' The man's face grew rosy with remembered happiness. 'I can't tell you how I felt at the sight of that case! Ten feet tall! That such a thing should happen to me! I felt like pinching myself to make sure I wasn't dreaming. I'd arranged with my firm to take my holiday, so that meant that I had my whole vacation entitlement plus another £500 I'd drawn out of the Post Office. I also had my passbook from the Halifax with over £2,000 in it. If I'd felt able to give the firm proper notice, I'm pretty sure they wouldn't have let me go without a nice bonus – I'd earned it – but I couldn't say a thing in case it got back to Mother. She'd gone to school with the mother of one of the directors – that was how I got into seedmen's supplies in the first place – and they'd stayed friends.'

'What were you planning on doing?'

'I wasn't worried. The mood I was in, I didn't care what I did. Digging ditches, sweeping the streets, anything that was far enough away from Spalding, so long as I had Annie with me. I even thought we might go to Greece – the wine-dark sea and all that. It all depended on Annie. Whatever she wanted, wherever she wanted, was all right with me. I want you to know, Inspector – ' modulating to a solemnity that, even in the circumstances, Jurnet could not help but find comical: it was self-evidently Endymion Mobbs's karma never to be taken with entire seriousness – 'that my intentions were strictly honourable. I was going to get a special licence. Annie and I weren't going anywhere except as man and wife. Holy matrimony or nothing, that's the kind of man I am. I think Annie appreciated that. Life hadn't been easy for her. I don't think men had always given her the respect she deserved.' There were tears in the salesman's eyes as he said: 'She kissed me several times, always very lovingly, but pure and gentle. She understood without a word being said that keeping myself pure for the right woman meant that I wasn't experienced.

180

"There's nothing to be afraid of," she used to say, before she kissed me. "Nothing to be afraid of."''

Jurnet reminded him: 'She left the green suitcase in your car. What then?'

The man took a deep breath.

'I drove along the road to the lay-by, as we'd arranged. She reckoned it would take her best part of an hour to finish up at the Caff, and then she'd join me there. She didn't want me hanging about in the car-park, it might have excited comment. It was our business, she said, nobody else's. People who wanted to gossip could find something else to gossip about.'

'You waited in the lay-by – '

'It was very peaceful. All that shrubbery between it and the road deadens the noise of passing traffic more than you would have thought possible. There was a pond in the field, with some sheep walking about and some cows sitting down next to the water, munching away like they were chewing gum. As it happened, I had some with me – chewing-gum, that is – and it put me in mind of it. I don't buy it often. Mother brought me up to think it was vulgar. I took out a stick and began chewing.' With a sudden sob, Endymion Mobbs said: 'Me and the cows, sitting there, chewing.'

'Did any other vehicles come into the lay-by during the period you were parked there?'

'Not one. While I was waiting I went over my figures, made sure my books were up to date and in order. I didn't want anyone getting the idea I'd gone off with some of the firm's money. The car was theirs, of course. I figured on leaving it somewhere safe, and then sending them the keys and the parking-ticket and a note to say where it was. I thought, before I do that I'll put it through a car wash, one of those with extra wax polishing that I don't ordinarily bother with. They've treated me well, my employers, over the years, and the one thing I was sorry about was letting them down. It takes years of personal contact to build up the kind of relationship I've built up with my customers.' Not without a certain complacency, the man finished: 'They were going to have a hard time filling my shoes.'

17

'Annie was earlier than I'd expected. To be honest, I could have done with another ten minutes to finish off my books, but of course I just put them away and hoped for the best.

'I'd never seen her looking so beautiful. She was a good-looking woman, you mustn't go by the way she must have looked dead. People look different when they're dead. But – and this you may not know – she had a rather yellowish skin. Well, sallow. It was her one bad point. But when she came into the lay-by that day and I got out of the car to meet her, she looked wonderful, sparkling like champagne.'

'What happened then?'

'She kissed me. Full on the lips, something she'd never done before. It made me feel quite dizzy. She made me open the boot so she could get at the bag with the blouson in it. When I saw what it was – well!' Tears welled up again in the sales rep's eyes. 'I knew this was the high spot of my life, the tops. I knew that nothing was ever going to come up to that moment.

'Annie made me try the blouson on. I thought it was a bit on the large side, but she said it looked lovely. She got a little mirror out of her handbag for me to look at myself in, best I could. We were larking about like a couple of kids. She got a bit upset when she noticed that the embroidery on the breast pocket had come undone a little, but then she smiled and said it didn't matter, she'd see to it when we stopped for the night. *When we stopped for the night!*' The man repeated the phrase in a tone of hushed wonder. 'I thought my heart would jump out of my chest! Can you even begin to understand what those words meant to me, that I was never to be alone again?'

'I can understand,' Jurnet said.

The seeds salesman stared at the detective for a moment, his face inscrutable.

'She made me put the blouson away. She didn't want to risk the stitching going any further. I must say I was sorry to take it off. In the few minutes I'd had it on I'd grown to love the feel of it, the new me. I reckon it's the way a snake feels when it casts its old skin and gets itself a brand-new one. Born again. Still, Annie was right to worry. Apart from anything else, I might have got some grease on it from the fish and chips.'

'Tell me about the fish and chips.'

Endymion Mobbs laughed out loud.

'You might ask, eh, what's the owner of a jacket like that doing eating fish and chips in a lay-by? Not if you saw what Annie brought, you wouldn't. None of your common cod or plaice! A halibut steak you wouldn't get better at the Ritz, and as for the chips – well, I can tell you as somebody who's eaten chips in more places than he cares to count, that the Caff chips are out of this world.'

Agreeing, Jurnet waited for what was to come next. A shadow had fallen across the face of the sales rep.

'I hope you didn't get grease on the anorak after all,' the detective prompted kindly.

'I told you, I took it off. Annie folded it up and put it back in the carrier bag, then put it back in the boot next to her case. Not that there'd have been any danger – she'd brought along a whole packet of serviettes. And a plastic knife and fork. And a sachet of ketchup in case I liked it with my fish, which I didn't, only she wasn't to know. Mother always said only common people drowned their food in ketchup. Stupid, wasn't it, but if you've heard that said from as far back as you can remember, it's bound to become part of your thinking. I told Annie what Mother said and we had a good laugh.'

But the shadow had deepened.

'What happened then?'

The man raised his head so that his face, in all its inadequacy, faced the detective squarely.

'What happened then was that she suddenly said she'd forgotten something. I said if it was tights or soap or something like that not to worry. We could always pick some up on the way.'

'On the way to where? You haven't said where you'd decided to make for.'

'Annie said she'd never been to Brighton, and I said, Brighton it is then. Anywhere that wasn't Spalding was OK with me. We were going to stay there until the licence came through and then, once we were man and wife, we'd have the whole world to choose from.' The man's chin trembled. 'She said what she had to do might take a little while or it might take a little while longer, but not to worry, she'd be back as soon as she could and why didn't I take a snooze while she was gone? She kissed me again – but on the cheek this time, not the lips – took the wrappings the fish and chips had been wrapped up in and got out of the car. "I'll put them in the litter bin," she said. Romantic, wasn't it?' Endymion Mobbs ended, bleakly staring. 'Those were the last words she said to me: "I'll put them in the litter bin."'

'Which way did she go?'

'Back to the Caff. In that direction, anyway. I offered to drive her, but she said no. I was disappointed, I won't deny it. I wanted to get the show on the road, as they say. I couldn't wait for the happy-ever-after to begin. But don't misunderstand me – not in an angry way. In a way I was even pleased. I don't know if I can make you understand – '

Jurnet said: 'Try me.'

'All my life', Endymion Mobbs explained, 'people have told me what to do. I don't say that in any complaining way, it's just that I'm more comfortable being told than doing the telling. Annie suddenly going off like that only proved what I suppose, in my heart of hearts, I already knew – you might even say it was part of the attraction – that she was going to be the boss, just like my mother. Only not like her. Annie wouldn't have taken advantage.' The voice became dark and intense: 'She wouldn't have, either! I'd stake my life on it. But all I could think of then, God forgive me, when she didn't come back, waiting and waiting and bloody well waiting, chewing gum like those bloody cows in the field till I could have turned into a bloody cow myself, was that she'd let me down.'

'Did it never occur to you that she could have met with an accident, or been physically prevented?'

The man stood up.

'Look at me,' he commanded in perfect simplicity. 'Take a look and then ask yourself why a good-looking woman, full of life and energy, should choose of her own free will to hitch up with somebody like me. The very thought is still the miracle that keeps me going. But that afternoon, that evening, waiting out there in that lay-by, what else could I believe but that, when it came to the crunch, she suddenly couldn't bear to go through with it?'

'You might at least have given her the benefit of the doubt.'

'Don't you think I know that now? Don't you think I know I should have gone looking for her – back at the Caff, in Lanthrop, I don't know where – anywhere rather than sit there feeling sorry for myself? Who knows, I might have got there in time to to save her.' The man moved his head from side to side like a caged animal. 'Instead, what did I do when it seemed ridiculous to go on waiting any longer? I fetched her suitcase out of the boot, tipped it over the fence into the field. Only that wasn't enough. She might have come looking for it. She didn't deserve to get it back, letting me down like that at the last minute. So what I did, I climbed over the fence after it. There was a strand of barbed wire I hadn't noticed that tore a piece out of the front of my shirt. "Mother won't half like that!" I remember thinking, and it only made me angrier with Annie. When I came down into the field the cows got up and walked away slowly, insultingly, like they were on Annie's side too, or so it seemed to me. I must have been insane. I threw the suitcase into the pond, watched as it sank below the surface. Climbed back over the fence, and drove home to Mother.'

'You hung on to the anorak, though,' Jurnet pointed out. 'You didn't dump that in the pond along with the case. Why was that?'

'I don't know.' Endymion Mobbs looked confused. He touched the blouson with both hands, anxiously. 'I suppose it looks bad?'

Jurnet said impassively: 'It does, rather.'

The news from 47 Lensmure Road, Spalding, was moderately cheering. Mrs Mobbs had been found trussed up with positively devilish ingenuity, her face smeared with chocolate. Apart from a bump on the back of her head she appeared little the worse for her ordeal.

Her story was that a gang of masked and gloved men – four of them, she alleged, one of them black, she could tell from the whites of his eyes – had burst into the house, tied her up and left her imprisoned in the larder. When the detective-sergeant in charge of the rescue had pointed out that, so far as he could see, there was no sign of a forcible entry and nothing appeared to be taken, Mrs Mobbs had merely shrugged her shoulders, said, 'That's your business,' following it up with some choice remarks about policemen who marched all over one's premises without first thinking to wipe their feet on the doormat.

She had shown no curiosity as to what had brought them to her address in the first place and rejected outright an offer to call in a doctor or, alternatively, of transport to the hospital for a medical check-up. When asked why she hadn't shouted for help as might have been expected, her reply had been that her son was expected home shortly, and he would take care of her if she needed any taking care of, which she didn't.

The Superintendent lifted a corner of the top page of Endymion Mobbs's statement as if handling a soiled dressing for which he could have done with a pair of rubber gloves.

Jurnet ventured placatingly: 'Not much to go on.'

'Less than nothing! If she'd named her son at least, held him responsible for her condition and for the theft of her money – which she obviously has no intention of doing – it would have given us an opening to hang on to him for the time being. As it is, we're going to have to let him go – to Brazil, for all we know: and that will be that.'

'Doubt he's planning to go that far any longer. The clockwork's run down, that's my guess. Doubt he's planning to go anywhere. His mother told the Spalding police he'd be home shortly. I think she knows her Endymion better than we do.' Jurnet smiled, glad to impart relatively good news. 'Two of their chaps are on their way down to pick him up and deliver him into her loving arms if he agrees to go – as I'm pretty sure he will, once he thinks it over. I asked them, and they owe us a favour or two.'

'That's something, I suppose. At least we'll know where to lay hands on him, if we need to.'

'We'll know all right! I could almost feel sorry for the poor bastard. After this, Mrs Mobbs'll watch him like a hawk.'

The Superintendent looked up from his papers, his patrician face alight with a boyish mischief that made his subordinate suddenly aware of how much he loved the man, blast his eyes. 'So long as she takes care not to turn her back.'

'And sticks exclusively to ready-sliced bread.'

The two smiled at each other and then the moment passed, as they invariably did, those brief hints of an intimacy never made explicit, but always there. Pushing Endymion Mobbs's statement aside with the gesture of a petulant child, the Superintendent demanded: 'Who's to say that Annie Chance didn't arrive at the lay-by to say she'd decided at the last moment not to elope after all? All those hours sitting in the car waiting – what credence can one attach to that? There could have been a quarrel. He tried to persuade her to change her mind and one thing led to another – '

'Except he'd never have run the risk of lugging her body across all that open sand in broad daylight – and that's assuming he knew about Lanthrop beach, which isn't all that likely.'

'I don't see that. Annie might easily have spoken of it. She might even have decided to postpone breaking the bad news; suggested that instead of eating their fish and chips in the car they drive down to the beach and have a picnic.'

Jurnet disagreed.

'I don't think so. Having once shaken the dust of the village off her feet, having been seen publicly departing with her suitcase, she'd never have suggested coming back a bare hour or so later and risk being seen by someone she knew. That fellow Gifford, for example. He'd have seen her when he came out to open the gate for Mobbs's car.'

'She could easily have ducked down.' But the Superintendent had begun to sound bored with his hypothesis. 'My purpose is simply to underline the inherent improbability of the fellow's story, a cobbled-up patchwork of implausibilities. Does it contain anything that makes it possible, at this distance of time, to test the truth of it?'

Speaking carefully, Jurnet said: 'It does open up one or two possibilities – '

Mrs Milburn did not look well. Over her absurd dress she wore, pulled closely round her body, a sacklike coat in which, for all the appearance of ill health, she looked younger than ever, a child dressed up in its mother's clothes. There was a greyness in her face that had the effect of making Jurnet's apologies for having kept her waiting more elaborate than he had originally intended.

'I hope WPC Hill has been looking after you – ' a remark which made the pert young policewoman who had been keeping Mrs Milburn company whisk away a used cup and saucer and a plate which had held some Rich Tea biscuits with quite unnecessary clatter.

'She has been looking after me beautifully.'

Not even the greyness returned Hannah Milburn to the self-possessed woman Jurnet remembered. Together with the reappearance of youth had come a touching vulnerability which the detective could not believe had ever been part of her previous incarnation. The transformation, which was astonishing, did much to explain Paul Abbott's outburst at the Museum, even if it explained nothing about Hannah Milburn.

'We're very grateful,' Jurnet said. 'Our lucky day, for once, that you decided to lunch at the Apple Tree.'

'But I didn't!' The dark eyes, opened wide, were not only definitely darker but, in some indefinable way, less knowing. 'I was on my way home. I had some dental work done yesterday under anaesthetic and I stayed in Angleby overnight as a precaution. I didn't want to risk driving – '

'Very wise!' approved Jurnet the copper; pleased, too, to have the greyness explained. 'Feeling OK now, are you?'

'Perfectly OK,' Hannah Milburn answered, a shade too quickly. 'Timmy will be wondering what on earth's happened to me. I'd have been back at Fastolfes hours ago if I hadn't seen it, at the traffic lights at the bottom of Bridge Street. I was held up there and I just happened to glance across at the car alongside, and there it was!'

'It?'

'The blouson! I was quite sure there couldn't be another one like it – not in Angleby certainly, probably not in England. I even thought – I couldn't be positive, but I thought I could see a thread still hanging. It had to be the same one! When the lights changed I let the car go ahead of me so I could get the number. But then I thought, why don't I follow him, see where he goes so I can let the police know? You could see, even sitting down, that the blouson was miles too big for him. He looked ridiculous. Just before the lights changed he turned his face a little and it looked so sad, not in the least dangerous.'

Making no comment on this last, Jurnet enquired: 'What did you do?'

'I kept behind him all the way to the river. I was afraid he'd notice he was being followed, but I think he must have been too busy finding his way. He kept slowing down at every turning as if he wasn't sure whether or not it was the one he wanted. He was obviously a stranger to Angleby. I was quite relieved when he turned into the Apple Tree car-park. At least it meant I'd have a chance to phone the police.'

'I understand you let the air out of his tyres.'

'Only the back ones.' The dark eyes brightened and some more of the greyness went out of Hannah Milburn's face. 'I used my nail file. I thought two would be enough. I didn't want to waste time before getting to a phone. Fortunately there was one in the bar.'

'We were very glad to get your call.'

'You took ages coming,' she complained in a childish way. 'At least it seemed like ages.'

'Mr Mobbs said the exact opposite – that we were very quick. Had you told him, then, that you had informed the police?'

'Of course not! What do you take me for? After I phoned I went straight into the dining-room, saw where he was sitting and told the man at the desk that the gentleman over by the window was expecting me. Ordinarily I'd have expected him to check the booking, but I think he was pleased to have someone take him off their hands. He was crying, you see; making people feel uncomfortable, which isn't what they pay for when they eat at the Apple Tree. A waiter was hovering about with a bowl of mushroom soup he must have ordered, not knowing what to do with it, whether to serve it or not.'

'What did you do?'

Hannah Milburn said: 'I told the waiter to leave the soup on the table, and then I sat down myself. I told the man to stop crying at once and eat up his soup before it got cold. It would do him good.' She added: 'I had to feed him the first couple of spoons and then he was all right.'

'Didn't he express any surprise, want to know who you were, what in the world you were doing there, ordering him about?'

'I told him I was a friend of Annie Chance.'

At the mention of Mrs Milburn's name, Endymion Mobbs came out of the depression which had settled on his narrow shoulders like a small personal fog.

'A lovely person! At first, when I saw her, how she was got up, I couldn't take in she was who she said she was. But at a second look, class written all over her. I couldn't get over running into her like that.'

189

'It's a small world,' Jurnet said.

'Yes,' the other agreed. 'When she commented on the blouson, I asked if she hadn't really meant it for Annie's son. I explained that I wouldn't want to have it under false pretences, especially at the expense of somebody who, I understood, was not all there. She answered that, whatever I'd heard, there was nothing wrong with Annie's boy and she'd given the blouson to Annie for her to do what she liked with, so that was all right. She said – ' Endymion Mobbs looked marginally happier – 'I looked very nice in it.'

'It's a small world,' Jurnet repeated. 'But not so small as all that. Not so small that someone who has just trussed up his old mum like a chicken ready for the pot and has her life savings in his pocket ready to buy himself a new life in Brazil, has no other choice than to travel via Lanthrop and Angleby, the two places where he is at obvious risk of discovery – travel, what's more, wearing the one distinctive article of clothing that could give him away. Maybe Keats could explain it; it's beyond me.' Jurnet spoke out of genuine bafflement. 'What I don't understand is why you didn't walk straight out of 47 Lensmure Road down to the local station, give yourself up and be done with it?'

The sales rep's lips began to tremble. 'What do *you* know?'

'Tell me.'

'What do *you* know, a fellow with your looks, the girls only waiting for you to crook your finger and they'll come running?' Eyes closed: 'Brazil, I thought – a new life, even a new love, who knows? And then I thought – ' the eyes opening to reality – 'who am I kidding? Brazil where the nuts come from – where they go to, you mean! A black hole of loneliness no different from anywhere else. A nothing like all the other nothings.'

'So how come you didn't turn yourself in and be done with it?'

'Do you know,' said Endymion Mobbs, looking surprised by the question, 'it never occurred to me. I've had so little to do with the police, perhaps that's why. One summons for parking on the double yellow line, that's all, and even that was a traffic warden, not a bobby. What I thought was, all this time they've probably been looking for a chap in a special kind of anorak called a blouson, and I'm it. I'll go to Lanthrop, to Annie's grave: I'll go to Angleby and walk up and down the streets so everyone can get a good look. If there's a God in heaven somebody will recognize what I'm wearing and that will be it. It won't matter any more whether my books are or aren't made up to date, I won't have to worry about returning the firm's car, I won't have to decide about anything ever again. If there isn't any God I'll go to bloody Brazil and serve me right.' The man leaned his arms on the table, buried his face in them and wailed: 'Mummy!'

18

The road to Lanthrop had changed with the changing year. The ambition had gone out of it; dank clods where the corn had stood brashly gold, leaves that looked as if they were only waiting for the next North Sea gale to put them out of their misery once and for all. Only the ruined church which, in sunnier times, Jurnet had got into the habit of acknowledging with a little nod every time he passed it, seemed to have gained in stature and solidity, to have come into its element, presiding over the dying land.

'"Season of mists and mellow fruitfulness – "' Ellers from the passenger seat unburdened himself of his favourite quotation. 'Don't ask me how the rest of it goes.'

'Send a postcard to Mr Endymion Mobbs, why don't you? He's the one knows all about Keats.'

'That whose it is? All I can remember is how Miss Duffield, our English teacher at Trefflyn Junior, had a wart on her nose which trembled when she recited poetry. Very sexy.' The little Welshman readdressed himself to the landscape. 'Mists OK, if that's what those dirty grey dishrags are, blowing about among the trees. But "mellow fruitfulness?"' With a shake of the head: 'The guy must have been pissed – I suppose what you could call poetic off-licence.'

'He probably wrote it somewhere in Greece or Italy.'

'You reckon? And I thought poets were always too busy starving in garrets to go on package holidays.' The detective-sergeant twisted his plump body so as to study his companion's profile in greater comfort. The handsome features looked severe, the lips compressed, unsmiling. 'For that matter, you're looking a bit autumnal yourself, if you don't mind me saying.'

'Anno Domini.'

Ellers shook his head again with a grin.

'It's that bloody third act, isn't it, that's got you down?'

'What's that supposed to mean?'

'The third act of the drama, boyo, the fucking denouement, as they phrase it in literary circles. The moment when the butler comes in and says, "I did it with my little bow and arrow."' Settling himself in his seat: 'I haven't known you all these years for nothing, Ben. If there's one thing that upsets you more than a murder it's fingering the sucker who done it.'

They came down the hill to the village, passing the turning to Fastolfes without stopping. Above them the trees that earlier in the year had turned this part of the road into a tunnel of green gloom had opened out to reveal a sky set about with odds and ends of cloud that looked like remnants left unsold for good reason after the summer sales. As always when they neared the sea, the wind began to blow: this time a wind with a nip to it. A skein of pinkfoot geese planed magisterially across the marshes as if to demonstrate, without boastfulness, how easy it was to fly once you had got the hang of it.

His spirits lightened by the sight, Jurnet turned the Rover right, past the village shop towards the police house, waiting by the church wall for an opening to cross against the traffic. When it came he drove the car into the police house driveway, relieved to note the patrol car already parked there, which meant that PC Wyatt was at home and they would not be exposed unbuffered to his good lady's lack of welcome. He immediately reversed out of it to park by the roadside facing the way they had come, and the decision encapsulated by this simple manoeuvre aroused in him a surge of pleasure. Rightly or wrongly, he was going *somewhere*. Anywhere was better than not going at all.

Not that PC Wyatt, when he opened the door to them, was all that welcoming either. The news that the elusive rep had been run to earth at last did nothing to bring a smile to the face of the village bobby.

'Don't tell me it's going to start up all over again!' was his appalled reaction. 'I was hoping we were shot of all that at last – I mean November nights closing in, people staying home in front of the telly, village settling down to what it used to be. What with the murder and the archaeology and the skeletons – ' the man spoke with the wrath of one recalling ancient wrongs – 'it's been some summer, I don't mind telling you. We've had everything here from Druids got up in sheets to Ancient Britons in woad and

193

not much else. There's been loonies sleeping out on the sandhill so they'll dream who done poor Annie in, and you couldn't go behind a bush for a leak without falling over a guy with a metal-detector. It's been a madhouse.' PC Wyatt took a revivifying breath and ended on a note of shock horror: 'There's even been talk of changing the name of the Hero to the Boadicea.'

'It must have been a trying time.'

'One or two done all right out of it. I reckon Ma Cobbold's made enough to go on a Caribbean cruise out of iced lollies alone. An' Bill Gifford, he's been running conducted tours of the Dune of Death – tha's what the bugger calls it – at 50p a head. Ruddy entrepreneur, I don't think!' With a chuckle, a sudden lightening of the large, good-natured features, the PC looked towards the shelf over the fireplace. Following the direction of his glance, the two detectives goggled with appropriate awe at the silver cup which shone there.

Jurnet observed, smiling: 'Not such a bad summer after all, then?'

At the Caff nothing had changed. Blanketed in the noise that spewed out of the loudspeakers the long-distance lorry-drivers sat chewing; recharging their batteries against the moment when they could once more heave themselves up to their cabs and be off transmogrified, pounding down the motorway in their eight-wheelers like mutant caterpillars.

Taking avoiding action so as not to cross paths with the manageress, the two detectives made for the end of the room where Ali, his cap and his white overall bright in the gloom, his single ear-ring gleaming, served his god, the frying machine, with dedication and humility.

Jack Ellers snuffled the air with ardour. 'Are we eating, Ben?' he asked hopefully.

'Of course.'

'Want me to order? Haddock and chips as usual, is it?'

'Haddock nothing! We're having halibut. Call it an Act III celebration.'

'Being a mite previous, aren't we? Hadn't we ought to wait till the curtain comes down before bringing on the bouquets?'

'Make sure, you mean, we haven't been performing the wrong play all along?'

'Something like that.'

'At least we'll have had the party. Just for the record, though – ' Jurnet went on, affectionately aware of the concern on his behalf which had called up the note of worry in the little Welshman's voice – 'I wouldn't want you to think I'm hugging some secret solution to my bosom. Trouble is, the last two or three pages of the script seem to have got stuck together. Some of the grease off all those ruddy chips, I shouldn't wonder – '

'Look who's here!'

After their cool reception at the police house, Ali's greeting, warm and apparently unequivocal, made them feel loved again. Obviously regarding an order for halibut twice as the highest compliment capable of being paid to man, he willingly took the photograph of Endymion Mobbs which Jurnet proffered and studied it carefully before returning it with a sigh.

'Poor Annie!' he said. 'To think that was the best she could do for herself!' His dark eyes melancholy with the recollection: 'One afternoon, my day off, I went over to the churchyard at Lanthrop. You'd think they were having the car boot sale of the century, the number of people. But it was pathetic! Her at one end, Joey the other. They shouldn't've done that.'

'That was Timmy. He knew his ma had had it in for Corvin. He didn't want her lying next to him for ever after.'

'I read something about it. Soft in the head he may be, still he shouldn't've done it. Two unhappy people. They could have kept each other company. Being angry is better'n being nothing.'

The man let his gaze stray back to the photograph.

Jurnet asked: 'Did you ever see the bloke yourself, here in the Caff?'

The other shrugged.

'How can I say? It's not exactly what you'd call a memorable face.'

'It certainly isn't that. Tell me this, Ali. I know time has passed, but please try and remember. Information that's come our way suggests that some time after Annie left the Caff she was seen returning, on foot, in this direction. Is it possible she came back here, around half an hour or so after she left?'

The small dark man shook his head decisively, his chef's cap bobbing.

'Out of the question! After what she did to Madam Muck the old bag would have scratched her eyes out if she'd so much as poked her nose in the door. You'd have heard the noise back in Angleby.'

There was an interval during which the fish fryer positioned the halibut steaks on their plates with a delicate precision, adding a garnish of parsley and a wedge of lemon to each. Watching, Jurnet commented: 'Same as you put up for Annie, eh, that last day?'

'The same, except no parsley and no lemon. That's strictly for the toffs and the flics. For the proles it's a sachet of ketchup. And a cardboard carton, if it's for taking out.'

'Two portions of halibut and chips. You're certain that was the lot?'

'I'd have added a bottle of bubbly if I'd had one by me. She deserved it. No – that was the lot.' Piling the chips on to a separate dish, Ali remarked: 'Never realized what stickers you lot are. When you stopped dropping in, I took it you'd closed the books and gone on to the next thing. *Goodbye Annie, got to love and leave you!* Tha's what I thought. Still at it after all this time – I must say I'm impressed. Like they say, the Mounties always get their man – right?'

'That's what they say.'

'It must feel great.' The fish fryer's tone was impeccably respectful: all the irony was concentrated in the large, heavy-lidded eyes. 'I bet it feels great, eh, when at last the moment you've been waiting for arrives and you pounce, catch the bugger like a wasp in jam.'

Jurnet looked down at his toothsome lunch, conscious of appetite draining away even as he picked up the loaded tray.

'Great.'

In the Baileys' front yard the gander, its blue eyes flashing, greeted the Rover like an old enemy. Oz Bailey, who had been unloading some rolls of carpeting from his white van, looked on in amusement as Jurnet, choosing the way of discretion, levered his long body across from the driver's seat and made his exit from the door on the passenger's side, where only a cockerel and a bunch of dishevelled hens disputed his passage. The detective was enabled to utilize this escape route since the passenger seat was empty, Jack Ellers having been dropped off at the police house to make a telephone call.

Bailey, who wore a torn khaki sweater over ancient jeans,

nevertheless radiated a self-confidence which annoyed Jurnet, despite himself. Gainsaying the evidence of his own eyes, the detective told himself that the fellow did not look in the least like him, whatever people said; or, if he did, only in so far as any dark-haired Mediterranean types were bound to share a certain similarity when dumped by some quirk of nature among a prevalence of pasty-faced Anglo-Saxons.

'Not by any chance in the market for a carpet?' the man called out, leaving the rolls leaning upright against the side of the van and strolling over in a leisurely way. 'Top grade Wilton, left over from a contract job. Going for a song. Could do yourself a favour.'

'No, thanks,' Jurnet returned curtly. As a copper he knew all there was to know about the fiddle of contract carpeting, the calculated over-estimation of quantities so as to leave a nice little bonus in the way of excess yardage available for disposal on the side. What was more, he could tell by the smile on the man's face that Oz Bailey knew he knew; that he was trading, in some obscure way, on that physical kinship between them.

The hell with it!

'Mrs Bailey at home?' the detective demanded.

The other began to laugh.

'Come to chat up my old woman, have you? Sorry to disappoint you. Brenda's not in.'

'You shouldn't be sorry,' Jurnet returned, unsmiling. 'You ought to be glad, because I'm here to have a few more words with you about Annie Chance. Your wife will have to know sooner or later, but for the moment, I imagine, you'd rather keep it private.'

'What are you on about?' There was no change of tone, no loss of assurance. 'Aren't you ever goin' to let that poor mauther rest in peace?'

'She's doing that already.' Jurnet put his hand on the white van, tapped the dented radiator. 'Useful pile of junk. Serves a whole shoot of useful purposes, I shouldn't wonder. Including picking Annie up that morning you went chasing after her to the Caff.'

'I told you. She'd been gone a good twenty minutes.'

'I know all about that. I'm talking about something different. I'm talking about later, after you left the Caff, when you were driving away. You saw her coming towards you down the road, didn't you? Unless she'd already reached the bus stop by the time you came along, and you found her waiting there.'

'Who been telling you bed-time stories?' Oz Bailey began, only for the brightness to die out of his eyes as the old grief took over. 'She weren't at the stop, nowhere near.' Jurnet's face showed no trace of his inner excitement that his shot in the dark had found its mark. 'What if I did see her? In't a crime, is it?'

'No. On the other hand, what it would seem to indicate is that, apart from her murderer, you were the last person to see Annie alive.'

'Somebody has to be last.'

Jurnet inclined his head in agreement.

'True. Except that, for some reason I am waiting for you to explain, you never saw fit to mention it to the police. You must see for yourself it gives rise to questions.'

'On'y one, which you know the answer to without giving me the trouble of saying. Brenda. As if I hadn't already got into enough trouble with her over giving Annie that lift to Angleby and letting her have the cash for her shopping – use your imagination! What kind of hell d'you think she'd've kicked up if I let on as I'd given Annie another lift the very next day, right arter promising on the Bible t'mend me sinful ways?'

'Gave her a lift where?'

'Gave her a lift back home. She said as how she'd forgotten something, and would I drop her off at Baynard's Lane. She didn't want anyone to see her. Which suited *me* down to the ground, I don't have to tell you.'

'Did she say what she wanted to go back for?'

'I got the impression she'd left behind some of her sexy undies – probably paid for by me at that, tha's a laugh. I was in a state, I don't mind telling you. All the way back to Lanthrop, with her there in the van smelling – would you believe? – of scent I'd paid a bomb for, French, none of your Old English Lavender, I kep' begging her, fer Christ' sake, think what you're doing, gal! Don't go off with some shit what's never even noticed what he's got down his trousers. If yer can't stand Lanthrop any longer, go off with me. I'll leave everything. We'll go together. I meant it, every word.' In a voice that had become hoarse with emotion the man said: 'I know it sounds hearts an' flowers, you'll split your sides laughin' – but I honestly didn't know how I were to go on living without her.'

'I don't see anything to laugh at.'

'Annie did. Laughed an' told me not to talk daft. I could easily

198

ha' strangled her there an' then, the bloody bitch.' Oz Bailey's features repositioned themselves in their habitual contours of ironic amusement. 'There's an admission fer you, Inspector! Take it down quick afore I deny I ever said it. But she were right to take the mickey. *Can't live without you, my Aunt Fanny!* You can put up with anything and everything if you have to.'

'What happened when you got back to the village?'

'I dropped Annie off at the top of the lane like she asked. She said she'd on'y be a few minutes an' would I be a dear an' wait and then take her back to where she'd come from? She had a nerve! What did she think I was made of – stone? I told her where to go an' she said ferget it: anyway, on second thoughts she didn't know how long she'd be an' she'd make her own way back somehow. She leaned over to kiss me goodbye – ' Oz Bailey's fists clenched. 'I couldn't trust myself to let her get that close an' I tole her to bugger off an' be done with it. I could feel my hands itching to get round her throat an' pay her back good an' proper for what she done to me. I backed out of the lane afore she were hardly out of the van door – a bloody Saab coming down the road nearly did its nut – an' drove around for the rest of the arternoon, I couldn't tell you where if you paid me.'

'When she got out of the van was she carrying anything with her?'

'On'y her handbag. Another present from yours bloody truly.'

'Nothing else? No carrier bag, for instance?'

'On'y the bag. She'd never need anything else, with that one. Tapestry design with a big gold chain to go over yer shoulder. Big enough to take a gran' pianner's what I said when she picked it out at M an' S.'

'Ah. Did you happen to notice any smell?'

'The scent – I tole you. She smelled like she'd poured on half the bottle.'

'Quite a story.' After a moment's silence Jurnet said: 'Assuming you're telling me the truth – and it is only an assumption – you realize the likeliest implication of what you've been saying?'

Bailey returned soberly: 'I realized the minute you told me you'd found her.'

'Yet all this while you've said nothing. How could you have let it go on, knowing what you knew?'

'You'll never know, back there in the police house, how close I was to spilling the beans. Sometimes I'm sorry I didn't. Other times I ask meself, who am I to start acting God Almighty when I'd have cheerfully done for her meself, on'y I hadn't the guts? Besides, I reckoned keeping my mouth shut was what Annie would have wanted. It's funny really – ' the man spoke hesitantly, discovering his own feelings in the articulation of them – 'all them weeks I thought she were living it up with that wimp I had only to think her name for my hands to get that itch to be at her throat. I'd hear her choking for breath, see her eyeballs pop – hear it so clear an' see it so real that when you actually found her dead in that dune, I wondered for a bit if I hadn't done her in after all, done it that arternoon when I'd driven round like someone crazy. Part o' me was glad she was dead – still is, if you want the truth. If I ha'nt got her, that preachy pillock han't either. Part o' me says serve you right, you ruddy bint, that'll teach you you can't walk out on a person without paying for it. The other part – ' Oz Bailey broke off, the mask of ironic amusement only slightly askew – 'says love. Not the first time, as I recall, you an' me have had a chat about that one little word; four bloody letters too long, if you want my opinion. Love – ' he rolled the word round his tongue – 'somethin' you catch if you aren't careful, 'cept you can't get it treated on the National Health like you can measles or the clap, not even if you go private. I think Annie an' I think love. No – ' the man corrected himself – 'not think. Feel in my bones like the weather, or rumbling round inside my skull like dominoes going click when they knock up against each other.'

Head thrust forward like the gander still venting its spleen on its reflection in the Rover's coachwork, Oz Bailey said: 'You've heard what they say – as how it's better to have loved an' lost than never to have loved at all?'

'I've heard.'

'Load o' balls!'

Jack Ellers came into the yard on the run, red with haste.

'The answer's no,' he got out, not waiting to get his breath back. 'Mobbs says he ate on his own. All Annie took was one of his chips. Said what with all the excitement she wasn't hungry.'

Jurnet received this information without surprise. Only wondering aloud: 'How did they come to be out on the beach, then? That's the question.'

'Maybe they had a picnic.'

200

19

Along the Fastolfes driveway the beech leaves drifted down from the trees, a few, and then a few again; down to the tarmac where a sadistic little breeze, operating at ground level, whipped them into reluctant dance before abandoning them any old where.

'Boy's got a bit behindhand,' was Sergeant Ellers' observation as the Rover's tyres slushed their way through the drifts towards the forecourt in front of the garage.

The garage doors were open, disclosing emptiness.

'Just as well she's not here.' Jurnet braked the car to a halt. 'Let's hope she hasn't taken him with her.' The two detectives alighted from the car in the same moment, both coming to a puzzled stop as they took their first steps up the path, brick-paved and sunken between banks of periwinkle, that led to the front door.

'What the – ?'

There were no banks. The periwinkle that Jurnet had last seen as a glossy green mass spiked with mauve-and-white stars lay uprooted among gouts of soil and the lumps of stone which had provided its invisible support. Branches of the wisteria which in spring had covered the front of the house with a honey-scented curtain, lay strewn about the ground, their naked ends hacked without mercy. On either side of the wide-open front door two Chinese lions lay decapitated, their serene Oriental countenances contemplating the sky with a complete absence of surprise.

Indoors, the house was its usual tranquil self, nothing out of place save for a single chair, a pretty thing inlaid with mother-of-pearl, overturned in the sitting-room and missing one leg. To Jurnet who, with Ellers at his heels, had run through the house calling to no avail, this single infraction of the elegant calm of the place was more ominous than any general havoc.

Taking separate paths and impelled by a growing sense of time passing, they scoured the grounds with no other success than to have retrieved the leg of the mother-of-pearl chair lying abandoned in a smashed cucumber frame. Some kind of poison must have been tipped into the pond, for even as they ran round its edge calling, always calling, fat bubbles rose to the surface and golden fish floated belly up among the browning lily-pads.

The Portakabins had gone from the paddock, the ground filled in where once the Romans had burned down the sacred grove in order to make a point about who was master. Encircling the wood where the Druids had buried their treasure, a fence topped with incurving spikes conveyed much the same message.

'We'll give the wood a miss,' Jurnet decided. 'The car's gone, that's the main thing.'

'So what do we do – go looking, or wait for them to come back?'

'Wait.'

Even as they spoke, they both knew waiting to be impossible.

'That woman in the shop knows everybody's business,' said Jurnet; and so they got into the Rover again and drove back over the fallen leaves, downhill to the village shop where Mrs Cobbold did not disappoint them.

'A picnic!' she exclaimed, shaking her head at the foolishness of some people. 'In this weather! This time o' year! Ham an' Cornish pasties, sugar mice and cupcakes, and I don't know what else. Anything his lordship asked for, he got. You should have heard the carry-on that there weren't no more raspberry ripple! "Carry on all you want," I said. "It's all one to me. I never keep no ice-cream after the 25th of September – never have and never will."' Mrs Cobbold gave the detective what could only be described as an ambiguous look. After all, Jurnet reminded himself, Mrs Milburn must be one of her best customers, she had to mind her p's and q's. She said: 'Haven't seen you down here in quite a while. You seen Mrs Milburn lately?'

'Not all that lately,' Jurnet answered, all transparent innocence. 'Why do you ask?'

'No reason. Jest that – ' abandoning commercial prudence – 'if you han't seen her lately, you're in for a surprise.'

'Oh ah.' Jurnet did not wait to be told its nature. 'We'll have to have a little talk.'

'At the gate, Bill Gifford took his time coming. That time of year, that weather – Jurnet tried hard to be charitable – there couldn't be all that many demands on his services. Probably watching telly, in which case he wouldn't be best pleased to find it wasn't even a paying customer he was called to bestir himself for. Hannah Milburn, as a resident of Lanthrop, would have gone through equally free, if indeed she had passed that way.

She had.

'I'm sure I don't know what's got into that woman!' the gate-keeper complained, lips pursed. 'She'll catch her death. That Timmy in't the on'y one needs his brains examined. Dress up to her hips, not so much as a cardigan, an' the two of 'em giggling like a pair of idiots. I told her it was bound to be a rough ole tide with all this wind behind it, but would she listen?'

The sky over the marsh had lowered perceptibly, bringing the clouds down with it. Another few feet, by the look of it, and they would squash flat the tops of the pine trees which stood between it and the beach.

Gifford called after them: 'If you see them, you tell 'er. Maybe she'll listen to you!'

Tell her what, for Pete's sake? To stop giggling like an idiot, start acting her age? Tell her about love, that little word which was four bloody letters too long? Jurnet put his foot down hard on the accelerator. Swish, swish, went the Rover between the pop-lars that lined the road, their green and silver frayed to a ragged yellow.

Hannah Milburn's hatchback was parked carelessly, a window left open, a door imperfectly shut. The two detectives parked alongside on the grass, sprang out and ran through the wicket on to the duckboard path through the pines.

Out of the wind in the shelter of the trees, they nevertheless felt its force redoubled, their very skeletons vibrating to the clamour overhead. Creaking like the spars of a three-master in high seas, the branches bent to the gale. Just the day, just the place for a picnic!

Emerging on to the beach they met the wind full on: the wind and the sand which set upon them like a swarm of stinging insects prior to taking up residence wherever an eyebrow, an ear, a gap between neck and collar offered lodgement.

The wind and the sand and the cold.

The cold was damp and salt and deadly, penetrating to the heart's core. The beach, so far as Jurnet was able to survey it through eyes caked with the stinging sand, had grown narrower, the sea nearer, thunderous.

What was it Gifford had said? *She'll catch her death.*

Jack Ellers shouted, his words barely audible above the racket of the elements: 'They're never here!'

'Yes, they are!'

Veiled in spindrift, the ring of dunes lay on Lanthrop beach like gigantic cattle ruminating, in their midst Katie Milburn's Castle, Annie Chance's sepulchre, the temple of love where Miriam had said, '*You* are my heart's desire.' Daring the wind to prevent him, Jurnet flung himself across the intervening space, his panting companion keeping up as best he could. The sandhill had entirely reconstituted itself, the rampart protecting its secrets back in place; though even as Jurnet took this in, the tell-tale wind whisked an empty box off the hidden summit, let it plane through the air in a moment of glory before depositing it at Jack Ellers' feet. 'Lyons Chocolate Cupcakes' proclaimed the label, before the sand covered it.

In the secret bowl scooped out of the top of the sandhill Timmy Chance, his face full of a beautiful mischief, lay laughing whilst Hannah Milburn, a plastic picnic box her tool, heaped sand on to his body. The woman had taken pains with her task, smoothing the sand as she went along, modelling it to the lanky shape prostrate at her feet. The boy was covered up to his chin, but it was clear to the two detectives, in the instant their heads cleared the rampart and their eyes, staring incredulously, took in the sight before them, that the deadly game was not yet quite over. The plastic box was full, the woman's body poised with unconscious grace as she hoisted it ready for the throw. Her curls serpentine in the saturated air, her exiguous dress plastered against her body so as to render it more naked than naked, she looked timeless, a nymph, a Grecian goddess out of legend.

A murderess.

Hannah Milburn paused in her graceful progress, looked at the intruders with exasperation. Said, 'Go away!' and flung the sand over the boy's face.

20

'I could say that it was a game. I could go on saying it was a game and there is no way you could prove it was anything else. Timmy will bear me out. We were having a picnic, we were playing games.

'I could deny throwing the sand in his face on purpose. I could say the picnic box was heavy – which it was – and that, surprised by your sudden appearance over the rim of the sandhill, my hand slipped. Even with you and your Sergeant swearing the contrary, I don't believe a jury would find me guilty. With my hair done the way I used to do it, and wearing the kind of clothes I used to wear, I think I would make a good impression in court.

'I could go on saying that it was a game: but I do not choose to go on saying it. I could also go on saying that I know nothing about Annie's death, but I do not choose to go on saying that either. I am by nature an honest person and I am sick of lies.

'Most of all, I am sick of love.

'It was not a game.

'If I ever go back to Fastolfes – which isn't very likely – the first thing I shall do is go down to the pond and root up the waterlilies, especially the *Gladstoniana*, the big ones that Timmy made a hat out of that day he sat in the water, smiled up at me and made me feel the world hadn't come to an end because my husband had been unfaithful and my child was dead, dead, dead. The weed-killer I put in the pond killed the fish but not the waterlilies, unfortunately. I am sorry about the fish. I had meant it the other way round.

'About Annie first. Mrs Cobbold at the village shop told me she'd seen her catching the bus carrying a suitcase. All I'd popped down to the village for was to get a loaf of bread. Timmy had gone back home long before. I pretended I knew all about

Annie's going, but of course I didn't – the two of us were never on terms of that kind. If it hadn't been for Timmy the only thing that would have concerned me about her leaving Lanthrop for good was where was I going to get another daily help as good as she had been.

'As it was, after hearing what Mrs Cobbold had to say I came out of the shop quite forgetting about the bread and trembling with joy, even though at the same time another part of me was telling me I must be crazy to feel so happy that Annie had taken herself off and now Timmy would be mine.

'Timmy! I don't have to tell you that he is scarcely the lovable bundle most people visualize when they think about adopting a child. I myself still find it astonishing that I ever wanted him. You couldn't hold anything you could call a civilized conversation with him, and his lack of table manners revolted me. Yet I never tried to alter him, to teach him things. That would have been cheating, false to my vision of the mischievous imp sitting in the pond with a waterlily on his head. God, I felt sure, meant me to take him the way he was – as found, as they say in the auction catalogues. Sometimes – water under the bridge – I can't help thinking that if only I had been able to take my husband Alan as found, including a mistress who bought him blousons and put loving messages in them, instead of shouting and screaming and sending him shooting off down the bypass blind drunk in his Jaguar, Katie would be alive today. So, in taking on Timmy, was I punishing myself for her death? I don't think so, but I honestly don't know. It didn't feel like punishment, is all I can say.

'What was Timmy doing with his mother gone? Waiting for her to come home with his dinner? I got into the car to drive over to Annie's to find out, only as I came up to Baynard's Lane, there was Mr Bailey's van, that old white banger of his, parked in the turning, and there was Annie just getting out of it. She didn't see me and went off down the lane. I went on a little way and parked, wondering what to do. While I was sitting there the van came past, Bailey driving like a madman, the van clanging and banging as if it would fall to pieces at any minute.

'I was banging and clanging myself, inside. Annie hadn't been carrying a suitcase. Perhaps, I told myself, she had only come back for something she'd forgotten.

'I had to know. I reversed back to the lane, and drove up it at speed, scratching the car dreadfully on the old brambles that hadn't been cleared away from last year. Annie could easily have been home by then, but she wasn't. She was walking along slowly, head bent as if she was thinking. Once she heard me coming, though, she lifted her head and waited. She would have recognized the car. I stopped, got out and ran to her; told her what Mrs Cobbold had said and asked was it true. Was she really going away?

'To my amazement I saw that she had been crying. There were smears of mascara on her cheeks. Annie Chance crying! It was like hearing th Sphinx speak. And when she spoke, it was even more amazing.

'She said yes, it was true – or rather, it had been. She *had* been going away, she had only come back on an impulse to bring Timmy one last lot of fish and chips, but now that she was back in Lanthrop she didn't know what to do for the best: she just didn't know how she could bring herself to walk out on him for good and all. She actually spoke of loving "that feeble-minded lout" (that was what she called him!) in spite of everything.

'In spite of treating him like dirt! In spite of beating him up so badly he'd had to come running to me for protection!

'Tears or no tears, I didn't believe her, any more than you would, I'm certain, if you had been there. She was lying in her teeth. Either the man she'd been planning to go away with had let her down at the last minute – I took it for granted there was a man involved – or she'd changed her mind about him, or else there was some other man back in Lanthrop – perhaps Oz Bailey, I don't know – that, when it came to the point, she couldn't tear herself away from. Her dreadful hypocrisy, the thought that I wasn't going to get Timmy after all – after the certainty of happiness I'd felt only minutes before, it was too much.

'Talking, we had walked past her bit of garden, past the lane's end and on to that grotty bit of land where the Council had once meant to build some houses and then decided against it. They had never cleared the place up and it was strewn with all sorts of builders' rubbish. I wasn't angry for myself, truly. I was sorry for Timmy, abandoned to his mother's tender mercies. Her mercies!

'It was more than flesh and blood could stand. When she repeated that, when it came down to it, she loved Timmy too much to leave him, I picked up a piece of brick from the ground and hit her. It was an unthinking gesture, no more than that, only unfortunately – no, fortunately: I am done with pretences – it caught her in the throat. She staggered, fell down and made some choking noises, and in almost as little time as it takes to write the words, she was dead.

'There was no doubt about it. I'd done a St John's Ambulance Brigade course and I carried out the proper tests without getting the slightest reaction. I am a law-abiding citizen, Inspector Jurnet, and my first instinct was to go and fetch PC Wyatt. To say I felt horrified would only be partly true. It had all happened so suddenly, so *naturally*. As to feeling guilty, I cannot honestly say that I felt guilty of anything worse than unladylike behaviour. My kind of people don't go in for hitting other people, whatever the provocation. When I decided not, after all, to go for PC Wyatt, it wasn't out of fear that I would be put in the dock for murder, or manslaughter at the very least. The possibility never occurred to me. Anyone, under sufficient stress, can lose their temper, and it was pure chance that the brick hit her where it did. It wasn't as if I'd specifically aimed for a vulnerable spot.

'I didn't go to the police, because of Timmy. I didn't want him upset. He was going to be upset enough as it was, once he found out that his mother had abandoned him. I may have been wrong, but that's what I felt.

'You will probably think it funny, you who must have had so much experience of people concealing bodies – or attempting to conceal them – when I say that the problem of getting rid of Annie's barely bothered me. I certainly wasn't afraid somebody might come along and catch me *in flagrante delicto*. My guess is that such fears only arise where the people who have done the killing are themselves passionately attached to their own lives, determined to stay free: whereas, so far as I was concerned, ever since the day Alan's car hit that tree on the bypass, life was something I could either take or leave alone, I didn't much care which.

'If I'm seen, I'm seen, was my thought, in so far as I gave the matter any thought at all. I lifted Annie up, hoisted her over my shoulder and carried her back to the car, where I put her in the back covered up with an old blanket I use for leaving on the radiator in cold weather. I went back and picked up the large bag she'd been carrying. It had her purse inside and a package of what, from the smell, could only be fish and chips. The grease was coming through the paper. That afternoon I burned bag and contents in the Aga, where it smelled vile for a while but burned to the same fine ash as the solid fuel we ordinarily burn there, so that was all right.

'So far as Annie herself was concerned, I waited till teatime before attending to her disposal. The reason I waited was this. At that time the road down to the beach hadn't been open to the public all that long. Few people seemed to have heard of it, or, if they had, seemed willing to pay £5 to use it. It was still early in the season, anyway, and there weren't all that many trippers about. As for the Lanthrop residents who could get in free, very few of them bothered to take advantage of Lord Lanthrop's generosity. The beach was something you took weekend visitors to see. During the week you had better things to do.

'What with one thing and another, then, Mr Gifford, in charge of the gate, had a good deal of time on his hands. As it happens, he is a great watcher of television, especially of that afternoon show called *Punters' Paradise* which comes on every weekday and has competitions with prizes such as micro-ovens and weekends on the Costa Brava. Not unnaturally, Mr Gifford found it most exasperating to be interrupted, as occasionally happened, right in the middle of taking down some vital particulars to do with the current competition by somebody wanting the gate opened. To keep such interruptions down to a minimum he let it be known discreetly to Lanthrop residents with cars that between 4 and 5 p.m. – while the programme was on, that is – the gate would be left unbolted. Outsiders would have no idea, but at least residents could let themselves in and out without taking him away from the box.

'Accordingly, a little after 4 o'clock on what I suppose I should call that fateful afternoon, I drove Annie down to the beach, trussed up in the large polythene bag the lawn mower had come in. I strapped the bag, together with a spade, on to the toboggan that had been hanging unused from two nails on the garage wall since Katie's death. I'd often meant to give it away, but somehow I never had. It just goes to show, doesn't it, that some things are meant to be. Without it, my task would have been much harder. By folding down the back seats I got the toboggan into the car without any trouble.

'I drove down to the beach without seeing anyone, or, more to the point, without anyone seeing me. The gate, as expected, was unbolted. Mr Gifford's TV, I knew, was in his kitchen, at the back of his lodge. Even in the unlikely event that he looked out of the

209

window, he would still be unable to see whose car it was going through. It was laughably simple.

'There wasn't a single car parked at the end of the road. I dragged the loaded toboggan over the duckboard, through the pines and on to the sands as far as the large sandhill with the hidden dip at the top, Katie's Castle. The fact that I had scattered Katie's ashes there did not deter me. On the contrary, I felt they would be a charm, my darling guarding Mummy's secret, keeping it safe for ever. I reckoned without you, Inspector, didn't I, you and that lovely girlfriend of yours? What *were* the pair of you up to?

'Burying Annie was the easiest thing in the world. The only difficult thing was getting the toboggan up the slope. The sand kept sliding away under the runners. In case it could ever be traced back to me, I took off the polythene bag and buried her just as she was. My last sight of her, she looked quite pleased with herself, not angry or anything like that. You might almost have thought I'd done her a favour. Perhaps I had.

'When I got back to the car, mine was still the only one parked there. And when I got back to the gate it was still unbolted.

'And when I got back home, there was Timmy.

21

'We have been very happy together, Inspector, Timmy and I. Perhaps I should qualify that and say, at least I have. I can't speak for Timmy. Much as I love him, I have not got to know him very well. You would think that simple-minded people would be simple to understand: that they haven't so many brains so there isn't so much to know. But it doesn't work like that at all.

'They are mysterious. They may not be able to make sense of the world they have to live in, but they don't need to. Deep down, I've become convinced, they harbour senses which don't need to depend on the grey matter in their heads. Perhaps that was the way it was with primitive man back in the Stone Age, I don't know. I only know that underneath that surface stupidity which can be such a trial to one's patience, there is a terrible wisdom – terrible because it is walled in, it can't get out and exact the respect it deserves.

'One thing at least I can claim without false modesty. *I* have given Timmy the respect he deserves. I have accepted him as he was. I haven't treated him like a dog to be taught tricks against its nature. He is a wonderful gardener. In the garden I gave him *carte blanche*: anything he wanted, he had. And when he wanted a woman, I did my best to give him that too.

'Sandra Thorne would have made the ideal wife for him. Timmy's penis is so small, I guessed he was impotent; any other girl he might have married would soon have gone looking elsewhere for what he was unable to supply. I could not bear to think of him made unhappy in that way. But Sandra with her ridiculous breasts was in love with herself, a female Narcissus – perfect! All she wanted from a man was admiration from a safe distance, status and money. From her point of view, I felt sure, if Timmy was sexually inadequate, so much the better.

'You already know about my plans – how I was going to build them a bungalow in the orchard, set Timmy up in business as a nurseryman. How everything in the garden was going to be lovely.

'Until you, Inspector Jurnet, spoiled it all.

'I am not blaming you. You are a good man, you did what you conceived to be your duty. But if ever I wanted to kill somebody, it was you when, in a few brisk words, you destroyed my lovely new world as utterly as Alan destroyed my old one out there on the bypass. If only I could convey to you what I felt the afternoon you called round to tell me about what had been going on at the goat farm, and how Timmy had refused point-blank to be tested for HIV!

'I don't imagine you noticed anything.

'Naturally I defended Timmy's right to make his own decision. For me to put pressure on him to have the test was to set at naught our whole relationship. You were annoyed with me, I know, and disappointed. But after you left my mind was in a whirl.

'Give me credit, Inspector, for having a conscience. There was no need to spell out the implications of what you had come to say, and I give you credit for not having done so. I knew without being told that dedicating myself to Timmy's happiness did not give me the right knowingly to put Sandra, or any other girl, at risk of Aids. On the other hand, Timmy wanted a woman. It was as simple as that.

'There was only one thing to do.

'I became that woman.

'I hope I haven't shocked you, Inspector. As a police officer, I don't suppose you shock all that easily. I know Paul Abbott was appalled when I started curling my hair and wearing clothes that were fifteen, if not twenty years too young for me. He said I was making myself ridiculous – as if that mattered! Love was what mattered. If love had required me to put on a false nose and paint rings round my eyes like a clown, I'd have done it without a second thought.

'Love! If, instead of truth, jesting Pilate had asked what love was, he would have been well-advised not to wait for an answer, or the poor man could still be waiting. Where was the boundary between maternal love and love that was physical, sexual? *Was* there, in fact, any such boundary, or were the two kinds simply different aspects of the same thing?

'Certainly, for myself, I slipped across the border between them, assuming it exists, without difficulty. It could have been, I suppose – (writing this down has led me to examine my own motives as never before) – that, without my realizing it, my feeling for Timmy had been sexual from the word go; that I only fooled myself into thinking it was anything else. Perhaps it wasn't Katie but Alan I had been missing all the time, his the emptiness I looked to Timmy to fill. I don't know.

'I don't think I want to know.

'Let's leave it at this, shall we? That I did what I did because it was necessary to keep Timmy away from other women and because, given the circumstances, I wanted to make him happy. I was his consolation prize, as he was mine.

'You mustn't think, either, going to the other extreme, that I conceived a grand passion for what Annie called her feeble-minded lout. His equipment, poor love, was minimal. To achieve an erection was a triumph. My role, in bed with him, was chiefly to praise and to encourage, to bolster his self-regard in the face of repeated failure. To be – dare I say it? – maternal.

'On the medical side, so far as I myself was concerned, I did all the right things – I mean, had myself tested. I never let on to Sandra and Ian about the HIV thing; instead, I made up some nonsense about a congenital weakness which would have made it positively fatal for Timmy to marry. I don't know how much of it they believed, but the money I gave them spoke louder than any questions it might have occurred to them to ask – though even so, after Boudica's hoard was uncovered and the papers were full of speculations about how much Timmy was likely to get by way of reward, that greedy girl had the cheek to write to me suggesting that she was entitled to a share on the ground that she had often gone into the wood with Timmy and wondered aloud what was inside that old badger sett.

'As I've said, I had myself tested. It didn't take long for it to happen. The second time I went, I was found to be HIV-positive.

'Can you believe me when I say that I received the news with something approaching elation? I think that ever since the day, Inspector, you told me about the goings-on at the goat farm I had felt in my bones that Timmy had been harmed, and it was, if nothing else, a release of tension to have one's fears confirmed. Now, at least, I knew where we were. I could make plans.

'Of course I never said a word – never explained to Timmy that as I was HIV-positive it must mean that so was he; that I must have caught the infection from him. Even supposing he had taken it in, which was doubtful, what would have been the purpose? We were never going to grow old together, he and I. We were doomed, star-crossed lovers like Romeo and Juliet (I'm not entirely joking!) whose brief, incandescent love was worth a century of dull domesticity. The knowledge drew me even closer to him. I felt a great tenderness. The thought of the physical suffering which almost inevitably lay in store for him made me redouble my efforts to make such years as remained to him a chronicle of joy. Knowing the worst, the future seemed beautifully uncomplicated.

'Which it would have been, if I hadn't become pregnant.

'I couldn't believe it! True, I'd never even tried to get Timmy to use a condom and I'd been very slapdash about taking my own precautions because it was unthinkable that he could ever get anyone pregnant. But he had, and I had to make a decision. Was I going to have an abortion or a baby?

'It will probably surprise you, Inspector, that I should ever have considered the alternatives. Mother HIV-positive, father feeble-minded – not exactly the heredity one would pick for a child, was it? On the other hand, the thought of what it would mean to Timmy in self-esteem to know himself capable of fathering one was intoxicating. As for the HIV, I read all the literature I could lay my hands on and found out that only twelve to fifteen per cent of babies born to HIV-positive mothers were born infected. In other words, there was an eighty-five per cent chance of bearing a healthy child – mentally retarded, perhaps, like its father, but that didn't mean it couldn't live a happy and fulfilling life.

'You may think it wicked of me, but I decided to go ahead with the pregnancy, even though Timmy, when I told him, wasn't as pleased and proud as I'd expected. Either he wasn't capable of envisaging himself as a parent, or perhaps he *was* capable and was a little jealous at the prospect of having to share my attentions with another child – for, in spite of everything, a child was what he still was, and what he would remain till the day he died.

214

'Disappointed as I was by his reaction, it didn't make me change my mind. I must admit to skating over what would happen to the poor little thing if and when I myself, let alone Timmy, developed full-blown Aids. There was no shortage of money, I told myself: I would make arrangements. It would be all right. I rather think, at bottom, I must be what one might call a primitive woman, programmed, at the cost of every other consideration, to bear children. If Alan hadn't been against it I'd have had as many as we were capable of producing together. The very mention of abortion always made me feel physically sick. I would take the eighty-five per cent chance.

'That was before the night they showed a film on Channel 4 about the babies with Aids in a hospital in Romania. I can't bear to speak about it, so I shan't.

'When I saw you in Angleby I said I'd been to the dentist. I hadn't. I'd had an abortion.

'Endymion Mobbs – what a name! And what a pathetic little man to go with it! If he and Annie Chance had really gone off together she'd have made mincemeat out of him. On second thoughts, maybe not. He obviously adored her. As you may have discovered for yourself, it's lovely to be loved.

'I suppose I really ought to apologize, Inspector, for phoning the police to come and get him. After all, nobody knew better than I that Mr Mobbs was a red herring. My excuse has to be that I was feeling most peculiar as I left the nursing home where the abortion took place – unreal: or perhaps "surreal" is closer to it. The last thing I ought to have wanted was to stir things up all over again. I felt, not exactly feverish, rather on a high, the way I imagine people are who have been taking cocaine or one of the other drugs which stretch the perceptions.

'As I drove through Angleby, pointing the car towards home, along streets I'd known all my life, the outlines of the shops and the buildings, their textures and colours, seemed sharper than I'd ever known them. I felt their reality literally penetrating me. If I hadn't felt like that I don't think I'd have even noticed Mr Mobbs wearing Alan's blouson. As it was, it seemed positively pre-ordained, as if the purpose of all that sparkling clarity were to concentrate my attention on the garment which – one way of looking at it – was the prime cause of everything that had happened to me.

215

'By the time I telephoned you to come to the Apple Tree I think I must have been a little crazy, because it truly had gone completely out of my head that I was the one who had killed Annie; the poor little rep had had nothing to do with it. The possibility that my action might have the effect of setting you on the way to the truth never occurred to me.

'After you'd done with me, Inspector, I didn't go straight back to Fastolfes after all. The euphoria – if that's the right word for it – was rapidly wearing off. I became aware that I was bleeding. My stomach felt as if it had been scoured with steel wool. Most of all, I was overwhelmed with a sense of loss for the child I had deprived of its right to be born. As if it wasn't enough that Katie was dead because of me, here was this blob of tissue, whose very sex I would never know, washed down the nursing-home sluice as a sacrifice to my own criminal irresponsibility. Besides that crime, let me tell you, the death of Annie Chance was no more than the swatting of a mosquito.

'How was I going to break the news to Timmy that there wasn't going to be any baby? Justifying my putting off the evil hour by telling myself I was too ill to go on driving, I turned off the road and booked in at that motel outside Massingham; lay on the bed there the rest of the day and through the night, not eating anything, suffering: no more than I deserved. I found myself thinking about the Druids' hoard buried in Fastolfes wood – not so much the treasure which was going to make Timmy rich as about the skeletons, the human ones and the horse. What barbarians the Iceni must have been to value gold above life! And the horse which, according to Paul Abbott, they held in tremendous reverence – why did they have to slaughter that as well? But then, upon reflection I thought that, one way or another, we all slaughter the things we love, don't we?

'After Sandra's departure I hadn't got anybody else in to do the housework. I didn't want to provide the village with more cause for gossip than it had already. I'd left mountains of food for Timmy in the fridge, all his favourite things, so I wasn't worried.

'I left the motel next morning and drove back home, the ghost of my aborted child perched on my shoulder like a spectral parrot. I am sure that you and your beautiful girlfriend, Inspector, comfort each other in time of trouble. That wasn't how it was with Timmy and me. I was the one who had to provide whatever comfort was needed, expecting nothing in return.

'He was in the kitchen when I got back. With tears streaming down my cheeks I put my arms round him and told him there wasn't going to be any baby. His face heavy with stupidity, he broke away from my encircling arms and said: "Tha's all right, then. Now you're back can I have a hot dinner? I'm sick of all that cold muck."

'I made him a lovely meal – steak and onions, mashed potatoes, runner beans, with hot apple tart and cream to follow: all his favourite things. Whilst he was tucking in I went out into the garden, *his* garden, and destroyed it.

'I went into the tool shed and fetched a fork, an axe, and that flame gun thing Timmy used on the weeds, and I went to work. What I couldn't cut down or burn I trampled on. I went through the rose garden with the flame gun like the wrath of God. It had been such a wonderful summer, so prolonged, that there were still plenty of blooms on the bushes. By the time I had finished there was only a wilderness of charred sticks.

'I meted out the same treatment to the chrysanthemums. The flowering season generally was long over, of course, which was just as well. I don't think I could have done what I did had the garden been blooming in all its glory.

'I went back to the shed and got some weed-killer which I poured undiluted into the pond. Timmy was always meticulous about his dinner break, never taking a minute over his hour and a half, never a minute less. I'd had a television set put in the kitchen where he ate his midday meal and when it was time to go back to work he'd turn it off in the middle of a sentence, the middle of a word, if his time was up.

'It's amazing how much damage you can do in an hour and a half once you put your mind to it.

'I was quite prepared for Timmy to kill me for what I had done. I'm not at all sure that that wasn't the point of the whole exercise. To be out of the heartache for ever – dead like those skeletons in the wood, dead as Katie and the small aborted ghost who still sat on my shoulder, thanking its lucky stars, if it had any sense, that I had saved it from the human condition – it would have been the tenderest token of love he could have given me. But no. What he did was look about him unbelievingly and then begin to cry as if his heart would break. Entwined in each other's arms – this time he did not repel me – we cried together.

217

'I had, I think, never loved him more purely than I loved him at that moment, lover and mother, mother and lover. I pushed his hair back from his forehead, took off his spectacles and kissed his swollen eyelids. I promised he should have a new garden better even than the old one, every single plant in it his own personal selection. It would be the best garden in England. People would pay money to come and see it.

'When he had calmed down a little and was already looking about the landscape like a new Capability Brown assessing its potential, I completed the cure by suggesting a picnic. Timmy loved picnics and even after the big dinner he'd just eaten I could see his pale, foolish eyes brighten. I said we would stop off at the village shop and buy absolutely anything he fancied, even things like sugar mice I usually refused to let him buy because they were bad for his teeth. I had by then, you see, decided that he had to be dead, so he wouldn't be needing his teeth much longer.

'Looking back, I believe that this – the subconscious recognition that Timmy couldn't be allowed to go on living – was why I'd been so reluctant to hurry back from the nursing home. It wasn't the bleeding, the pain in my stomach, not even the grieving over my child that never was and never could be. What if I developed full-blown Aids and died before he did? Who then would be there to stop him from spreading the infection to some other woman or women, fathering some other child who should never be born?

'Do you remember, Inspector, saying to me that trails never grow cold? Then, you sent a cold shiver down my spine. However, as, I presume, a student of crime, you may find it interesting to learn that murder isn't necessarily the solemn, not to say sordid, ritual one would expect it to be. I've read somewhere – I don't know whether it's true – that a scorpion's bite can drive people mad in a rather wonderful way. Up to the moment they fall down dead they dance, they sing, they tear off their clothes and make love with an intensity of passion beyond anything they would be capable of in the ordinary way of things. St Paul, doesn't he, in one of his Epistles, says: "Death, where is thy sting?" so perhaps he too saw it as a kind of scorpion.

'Whatever death is, or isn't, I think both Timmy and I were bitten by it that afternoon. I don't know what Mrs Cobbold at the shop, or Mr Gifford on the gate, could have thought of us, but I couldn't have cared less. We were feeling wonderful – not just me, Timmy as well. He positively glowed, and not, I'm quite sure, just because he had half a dozen sugar mice in a paper bag on his lap. He had become beautiful, the way you may have noticed he did sometimes; breathing deeply, like an athlete warming up for a special event. I think, with his special way of knowing things, he knew it was a picnic to end all picnics. And, without knowing how I knew, I think he was glad.

'As we drove down the road to the beach we sang, we laughed, we shouted for no reason. It was, you'll remember, a chill, blustery day and the wind snatched our noise away and tossed it up in the air like a ball for the gulls to squabble over. Under the pines it was quieter, but once we were out on the sands – pandemonium! Only in the bowl at the top of Katie's Castle was there peace and quiet, and even there you could hear the wind prowling round the rampart like a wild beast kept at bay by a camp fire. But within we were so cosy, it was lovely.

'After we had eaten our picnic – Timmy put away *four* of the sugar mice, one after the other! – we even made love, me still bleeding my HIV-positive blood and in pain, as if that mattered. I would have stood it however badly it hurt. In fact, the more it hurt, the better. It was only fair. The wind had blown away the ghost on my shoulder, but I could still hear its tiny voice, louder than all the wind's hullabaloo, the voice of silence.

'I began to cover Timmy up with sand, a game. How happy we were until your untimely arrival interrupted us! Five, ten minutes more and he would have been dead. How even happier we would have been then, both of us! Why, oh why, did you have to be in such a hurry?

'For what have you now? An HIV-positive moron who has steadfastly refused to be tested, so you have no way of knowing officially what a menace he is. Perhaps you think I am lying? Perhaps you think that I picked up the infection elsewhere, a one-night stand, and I'm putting the blame on Timmy without cause? As judges seem to be fond of saying to juries, it is for you to decide.

'*Postscript*: In case you are wondering whether, if you hadn't turned up when you did, I would have killed myself as well as Timmy, the answer is an emphatic no. That would indeed have been unforgivable, even by that God whose mercy is notionally without limit; an attempt to avoid payment – not for Annie Chance, not for Alan, but for my three beloved children – for Katie on the bypass, for that darling blob of tissue down the sluice, and for Timmy.

'For Timmy.'

22

The Superintendent was shocked. The profile presented to Jurnet and Ellers, waiting in the large, seigneurial room where the November afternoon pressed dourly against the window panes, was pale and stern, an antique cameo. If the man had professed himself appalled at his subordinates' grotesque misreading of the Annie Chance case, Jurnet would have been the first to understand, bow his head and wait for the storm to pass, the aftershocks to stop rattling the electric-light fittings. Once over his initial disorientation, the Superintendent would have been the first to recognize that you had to make do with what you had, and that business as usual was all that stood between order and chaos. He would have abandoned his classic pose at the window, retracted the unforgiving glare directed downwards at the people moving about the Market Place as at some noxious species of black beetle, resumed his throne – his seat at his desk, that is – and, his gold fountain pen *couchant* in front of him, got on with it.

That, as things had turned out, his two henchmen, to their unbounded astonishment, had surprised Hannah Milburn in the act of polishing off Timmy Chance instead of vice versa as expected, was no more, you might say, than a quirk of history. Arriving in the nick of time like the Fifth Cavalry, they had delivered the goods. So why the drama?

The trouble was obviously deeper, Jurnet realized, divided as usual between uncritical affection and impatience that an intelligent being could at the same time be such an arsehole. More than the earth had moved. Moral underpinnings normally immune to seismic activity had been turned arsy-versy. How did the Richter scale register the shock set off by the fall from grace of an English gentlewoman?

Whilst Jurnet was turning over in his mind the wisdom of

221

pointing out, by way of comfort, that Mrs Milburn, whatever else you might think of her, had, true to form, expressed a lively concern for the fate of Boadicea's horse, the Superintendent turned back to the room and, as so often in the past, shattered in a sentence the other's cocky conviction that he could read the bugger like an open book. In a voice taut with suppressed feeling the Superintendent demanded: 'What in the world can we do about that boy?'

Not fully understanding the question, Jack Ellers offered: 'They reckon he's set to pick up a packet. He won't be short of mates to help him spend it.'

'Only too true, alas! Colton checked him over, to make sure he was all right after that near-burial in the sands, but that was as far as he could go, keeping to the rules. For reasons I needn't elaborate, Colton could neither take a blood sample nor, assuming he had the expertise to do it, undertake a psychiatric assessment. As it was, he told me off the record that the impression he got of the boy is that he would certainly be judged capable of independent living – and capable, consequently, of being as deadly as the plague to any woman – or man, for that matter – unlucky enough to come into carnal contact with him.'

Jurnet said: 'That's what worried Mrs Milburn.'

'Understandably! However – ' A ghost of frosty amusement had appeared in the deep-set eyes. The worst is over, Jurnet inwardly rejoiced – 'murder, fortunately or unfortunately, is not an option open to those of us on this side of the fence. One of the glories of the law, you might say – or alternatively, its chief idiocy – is its utter rejection of convenience as an adjunct of justice. I suppose it can be expected that once the juicier titbits about the goat farm get into the papers, and assuming the jury accepts Mrs Milburn's word for it that Timmy Chance was the source of her HIV infection, the number of candidates applying for the post of his live-in companion will be substantially reduced – but for how long, that's the trouble? Memories are so damnably short – '

'The lives of people who are HIV-positive,' Jurnet pointed out, 'tend not to go on all that long either.'

'True! We'll just have to go on hoping, won't we?'

Hope! Hope that Timmy Chance would develop full-blown Aids without hanging about – kick the bucket and that would be the end of the matter. Hope like that, fumed Jurnet, bogged down in the one-way system that often seemed to him a personal act of spite on the part of the city planners designed to keep him from his love, gave hope a bad name.

Hope that Miriam would be back at the flat, waiting for him – that was another kind of hope altogether. Fantasy, wishful thinking by somebody old enough to know better. He had already phoned her glitzy pad down by the river to let her know the Chance case was sewn up, or screwed up, whichever way she cared to look at it. She could return without further fear of putting him off his strike.

The answer he got was recorded in a voice he did not recognize: *'Miriam Courland is away for an indefinite period. Messages will be forwarded and dealt with as soon as possible. Please speak when the signal tone ceases.'*

'Where are you?' he had shouted down the mouthpiece, repeating the demand over and over until the Ansaphone, he surmised, either ran out of tape or shut itself down out of sheer boredom. *'Where are you?'*

Paris, New York, Hong Kong, Jerusalem? She had, from time to time, disappeared to all those places, and more, in the interest of her knitwear business. Waiting at a red light, Jurnet's hands on the Rover's steering wheel trembled at the thought of all that loveliness adrift in a world full of men with everything going for them which he had not. The night before, desperate, he had called Rabbi Schnellman, rehearsing, whilst counting the rings, phrases of explanation as to why he hadn't been in touch earlier to continue his lessons in Judaism: only to ask, so soon as he heard the phone picked up and the Rabbi's 'hello': 'I suppose you don't happen to know where I could get hold of Miriam?'

The Rabbi had no idea. Out of breath from running up the stairs, he had cut short the stammered excuses which followed.

'My dear Ben,' he countered, 'no guilt, I beg of you, or I shall begin to wonder if you haven't been coming to the wrong shop. Here, as you know, we are not in the business of looking for customers.'

Taking in the breathlessness, Jurnet made the correct deduction. The Rabbi had been down in the synagogue hall where, with transparent guile, he had installed a magnificent table-tennis table in the hope of luring the young of local Jewry on to synagogue premises.

'Hope I didn't interrupt a game?'

'You did me a favour. Danny Platt is here – you know, from the University. I'm not in the same league. Nearer your mark – '

That was all: no voiced invitation. Only a warmth of spirit

which came over the wire almost palpable, a speaking without language. Loving the man, aching to get out of the house, Jurnet had driven over to the synagogue and allayed his loneliness for as long as it took to trounce Danny Platt, whom he had never before come near beating, in three successive games (was the God of the Jews, he wondered, trying to tell him something?) – only to find himself back at the empty flat, with the sweet savour of victory souring in his throat, lonelier than ever.

'You are my heart's desire,' he reminded himself, for what that was worth, parking the Rover – no sign of Miriam's Renault – alongside the bulging black sacks which, as ever, awaited the dustman. Tomorrow and tomorrow and tomorrow there would always be garbage, one of the eternal verities – but desire? The very word had something insubstantial to the sound of it, a butterfly on the wing. Careful when you caught it or it could come apart in your hands.

And even love – Hannah Milburn, if he recollected aright, had said love was as fragile as a Ming vase and as easily broken. Well, being who she was, she would, wouldn't she? Love, Jurnet amended, going down-market, was as fragile as the jug on his mantelpiece, the one he'd picked up at the Reject Shop, chipped when he'd bought it and consequently 75p off.

He got out his key and came into his kingdom, edging past the O'Driscoll pram, ascending past the joss sticks, the cabbage and the slow-simmered underwear, up to the second floor and home.

Home! The mockery of the word made his heart ache, brought tears to his eyes. Not manly, he chided himself. Out of character. Out of public character, anyway.

He was only too well aware of the way he looked, dammit: the smouldering Latin looks, the air of raffish adventure that, pillar of society though he was, God help him, he seemed unable to conceal. Bullshit, when all he wanted was to be a bloody bourgeois with a nice little house, a nice little garden, a nice little mortgage, a three-piece suite, a fitted kitchen, an avocado bathroom and Miriam.

Miriam.

Feeling low, lower, lowest, he dug into his trouser pocket for his door key, had some difficulty locating it. He was trying his jacket pockets instead, first one, then the other, when a small noise made him look up.

Dazed with joy, he watched the door slowly opening.